MW00416891

To Lynne,

All the best,
Freda Hansburg

TELL ON YOU

Freda Hansburg

Copyright © 2017 by Freda Hansburg

All rights reserved. No part of this publication may be reproduced, distributed, or transmitted in any form or by any means, including photocopying, recording, or other electronic or mechanical methods, without the prior written permission of the publisher, except in the case of brief quotations embodied in critical reviews and certain other noncommercial uses permitted by copyright law. For permission requests, write to the publisher, addressed "Attention: Permissions Coordinator," at the address below.

Micro Publishing Media
PO Box 1522
Stockbridge, MA 01262
www.micropublishingmedia.com

MICRO PUBLISHING MEDIA, INC

info@micropublishingmedia.com

Printed in the United States of America

Hansburg, Freda
Tell on You, Freda Hansburg

ISBN 978-1-944068-32-5

2017

Cover Design: Michael Yuen-Killick
Book Design: Jane McWhorter
Author Photo: Dana Cherubini

This is a work of fiction. Any names or characters, businesses or places, events or incidents, are fictitious. Any resemblance to actual persons, living or dead, or actual events is purely coincidental. If you think it is you I promise not to tell.

To Dan, and our lagoon.

Part One

"...he wanted to recover something, some idea of himself, perhaps...if he could once return to a certain starting place and go over it all slowly, he could find out what that thing was."
— F. Scott Fitzgerald, *The Great Gatsby*

ONE

"ALL RIGHT, LADIES!"

Jeremy Barrett clapped to get the attention of his second period Advanced Placement English class. When they continued talking, he barked: "Hey!" Eleven pairs of adolescent eyes turned toward him and the buzz of their conversations died down. The Forrest School demanded academic excellence along with the steep tuition. These daughters of wealthy New Jersey bedroom communities mostly rose to the challenge. Jeremy found them a pleasure to teach.

He scanned the room, mentally taking attendance and ticking off today's borderline violations of the school dress code. Here, a bit of exposed belly or cleavage, there, some serious piercing. He frowned, but not over the wardrobe issues. No one had called in absent today, but someone was missing.

"Anyone know where Heather is?" They were all enmeshed in a tapestry of tweets, texts and posts. If one fell off the cyber trail for more than fifteen minutes it drew the herd's attention. Cellphones were supposed to be turned off, but there were always a few cheaters. Probably more than a few.

But nobody offered an explanation for Heather's absence.

Jeremy shrugged off his unease about the missing girl and began his lecture. The Great Gatsby, one of his favorite novels. The latest movie remake, combining 3D and JayZ, had piqued his students' interest when he'd shown it in class. Personally, Jeremy considered the film an over-the-top, gaudy spectacle that turned Nick Carraway into a derelict and mangled Fitzgerald's gorgeous prose and dialogue. But his students ate it up.

"So, let's come back to our discussion of how Fitzgerald used water imagery." A loud rapping on the open classroom door interrupted. Jeremy looked over to see the principal's administrative assistant, Mrs. Marvin, wearing a prim suit and a pinched expression.

He scowled at the interruption. "What is it?"

"Mr. Donnelly would like to see you."

"Now?" Jeremy's tone bore the outrage of a surgeon interrupted in mid-operation.

Mrs. Marvin looked back at him, stone-faced. "Right away, he said. I'm to stay and monitor your class."

Her words provoked a chorus of murmurs among his students, which Jeremy put a stop to with a loud "Shhh! Start reading the last three chapters. I'll be back in a few minutes."

A prickle of anxiety clenched Jeremy's stomach as he walked down the hall to the principal's office. Nothing to do with any childhood memories of disgrace, for Jeremy had been a diligent, rule-abiding student. His peccadilloes—well, transgressions—a recent development. He'd promised himself he'd get his act together. But—Donnelly. What did he know?

The principal rose as Jeremy entered his office.

A room designed to elicit tranquility rather than fear, it boasted a pastoral view of the green athletic field through French doors that led out onto a small balcony. Set on an estate, the Forrest School resembled a plantation more than an institution. Still, as Mr. Donnelly pointed him toward the sofa, Jeremy's hands felt clammy. He mentally prepared defenses, but kept coming up short.

"Thank you for coming so promptly, Jeremy." The principal wore a gray pin-striped suit today, dressing the part of CEO. Probably to stay on a par with the parents, many of whom were CEO's.

"Of course." Jeremy nodded. "What did you want to see me about?" He winced inwardly. An English teacher, ending a sentence with a preposition.

Mr. Donnelly didn't appear to notice. He drew up his hands to form a steeple, touching his lower lip. Sunlight from the French doors reflected off his glasses. He looked like a church. A folded piece of paper rested on his lap. "It's about Heather Lloyd."

Jeremy drew a breath. Bad, but not the worst. "She's absent this morning," he said. "Has something happened?"

"That's what I'd like to understand." The principal passed the paper to Jeremy. "I received this email from Heather's mother this morning."

Jeremy unfolded the paper and read the message, his mouth turning to dust. Finishing, he looked up at Mr. Donnelly in silence.

"Jeremy," the principal demanded, "what is this all about?"

TWO

STEELING HIMSELF, JEREMY BEGAN.

"Sir, the thing with Heather built up for a while…"

"Thing?" The principal frowned. "What kind of thing would that be, Jeremy?"

"You know. We're reading Gatsby. Love stories—they give girls ideas sometimes."

"Go on. Explain it to me."

So Jeremy did. The problem, he told Donnelly, first became obvious during a particularly animated discussion about the novel.

Jeremy explained how he'd challenged the class. Jay Gatsby—steadfast knight, or obsessive fool? Did Fitzgerald want the reader to admire or pity him? Jeremy described how he'd drawn out their responses—at first, halting and tentative, then turning rapid and eager—and stoked their debate. Hip to be cynical in their world, yet most of them defended Gatsby. Something of a romantic, Jeremy had always identified with the character.

He didn't mention that part to Donnelly.

"So there they were, getting into it," Jeremy continued. "And I looked over at Heather." An uneasy chuckle. "I could see she was in la-la land."

She'd been looking his way a lot lately, Jeremy explained, but that day her stare was—hungry. Hungry as Gatsby's gaze at Daisy's small green light across the blue water. "I tried to avoid looking at her," he told Donnelly, shuddering inwardly as he pictured Heather's moon face. No mistaking the way she'd hung onto his every word. "Not like that's never happened before," Jeremy went on. He'd seen that look on plenty of schoolgirls. It came with the territory.

Jeremy didn't mention how Heather's lovestruck stare had pissed him off. Or that, as a rule, he kind of got off on those looks. At least coming from prettier girls than Heather. Riffing on love and literature brought Jeremy as close to rock star status as he'd ever get. An English teacher served as high priest, guarding the secrets of the heart and initiating eager young women to its mysteries. Exhilarating, but harmless—awakening their innocent passion for literature. No harm, no foul. But under the ardent gaze of awkward, pudgy Heather Lloyd that morning, Jeremy's irritation had mounted.

"So," he told Donnelly, "I wrapped up the discussion and assigned them a short paper, due that Friday. Five hundred words on the question: Why does Daisy stay with her husband, Tom, instead of running off with Jay Gatsby?"

As Jeremy concluded his narrative, the principal regarded him with narrowed eyes. "So that was when you realized Heather was attracted to you. And what did you do about it?"

"Nothing." Jeremy shrugged, playing it light. "You know, adolescent girls read love stories and get crushes on their teachers. It happens."

Mr. Donnelly absorbed this information in silence.

"Anyway, I've found it best to ignore it. Sooner or later, they move on to their next infatuation." Too cynical?

The principal frowned again. "So that's what you did? Ignored it?"

Jeremy paused. "Until I read what she wrote in her paper."

He'd graded more than half their essays, Jeremy explained, before coming to Heather's. Her usual pedestrian prose, until that startling paragraph. He remembered it well enough to quote to Donnelly verbatim:

Daisy was selfish and materialistic. She didn't deserve a man like Gatsby. Real love means seeing past superficial things, like money, cars and houses. It means seeing someone's inner beauty. Like I see yours. I'm watching for your green light to shine for me, Mr. B. (Hint, hint.)

Jeremy remembered the sudden heat flushing his face, the combustible mix of emotions. Did that silly, presumptuous sixteen year old really imagine he'd be aroused by such sophomoric crap? He refrained from sharing that with Donnelly. Nor did Jeremy admit that he'd felt a tiny bit flattered, angering him all the more. Damn the twit. Heather, the last girl in the class from whom he'd want this type of attention. Light years from…

Jeremy remembered snapping his pencil in half.

"Jeremy?" Donnelly stared at him.

Jeremy startled back into the moment. "So then I realized I had to put a stop to it, sir." Nip it in the bud. "So I checked though the rest of Heather's essay, then gave her a grade."

"And the grade…?"

"Uh, C+." Jeremy had scrawled it across the top of the paper—quickly—to be done with the matter.

"Anything else?" Donnelly asked.

Traces of perspiration rose at the roots of Jeremy's hair. "I wrote a comment."

The principal waited.

"Uh—not consistent with acceptable standards of scholarship. Something like that," Jeremy said.

Mr. Donnelly pursed his lips. "Why didn't you discuss this situation with me after you read Heather's paper?"

Jeremy wracked his mind. "I didn't want to blow things up and embarrass her even more." Or myself.

"So, these allegations of Mrs. Lloyd's—" The principal took back the copy of the email from Jeremy. "—that you made sexual advances toward Heather…"

"Completely untrue. Never even alone with the girl." Jeremy shook his head. "God knows what she may have told her mother. But, no, absolutely nothing to it."

Mr. Donnelly nodded. "I want a copy of that paper."

"Of course," Jeremy agreed. "I archive all their papers until the semester is over."

"There'll be an official inquiry."

Jeremy's jaw went slack. "Is that really necessary?"

"I'm afraid so." The principal's mouth twitched as if he'd tasted something sour. "I must say, it sounds like you were unduly harsh with the girl."

Jeremy swallowed. Perhaps he had been.

"I'm putting you on suspension, effective immediately," Donnelly said.

"Suspension!" Jeremy protested. "That's crazy! I didn't do anything."

Mr. Donnelly put up a hand to silence him. "I'm sure we'll wrap this up quickly, and everything will get back to normal."

"But how will I support my family?" Jeremy fought a wave of panic, picturing Melissa's reaction. And, worse, her parents'. His in-laws hardly held him in high esteem.

"If—when you're cleared," Mr. Donnelly corrected, "you'll be paid retroactively for administrative leave. I'm sorry." He didn't sound it. "But we can't ignore this kind of thing. We have procedures for these circumstances. Legally, morally and practically, I have no other choice."

Jeremy sat, speechless. They were already in a deep financial hole.

Mr. Donnelly stood. "Assuming everything you told me is true, I'm sure you have nothing to worry about."

Jeremy rose unsteadily to his feet. "Sir, I have nothing to hide. I'd never do anything to hurt a student, or the school."

"I'm relieved to hear that." Donnelly gave him a frosty smile. "Now, can I rely on you to collect your things and leave the premises immediately? Without the embarrassment of a security escort?"

Not much of a choice. "Of course."

He slunk out of the principal's office, his mind reeling. For all his bravado, he had plenty to hide, and everything to worry about.

THREE

IN HER BEDROOM, PLAYING Candy Crush on her faux bling-covered iPhone, Heather Lloyd had nearly cleared her mind of the mess she was in. Pretzels, her brown and white long-haired guinea pig, purred in his cage, doing his happy dance for love of her company. She smiled and clucked at him.

Her phone rang, displaying Nikki Jordan's name on the screen. Much as Heather craved solitude right now, she'd never have the nerve to blow off Nikki.

"Hi," she said tentatively.

"Why aren't you at school?" Nikki demanded. "You sick?"

"Uh huh." Heather's palms slickened with sweat. Nikki had that effect on her. "Kinda."

"But you didn't call in, right? In first period Mr. B didn't know where you were. Neither did I." The chill in Nikki's tone carried the message that Heather should have kept her better informed.

"I know. I'm sorry. Kind of a last minute thing."

"I'm worried about you, Heather. What's wrong?"

Something in Nikki's words gave Heather a spooky, woo-woo feeling. How did Nikki do that? Say the exact right words of caring and concern, yet make them sound like a threat? "I'm—I have a really bad headache. I took some Advil but it didn't even help."

"Poor Heather! I hope it's nothing ser-i-ous." Drawing out all three syllables.

Heather's face burned. Making fun of her? They were supposed to be friends. Heather helped her with stuff, like replacing Nikki's cracked cellphone screen last week. "I'll be okay," she muttered.

"You know…" Nikki paused. "When Mr. B gave back our Gatsby papers the other day, you looked pretty sick then, too. I kind of wondered if there was a problem, or what."

How did she do that? Nikki always knew things. Like some kind of witch. "Well… he didn't give me a very good grade," Heather admitted.

Nikki waited, her silence as powerful as her voice.

"A C+." Heather's voice wobbled. "And he wrote some nasty stuff on my paper."

"Like what?"

"Heather?" Her mother's voice coming from the bedroom door made Heather jump. "Who's that you're talking to? Why aren't you resting?"

"Gotta go," Heather murmured.

"Call me later." Nikki hung up.

"Sorry, Mom." Heather slipped the phone onto her dresser. "Nikki got worried because I missed class."

Her mother eyed Heather's Hello Kitty pajamas. "I think you should take a shower and put on some clothes."

"But—"

"I had a call from your principal, Mr. Donnelly. He said an investigator from the Division of Child Protection and Permanency will be coming over here to take a statement from you."

"Child—what?" Heather stared at her mother.

"The child welfare people," her mother said impatiently. "You know. They used to be DYFS."

Heather puzzled over it. "Why'd they change their name?"

"Heather!" Her mother got that harried look. "How should I know?" She rooted through Heather's dresser drawers, selecting a suitable outfit. "Whatever they call themselves these days, it's a good thing they're coming. Honest to god, the things that awful man did. It's a crime! My god, you're only sixteen." Her voice rose. "Of course DCPP is going to investigate! It's only right. So I want you to get ready." Her mom tossed clothing onto Heather's bed. "Here, this should be—"

A spasm gripped Heather's stomach. Groaning, she clutched her belly and sprinted for the bathroom, slamming the door behind her. Her mother droned on, but the closed door cut off the sound of her voice.

When Heather emerged, her mother had gone. The outfit she'd selected for her lay spread across the bed. Heather stared at the clothes for several moments before taking off her pajamas. She pulled the cotton sweater over her head and pushed her arms through the sleeves.

Smoothing the garment over her chest, Heather wished, as usual, for bigger breasts. A smaller waist. Anything but what she saw in the mirror. She hated the way she looked in pale pink. Mom had chosen an outfit that made her look innocent and girly. For a miserable moment, Heather wondered if her mother had selected the sweater in full awareness that pink wasn't her color. A statement for the DCPP worker: Look. She's not even that attractive. What a sick pervert that man must be.

Only he wasn't, Heather thought. Mr. B, a skeeve? So smart, sensitive, funny. Handsome, too, in a brainy sort of way that made her dream he'd notice someone like her. Heather grabbed a brush and jerked it furiously through her hair to keep from crying. Why did he have to go and make her feel like such a dork?

She hurled the brush across the room.

He'd led her on. He had! Glancing her way in class all those times, during his lectures about Jay Gatsby and Daisy Buchanan, about love and longing. She hadn't imagined it. Heather had been so sure, when she wrote that stuff in her paper, that he wanted her, too.

After all, what was Mr. B supposed to do, if he liked her? Teachers can't exactly come out and say: "Hey, you wanna hang out?" So he had to be careful. Subtle. And she, Heather, had gotten the message. Knew! But then he'd gone and written those mean comments and given her a lousy grade that her mother was bound to question and get all bent out of shape over. So what was she supposed to do?

Heather retrieved her hairbrush and placed it on her dresser. Her stomach clenched and made a hideous noise. She'd had to come up with some explanation when Mom insisted on looking at her paper. And so she'd stretched the truth a little—but really, only a little. She'd made it like Mr. B had actually said some of the things his looks were suggesting. That was all. She'd interpreted.

Like he'd taught them to do in English class.

Heather turned away from the mirror. If she hadn't done anything so bad, why did she have stomach cramps at the prospect of talking to that Child Whatever worker? Maybe getting Mr. B into a shitload of trouble. But he deserved it, right? And what would Mom do, if she admitted she'd lied?

The doorbell rang, and Heather raced back to the bathroom.

FOUR

NIKKI JORDAN STOOD, AN island of serenity in the packed school corridor, bustling with fellow students scurrying to their next class. She wore a small smile. Her intuition—which Nikki always trusted—smelled something funny going on with Heather, and Nikki wanted the 411. Well, she'd sure as hell get the full story out of her later.

Meanwhile, let French class wait.

Nikki's ice blue eyes scanned the hallway. The door to the principal's office opened. Mr. B walked out, looking positively sick. Jeez, his face was practically white. Something going on, all right. The tiny hairs on Nikki's skin prickled with anticipation. When Mr. B headed down the hall, she gave him a head start—not to make her pursuit obvious to any onlookers—then followed.

JEREMY LOOKED AROUND HIS office in confusion. What should he take home? Surely not everything. He placed his briefcase on the desk and opened it. The suspension couldn't be permanent. The more he took home, the more he'd have to bring back in a few days. Only a matter of days. A week, at most, right? He couldn't afford to be out of work longer than that. The thought made him queasy.

No. He stuffed books and papers into his briefcase. He hadn't said or done one untoward thing to Heather Lloyd. Not the Salem witch trials, after all. On cue, he picked up his copy of The Crucible. They'd studied the play last semester. He managed a wry smile. No trial coming here, at all. No arrest. It would all blow over.

He picked up a paperweight from his desk—a snow globe. A gift from Melissa, it displayed a tiny New York skyline within. Jeremy held it in his hands, flipped it and watched as white flakes fell on the city. How would he explain all this to Mel? He put the globe into his briefcase.

He reached for another memento—a baseball resting on a display stand. Passed on to Jeremy by his father, it bore the signature of the three-time Cy Young award-winning pitcher, Tom Seaver. Mike Barrett, a die-hard Mets fan, even before the team began logging wins, had wangled Tom Terrific's autograph on Fan Appreciation Day at Shea Stadium. One of his father's most treasured possessions, Jeremy kept the ball turned on its stand, signature facing down. An ordinary baseball made a less tempting target for theft.

Jeremy ran his fingers over the smooth leather, feeling a pang of regret. His father had encouraged Jeremy to share his passion for baseball, but he had remained indifferent. Beyond indifferent. Always the last kid picked by playground captains, Jeremy swore off sports early on. He'd never admitted the reason to his dad, left hurt and bewildered by Jeremy's rejections. Two years since his father's fatal heart attack, only a week before Jeremy turned thirty one. And he felt like shit every time he looked at that damned baseball. Yet he'd kept it there on his desk in plain sight, half wishing one of his students would steal it.

Instead of the jock he'd have understood, Mike Barrett wound up with a nerdy kid who devoured literature and wrote poetry. His father had loved him, Jeremy knew, but he'd recognized his dad's disappointment. When he'd married Melissa, Dad was probably relieved that his artsy-fartsy son wasn't gay.

No leaving the baseball behind.

Jeremy dropped the ball and stand into his briefcase. He eyed the Casablanca poster mounted on the wall. His favorite film. Rick and Ilsa. Here's looking at you, kids. He started toward the wall to take it down, but changed his mind. Carrying it through the corridors would only make his departure more conspicuous.

What else? He'd left his copy of Gatsby back in the classroom. Now he'd have to interrupt the next class to retrieve it, or risk the principal's wrath by hanging around until the period ended. He'd written his name on the inside cover. Maybe the book would find its way to his box.

He closed his briefcase, chewing on the inside of his cheek, an anxious traveler, sure he'd forgotten to pack something essential. And it hit him. Heather's paper. He had to email it to the principal.

He booted up the laptop furnished by the school. While he was at it, might as well email a few files to his home computer. Use the time off to get ahead on his lesson plans.

The login page came up, asking for Jeremy's UserName. He typed in jbarrett. Invalid UserName.

"Damn it!" he muttered, trying again.

Invalid UserName.

They'd already shut him out of the system.

Jeremy kicked his desk chair and sent it scraping across the floor. Then he remembered—he'd backed up the papers on a zip drive, to work on them at home. He still had a copy for Donnelly.

A soft rapping on his office door.

"What?" The last thing he needed right now was company.

The door opened part way.

"Mr. B?"

Round doe eyes, under a fringe of dark lashes, fixed on his face. "Talk for a minute?"

Those delicate features, etched with distress, pulled at his heart. Determined, he looked away. "Not now, Nikki." Not when I'm all fucked up like this.

She took a step into his office and leaned one slender shoulder against the door jamb. "Something's happened, right? Please tell me. I'm worried about you."

Jeremy smiled, in spite of everything. She worried about him. His resolve began melting. "I have to leave now," he said. And then not see her for—how long? He stepped forward, closing the space between them. "Anyway, we can't talk here."

She opened her mouth to speak.

Those lips! He murmured: "Meet me at the park on your lunch break. The regular spot."

She backed out of the doorway, flashing him a grin that took his breath away.

FIVE

"HEATHER? WHAT ARE YOU doing in there?" Her mother rapped on the bathroom door. "Hurry up and come into the living room. The woman from DCPP is here to talk with you."

"Be right out, Mom." Heather flushed the toilet and went to the sink to wash her hands. She splashed cold water onto her face and toweled off.

"Heather?" her mother called.

She made a face at herself in the mirror, wishing she had the nerve to do that to her mom. "Coming!" She opened the bathroom door to the sight of her mother's frown. "Sorry. My stomach's upset again."

"Let's go." Mom motioned her toward the bedroom door. "You don't want to keep the investigator waiting."

Do too. Heather trudged into the living room, her mother a half-step behind her.

A heavy-set woman with ebony skin that contrasted with her brightly-colored print dress, rose from the couch, smiling, when Heather entered. "Hello, Heather. I'm Ms. Price." She held out her hand.

Heather gazed at the pink-skinned palm for a moment, then shook the woman's hand.

"Why don't we sit down?" the woman said. "I have some questions for you."

"Uh huh." Noting the investigator's large tote bag already resting on the couch, Heather moved across to a chair on the other side of the coffee table. Her mother swooped into the chair next to hers and Heather felt an impulse to flee.

"Mrs. Lloyd," the investigator said, "It might be helpful for me to speak privately with your daughter."

Her mom pursed her lips. "I don't see why that should be necessary. Heather doesn't keep secrets from me."

"No, of course not," Ms. Price agreed. "But perhaps she would feel more comfortable if it were the two of us." She glanced over at Heather. "Since she's over fourteen, a parent's presence isn't required for the interview."

Heather turned to her mother, eyes beseeching. If she didn't have to deal with both of them at once, perhaps she'd get through this.

"I prefer to stay." Her mother's mouth set in a firm line.

Heather's eyes dropped to the floor.

Ms. Price nodded, her silver hoop earrings jangling. "Very well." She reached into her tote bag for a yellow legal pad. "I'll be making a few notes while we're talking. Okay?" She clicked a ball point pen, and Heather drew a breath.

"Certainly," Mrs. Lloyd said.

"Unhhuh," Heather mumbled.

"So, then. Heather, I've spoken with your principal at the Forrest School, Mr. Donnelly. He said your mother—" A slight nod of her head acknowledged Mrs. Lloyd. "Made a complaint about your English teacher, Mr. Barrett. Did you know about that?"

"Yes ma'am."

"Do you know what your mother's complaint said?"

Heather started to say yes, but hesitated. She hadn't read her mother's email. A trick question? "Um—I think so."

"Tell the lady what Mr. Barrett did to you," her mother ordered.

"Mrs. Lloyd, please," the investigator said. "I prefer that you let me conduct the interview with your daughter."

Heather's mom held up her hands in a gesture of surrender. Heather doubted she'd give up that easily.

"Heather." Ms. Price fixed dark eyes on her. "Would you like to tell me what happened between you and Mr. Barrett?"

Heather swallowed. Not really. "Well…he—he's a really good teacher. All the kids like him."

With a slight smile, Ms. Price jotted a note on her pad. "Why is that?"

Heather relaxed a little. "He's pretty hip. Like he doesn't talk down to us, and stuff."

"I see. So you liked Mr. Barrett."

Mrs. Lloyd sniffed. "His teaching wasn't the problem. Tell her how he stared at you all the time."

"Mrs. Lloyd…" The investigator's tone held an edge, punctuated by a few extra clicks of her ballpoint. "Heather?"

"What?" Her palms began sweating.

"What do you think your mother meant—about the staring?"

Heather took a breath. "He—looked at me a lot in class. We—uh, studied The Great Gatsby. Ever heard of it?"

Ms. Price smiled more broadly this time and nodded as she wrote. "I had to read that one in high school, too. How did you feel when Mr. Barrett stared at you in class, Heather?"

Heather rubbed clammy palms against her thighs, trying to figure out the right answer. "Kind of—embarrassed, I guess." Excited or flattered would have been closer to the truth. She glanced at her mom, hoping those compressed lips were on account of Mr. B, and not her.

"Mr. Donnelly mentioned…" Ms. Price paused, as if weighing her words.

Heather held her breath, waiting for her to continue.

"—an incident involving a paper you wrote for Mr. Barrett," she concluded.

Heather's face grew hot. She hoped she wasn't turning beet red.

"He led her on!" Her mother sounded shrill. "The man is a predator!"

The investigator clenched her jaw. "Mrs. Lloyd, I need to hear what Heather has to say. Perhaps it would be best if you left the room."

Her mother's eyes narrowed. "May I remind you that this is my house?"

Heather wanted to crawl under the sofa. Beyond terrible. She thrust both hands into her curly hair and pushed back hard enough to feel the roots pull against her scalp.

"Mrs. Lloyd." The investigator's tone turned frosty.

"All right!" Heather cried out. "I'll tell you." She had to end this. "He—he walked up behind me in class one time and started rubbing the back of my neck. And another time he patted my rear end when I was the last one out of the room." Keep going, keep talking! "He used to wink at me and give me these—these sexy looks! And he got me all—messed up and everything, so I wrote that stuff on my paper." Heather burst into tears. "Then he practically failed me and treated me like everything was my fault! But it wasn't me! It was him. Him!"

Ms. Price scrawled furiously on her pad as Heather jumped up and ran to her bedroom.

"Heather, get back in here right now!"

She slammed the door behind her, drowning out the sound of her mother's voice.

SIX

JEREMY LINGERED A FEW minutes in his office to make sure Nikki left the hallway outside. How had he fallen in so deep with her?

At first, his feelings had been a concerned teacher's for a gifted student, one whose frail shoulders clearly bore too much weight. An overdue assignment, coming after several weeks of pitch-perfect written work and class participation: the red flag. Nikki had come to his office, blue eyes brimming, to turn in her paper—three days late—offering an apology, but no excuses.

He'd coaxed the story out of her.

A recent divorce, an indifferent father. Mother working too many hours and, reading between the lines of Nikki's halting account, depressed, to boot. All of which left a sixteen-year-old girl playing surrogate parent to her eight-year-old special needs brother and burdened with who knew what other responsibilities at home. Jeremy had discerned no resentment in Nikki's description of the situation. If anything, she'd sounded guilty about not doing more.

He shook his head. She worried about him.

Without bothering to turn off the useless laptop, he snatched up his briefcase and went out the door.

Head down, eyes glued to the floor, Jeremy made his way down the corridor, praying he wouldn't meet anyone. He resisted the urge to jog. Hell, he fought the impulse to throw his jacket over his head like some poor slob doing a perp walk. Don't act guilty. Don't call attention to yourself. Don't—

"Jeremy! What's wrong?"

How tempting to keep walking and ignore his colleague Marge Peterson. But the concern in her voice, the kindness she'd always shown him, ruled out that option.

"Nothing serious." For a moment Jeremy's mind went blank. Then he pulled himself together. "A doctor's appointment." He smiled weakly at Marge's puzzled expression. "Sorry, gotta run."

"But everything's okay?" Her voice followed him down the hall.

"Fine, Marge." He waved without turning back.

Jeremy made it to the parking lot, spared any additional encounters. He opened his car door, threw his briefcase onto the passenger side and sank into the driver's seat.

Now what?

Of course he should go home and tell Melissa what had happened. Get himself a lawyer, maybe. But he stayed put, elbow resting against the steering wheel, chewing the cuticle of his thumbnail. Not yet. No facing Mel until he got his own mind around all this.

Jeremy glanced at the dashboard clock. Another hour and a half before he'd meet Nikki. He bit his cuticle again, savagely enough to taste the metallic tang of his own blood. Unthinkable to keep that rendezvous.

And yet.

He started the engine.

Jeremy made two cups of coffee and an English muffin kill an hour at the local diner, all the while reminding himself of the solid arguments against meeting Nikki Jordan. Teachers didn't tryst with their students. Not if they wanted to keep their jobs. He'd already been suspended and accused of sexual misconduct. Madness to take any more risks, even though he was innocent. Mostly.

All he'd meant to do was step up and be the concerned, supportive adult Nikki so plainly lacked—and needed—in her life. Encouraged her to come to his office and talk, unburden herself. And gradually she had. The day she told him how much she missed her father, tears rolling down those porcelain cheeks, Jeremy ended up giving Nikki his cellphone number. In case she needed help when her mother wasn't around.

A couple of weeks and she'd used it one evening, not so late as to be inappropriate, but late enough. No, she refused to ask her mother to take her to a therapist. "No one else listens to me like you do," she'd told him. And he'd been touched.

Jeremy hadn't known the real Nikki Jordan then. And didn't, even now. That discovery lay ahead of him. In the end, he drove over to the park early and waited at their regular bench.

The small suburban park stood only a few blocks away from the Forrest School, but thanks to the lush athletic field and ample outdoor gathering space on campus, students had no reason to trek over there during the school day. No legitimate reasons, at least. An occasional pot smoker might lurk behind a tree, but rarely. Easier for the stoners to slip into the spectator stands on the athletic field.

A few weeks from now, when April lengthened the days and opened early blossoms, mothers with strollers would populate these benches. But today, during the second half of March, the wind chill kept them away. Jeremy had relied on the cold to furnish privacy over the past six weeks, using the park as his secret meeting place with Nikki. Foolhardy, he knew. And very, very wrong. Teachers don't tryst with students. His eyes darted around the empty grounds and benches while he waited for her.

He heard her footsteps before he saw her, the crunch of a dead leaf signaling Nikki's approach. He sprang from the bench and turned, his stomach doing a tiny flip flop.

She came toward him, wearing that smile that reduced all his concerns to dandelion fluff, scattered into the wind. Drawing closer, Nikki raised her arm and held out a book.

His copy of Gatsby.

"You left it in the classroom." Her voice tinkled like sleigh bells, and held a captivating hint of shyness.

"Thank you," he murmured, reaching for the book. She took a step toward him, then another, passed him the book and rested her head against Jeremy's chest. Did she hear his heartbeat? He stepped away and saw a ripple of disappointment cross her face.

"What happened?" she asked. "Why did Mr. Donnelly want to see you? Why did you leave school like that?"

Jeremy hesitated. He ought not to burden her with this. Nikki had enough on her shoulders at home. Being the protector was his job, not hers.

"Tell me," she urged. "You looked so upset when you came out of his office." She touched his shoulder. "You don't have to deal with this alone, you know."

"Nikki." Jeremy pulled back and cupped her chin with his hand. "I don't want you worrying about me." He looked into her light blue eyes, certain they were the color of glaciers—even though he'd never seen one firsthand. Yet glaciers were frozen and Nikki's eyes warm, radiating devotion. Those eyes made him want to write poetry again.

"It has something to do with Heather, doesn't it?"

Jeremy drew a swift breath. So bright, so perceptive. An old soul inside an elfin teenaged body. He smiled. "Now, how did you figure that out?"

She gave him back a hint of a smile. "I have my ways." Her expression turned somber. "Are you in some kind of trouble, Mr. B?"

"Nothing serious," he assured her, striving for an easy, confident tone. "Heather got some crazy ideas in her head."

"But—why did you leave the school all of a sudden?"

"I—I'll need to take some time off. Only for a little while," he added. "Don't worry. Everything will work out fine."

Her eyebrows arched. "Will I still be able to talk to you?"

He gazed at her hair, so dark that it shone blue-black in the midday sunlight. "Of course you will. I'll be in touch." He fought the urge to kiss her once, gently, on those soft, pink lips. "You'd better get back now." He held up his copy of Gatsby. "Thanks for rescuing my book."

She nodded. "Bye, Mr. B. Be careful."

He watched her make her way between two bare trees, nimble as a fawn. Watched until she left his sight.

A gust of cold wind roused Jeremy, sent him walking briskly toward his car.

What kind of shit would pour down on him if people knew? The line had blurred so gradually that the point of no return had come and gone before he realized it. One day he'd been Nikki's teacher; the next, her confidante. And then…

No one else listens…

Sixteen might be the legal age of consent, but teachers occupied a position of trust. Intimacy with a student? Illegal. But how illegal, in his case? He knew she had a crush on him. And knew he shouldn't enjoy it as much as he did. Intoxicating to have a beautiful young girl look up to him. Still, he'd exercised restraint, hadn't he? Only some hugs, first supportive and sympathetic, then, admittedly, more ardent. Always with Nikki the one to initiate them, as if that made it all okay. At first they'd met in his office or an empty classroom, then progressed to the park—or, on a couple of really cold days, his car. Imagine seeing that on page one of the newspaper. But he'd wanted to be alone with her, to drink in the sight of her.

No one else…

Shivering, Jeremy pulled his keys from his coat pocket.

Yeah, guilty enough. Jeremy had drawn Heather's attention and brought on her bogus complaint, as surely as if he'd groped that pathetic girl. Heather sat next to Nikki in his second period English class, and he'd let his gaze wander off in that direction one too many times. Heather's dumb love note had shattered his denial, the flood of his own shame catching him all unprepared. So Jeremy had overreacted and turned on Heather.

Now he only hoped to survive the coming storm.

SEVEN

WITH NO CONSCIOUS PLAN to pretend things were—routine, Jeremy loitered at the local library and arrived home at his regular time. Mounting the stairs to their garden apartment, he still had no clue how to break the news of his suspension to Melissa.

When he opened the door, she stood there grinning at him.

"Guess what?"

Whatever, he could top it. "Mel, I'm not much in the mood for guessing games."

"I'm pregnant."

Oh, shit no.

Melissa beamed. The smile, a bit—forced? She scanned his face for a reaction. He closed the door behind him—slowly, buying time. Pregnant. Now? "What happened?"

Melissa rolled her eyes, like he'd said something funny, which Jeremy didn't think he had. "A wild guess? I'd say one of your little guys was a champion swimmer."

Not amused. "You know what I mean. I thought you were on the pill."

Melissa's smile withered. "They don't always work."

Jeremy searched for a response. "Well! That certainly is news."

Her eyes remained glued on him. "You don't sound very happy."

Here was the moment to tell her about the suspension, he knew. "No! I'm—surprised, is all. Uh, congratulations."

She flung her arms around his waist. He felt her exhale. "You, too."

"When are you—uh, we due?" Jeremy drew back to face her.

"Around Thanksgiving? I see my gynecologist tomorrow. My obstetrician, I mean." She giggled. Melissa was not a giggler. "He gets a promotion, I guess."

Jeremy nodded mutely, thinking: Wake me up. Shit, beam me up. He took in the living room of their rented garden apartment. The same room he'd left that morning—taupe pleather sofa with Melissa's jacket laying on it, brown and beige striped fabric-covered chairs—her sneakers on the floor between them—the wood and glass coffee table piled with her books and handbag. The right apartment. Except in some parallel universe, where a Supreme Being with a sick sense of humor had played a cosmic joke on him. Twice, yet, in one day. If he walked out the door and came back in again, would everything return to normal? A reboot?

"Jeremy?" Melissa stared.

"Yeah!" He smiled, having no idea what else to do. "Wonderful, honey. Really. But—uh—what about grad school?"

Melissa raked her fingers through her dark mane of hair. "I don't know. I've hardly had a chance to think about it." She shrugged. "I mean, I'll still apply. If they accept me, there's always the option of starting in January, instead of September. Right?"

"Sure, makes sense." He trailed off, imagining three Barretts to feed, instead of two. Technically, two Barretts and a Milton-Barrett, a bit of nomenclature Jeremy had come to resent. To Melissa, the hyphen conveyed feminism; to Jeremy, it meant her parents were part of the marriage. Still. "Uh, Mel, there's something…"

"Hey!" She eyed the khakis and sweater he'd worn to school. "Go change, babe. My parents are taking us out to dinner, to celebrate! The Moreland Inn."

Celebrate? Her parents?

Melissa tugged at the neck of her sweatshirt and laughed. "Guess I'll put on something sexy, while I still can."

Jeremy frowned. "You told them already?"

Melissa looked away. "Mom was with me yesterday when I bought the home pregnancy test. She called this morning to find out the result." Her brown eyes were wide, innocent. "I had to tell her, didn't I?"

Jeremy stood in the shower. Maybe he'd stay there all night. A celebratory dinner with the fucking Miltons. How could he rain on everyone's parade?

Melissa, pregnant. Not that pregnancy was unheard of, or even unexpected, after four years of marriage. God knows, his mother and in-laws had dropped enough hints about grandchildren. In their first couple of years together, he and Melissa had visited the topic in a vaguely positive way. Sure, they wanted a child—eventually. The way you wanted life insurance—a good idea, and one day you'd get around to it.

But—now? Their financial situation was beyond dismal since Melissa was laid off from her job at the publishing company. A "job" job, not a career job, one she'd fallen into through a girlfriend's connections. Lately, Melissa had been talking about moving in a new direction, maybe graduate school. She'd debated between law and social work. Not the corporate kind of law, where people actually made money, or used to. Something more activist, pro-social.

Maybe environmental or feminist law. Nothing that promised to put a dent in their credit card debt, which only Jeremy seemed worried about. Now neither of them would be bringing home a paycheck.

"You gonna let me have a turn in there?" Melissa called out.

"In a minute." He turned off the water and reached for a towel. Pulling back the shower curtain, he stepped from the tub, to see his nude wife twisting her hair up into a clip in front of the mirror. He observed her toned, almost boyish body while he dried off. She didn't look pregnant.

"How accurate are those home pregnancy tests, anyway?" he asked.

Melissa sidled past him, swatting him on the butt as she stepped into the shower. "Over 99 per cent."

"Huh." A sinking sensation in his stomach. "That's really amazing," he said.

EIGHT

BY THE TIME THE entrees came, Jeremy had downed a martini and two glasses of Cabernet, already over his limit. Caught up in the festivities, his in-laws scarcely noticed, but Melissa shot him sidelong warning glances.

"Have you told your mother yet, Jeremy?" Howard Milton refilled his own glass and held the bottle above his son-in-law's. "More Cabernet?"

Jeremy nodded, chewing roasted pork loin.

Howard poured. "Bet she was over the moon."

"No, Dad." Melissa corrected. "We haven't told her."

Jeremy swallowed. "I meant, yes about the wine." His third glass. Better slow down. "We tried calling her before we left, but she didn't pick up."

"Not the kind of message you leave on voicemail," Melissa said.

"I'm sure Gail will be as thrilled as we are." Beth Milton grasped Jeremy's hand before he could pull it away. "If only your father were alive to share this with us."

Jeremy nodded and extricated his hand. He glanced around the room, taking in the gleaming hardwood and crystal décor of the Moreland Inn. Imagine his old man in a place like this. Mike Barrett, a humble, hardworking insurance salesman, would have been more at home at the local diner.

Jeremy gulped the pricey Cabernet, trying to wash away the familiar taste of guilt and resentment his father's memory evoked. A jab to his ribs commanded his attention.

"Try some of this red snapper. It's awesome." Melissa offered a forkful of her entrée.

Jeremy took a taste. "Terrific. A Chardonnay would go great with that." He flashed her an evil wink. "But Mommy isn't drinking now, right?"

Her lips pursed. "Thanks a lot. I didn't think about it until you said that." Melissa sipped her water. "A small enough price to pay."

"Don't worry," Jeremy said, topping off his wine glass. "I'll drink for both of us."

"See what a good mother she'll make?" Beth Milton chimed in. "Have you thought about names? Oh!" Her eyes widened. "If it's a boy, how about Milton? The family name!"

"Or Melatonin, if it's a girl," Jeremy deadpanned, drawing a black look from Melissa. Time was, she'd have laughed at that line. They'd be co-conspirators against her parents. If a conspiracy existed nowadays, he was the outsider.

"Mom," Melissa said, "I haven't even seen my gynecologist—uh, obstetrician, yet. It's too soon to be thinking of names."

"Well, I'll tell you what it's not too soon to be thinking about." Howard leaned back in his chair and looked around the table, ensuring he had their attention.

Tempted to tap a spoon against his water goblet, like people did when the best man rose to speak at a wedding, Jeremy swallowed more wine instead.

"It's time the two of you bought a house," Howard announced.

"Oh, yes!" Beth agreed. "You can't raise a baby in that tiny apartment."

Jeremy caught Melissa's warning glance, but spoke up anyway. "We're not ready to buy. We might not even stay in New Jersey. Besides, an apartment is probably the most convenient place to take care of a newborn."

"Son," Howard began.

Jeremy loathed it when his father-in-law called him that.

"You have to think long term," Howard said. "Now is the time to buy, before the real estate market rebounds. The recovery has already started." A successful real estate developer, Howard spoke with authority. "You and Melissa can't afford to wait." He smiled. "Besides, you think we'd let our first grandchild grow up in a rented garden apartment?"

"Dad!" Melissa leaned across the table to catch her father's eye, preempting Jeremy's response. "You know I've been thinking about grad school. We can't possibly afford a house now. Besides—"

"But surely you're not going to start graduate school with a baby on the way!" Beth stared, aghast, as if her daughter had proposed taking up skydiving.

"Why not?" Melissa shot back. "Just because you were happy as a stay-at-home mom doesn't mean I have to—"

"Oh! So you're going back to work, after all!" Jeremy raised his glass. "I'll drink to that."

"Jeremy," Melissa said through gritted teeth.

"The point is." Howard spoke over both of them. "It will be our pleasure—our privilege—to take care of the down payment on your new house." He raised his own glass in a salute and drained the last of his wine. "And that's settled."

Furious, Jeremy lurched forward, nearly capsizing his half-full wine glass. "Wait a minute!"

"Jeremy!" Melissa hissed.

"No, hey! Don't I get a vote?"

"Son." Howard pulled Jeremy's wine glass out of reach. "That's enough."

"Oh yeah?" Jeremy wanted to grab back the wine and fling it in his father-in-law's face. "Well, I vote the three of us move in with you guys. You all can change little Milton's diapers while Melissa sleeps in and I look for a job. Won't that be fun?"

In the awkward silence, three sets of eyes glared back at him. Jeremy yanked the napkin from his lap and tossed it on the table. "Come on, Mel." He stood too quickly, swaying. "Maybe you better drive, huh?"

NINE

HALFWAY BACK TO THE apartment, Jeremy broke their seething silence. "So—what? I'm the bad guy here? Is that it?" He waited. "Mel?"

"Not while I'm driving," she growled.

"Fine." He turned and cracked his window, letting the cold night air finish the job of sobering him up.

"Will you fucking close that?" Melissa snapped. "It's freezing in here."

"Of course, Your Highness," he muttered.

"I said, can it while I'm driving, okay?"

Jeremy shut his mouth and his window. He stewed through the remaining minutes of the ride home, stealing sidelong glances at Melissa's tight-lipped face. Already he regretted his outburst at the restaurant. Yet, resentment of his father-in-law still burned, a slow, steady flame. How dare he play the CEO of their lives?

Pulling into a space by their apartment building, Melissa hopped out of the car, slammed the door behind her and headed upstairs. Jeremy took his time following her, bracing for the showdown.

Melissa stood in the living room, arms crossed over her chest, ready for battle. "How could you?" she demanded when he walked in.

"How could I? What, we're supposed to hand over our future to Howard the Great in exchange for buying us dinner?"

"They were being generous," Melissa said. "It was a celebration. Which you turned into a—a drunken brawl!" Her dark brows nearly met in a chevron of anger.

"I wasn't drunk!" Jeremy protested. "Especially with your father snatching away my wine glass."

"Every time my parents try to do something nice for us you get threatened. What the hell is your problem, Jeremy?"

"My problem? My problem?" Nearly sputtering. "Let's see, besides your father trying to run my life? Besides you springing a baby on me? How about the fact that I got suspended from my goddamn job today?"

Melissa stared. "What?"

Shit. He hadn't meant to break the news that way. "Well, temporarily," he said, backpedaling.

"Jeremy! What happened?" Her fury gave way to a look of alarm.

"There was—a student, her mother, really—made a bogus accusation that I, uh, harassed her."

"Sexually harassed her? A student?" Melissa stared at him in horror. "Jeremy, my god!"

"Look," he said, desperate now to reassure her. "It'll be okay. The girl had a crush on me and wrote a love note on her paper. I gave—I graded her work accordingly. Next thing I know, Donnelly hands me an email from the kid's mother claiming I molested her. It's bullshit, Mel. There'll be an investigation, and—"

"Investigation?" Melissa blanched. "Jeremy, you need a lawyer, right away."

She might have a point. "Well..."

"Are you still getting paid?"

He could tell the question had only now occurred to her. "Uh, not while I'm on, uh, leave," he said. "But retroactively, yeah, when it's settled."

Melissa shook her head, shell-shocked. "Jeremy, I should call my father right away about a lawyer."

His back burner pot of resentment boiled over. "Christ, Mel, can we keep your fucking father out of this, please!"

"But—we need help." Her eyes filled with fear. "Of all the times for this to happen. With a baby on the way."

"Yeah, well, maybe now you get that this might not be the time for us to have a kid." He knew that for a low blow as soon as he'd said it.

She looked stricken. "Don't you want this baby?"

He struggled for the words. "It's just—so sudden. It's not like we planned it, or talked. I mean, aren't you even a little bit—ambivalent?"

"How can you say that?"

She had to ask? What the hell was birth control for? "I don't get it," Jeremy said. "Yesterday you were hell bent on grad school. Today you're all gung ho on motherhood. I thought we agreed you'd start bringing in a paycheck again."

"And I thought you promised to find a decent job. My father says..."

"Fuck your father!" Jeremy exploded. She cringed and he took a calming breath. "Look, don't change the subject. I asked you to help me understand your feelings about being pregnant. To explain to me how—overnight—your plans and goals completely changed. Don't make this about your parents. It's about us."

Melissa's lip trembled. "You're the one who changed the subject." Her eyes welled. "Jeremy, I'm scared. What are we going to do?"

Surprise, followed by a wave of guilt, swept over him. Unlike Melissa to show such vulnerability, especially in the midst of an argument. Maybe pregnancy affected her that way? The notion ramped up his guilt another notch. He stepped forward and reached for her, but she turned away. He felt like a heel. Maybe that was the whole idea. He chided himself for his cynicism.

"Melissa, I'm sorry." He massaged her shoulder, knots of tension there. His fault. "Don't worry, sweetheart. Everything will be okay." He wished he believed that. "And it's not that I don't want the baby." Just not now. "But can't we talk about it? Be open with each other?" He turned her to face him.

Her eyes brimmed. "Honestly, Jeremy?"

"Yes!" Already he had doubts.

"I've been so—confused about things," she said. "Torn. And now, this pregnancy, coming out of the blue, it's—I don't know—it's like some kind of sign, or something."

"A sign? When did you start believing in signs, Mel? I thought you were an atheist? Or at least a secular humanist." He tried for a lighter note.

She wiped her eyes with the heel of her hand, leaving raccoon smudges of mascara. "I don't mean I've found religion. Just that—fate, or something—made the decision for me. Us."

"So now you're a fatalist? What is this, a Russian novel?"

Melissa laughed through her tears. "No. Oh, I don't know, Jeremy! Suppose this is where we're meant to be right now? Maybe Mom was right about grad school. You know?" She flung her arms around his neck. "Can't you please, please be happy about the baby? And I'll have faith in you. And we'll work out all the other stuff."

He patted her back, drained. "Sure. But, please Mel, don't go calling your father tonight. Okay?"

Her head nodded against his chest. "Uh huh."

She'd end up calling him about the lawyer, sooner than later, Jeremy knew. Once again, Howard Milton would charge to their rescue. And yet again, he, Jeremy Barrett, Royal Fuckup, would roll over and let him. The Miltons always prevailed. None of them thought him important enough to call the shots, himself included. Compared to his own hard-working father, Jeremy felt like a slacker. Compared to Howard Milton—a joke. So he surrendered and stroked Melissa's back, pushing aside the image of Nikki Jordan's lovely face that stole, unbidden, into his mind.

TEN

"OWW!!" EIGHT-YEAR OLD Brandon Jordan screeched as his sister Nikki twisted his arm in an Indian burn. "Nikki, stop!"

His cries brought Mom crashing into Nikki's room. "Nikki, I won't have you bullying your brother again. Let him go this instant."

"But I caught him in here messing with my stuff!" Nikki gave Brandon's arm a final wrench before releasing him. Pouting, he scurried from her room.

"I don't care what he did. I told you, keep your hands to yourself." Her mother turned away, judgment delivered.

Probably in a hurry to get back to her vodka and reality TV. "At least when Dad was here, somebody stuck up for me," Nikki called after her.

Mom's angry face reappeared. "Stuck up for you?" A bitter laugh. "Stuck it to you, and all of us, is more like it."

"Wasn't me he left," Nikki said.

"Really? When's the last time he even phoned you?" Her mother walked off with that parting shot.

"Like you'd know, bitch." Nikki said it under her breath, but not under enough.

"Who do you think you're talking to?" Mom stormed back into the room, got right up in Nikki's face, breath boozy. "You're grounded for the next three days, kiddo. Give me your car keys, right now."

"Maa!" Nikki protested. "How will I get to school?"

Her mother held out her hand for the keys. "Get up an hour early and I'll drop you on the way to work."

"No way!" Nikki fished the keys from her bag and dropped them into her mother's open palm.

"Then walk." Her mom headed out of the room, turning back for one last jab. "Or call your father."

This time Nikki closed the bedroom door before cursing her out. Walking to school sucked, and tomorrow's weather forecast called for cold. Call your father. Very funny. Dad lived in Austin now. But it gave her an idea.

Nikki picked up her phone to make the call, rehearsing the pitch in her mind.

I'm so lonely, Mr. B. I'm taking care of my brother again because my mom went out. And she forgot we were supposed to take my car in for a new battery. And I was wishing…I know I shouldn't ask you…but if you met me and gave me a ride to school tomorrow, I'd get to see you. You wouldn't have to take me right to school, just drop me nearby.

She'd sell it to him. And after that, she'd see about getting even with her mother and brother. Maybe steal Brandon's Game Boy batteries and hide them. And see how much distilled white vinegar she could add to Mom's vodka bottle before the bitch actually noticed. Nobody, but nobody, got to score the winning point against Nikki Jordan.

ELEVEN

"MELISSA, DARLING!" BETH MILTON'S voice trilled through the telephone receiver.

Melissa leaned back against the pillows and stifled a groan. The other side of the bed was empty. She looked at the clock on her night table. "Mom! It's barely nine. What's the matter?"

"I wanted to make sure you were all right."

The way she said it conveyed disapproval of Jeremy, pity for Melissa, distaste for last night's debacle at dinner—or maybe Melissa read too much into the comment. "I'm fine, Mom." She burped. "Just nauseous."

"Oh, sweetheart! What's the matter? Are you having morning sickness?"

"Uh huh."

"Melissa, saltines! They're the best thing for that. Do you have some in the apartment? I'll stop at the supermarket and bring over a box."

Like having a well-meaning locomotive charging through her bedroom. "Mom, I'll be fine. I'll have some dry toast. It'll pass."

"Sweetheart, I had my friend Joyce Robbins scan the local real estate listings. You know how she stays on top of the best areas." Melissa's father might be the real estate professional, but her mother plied the field vicariously, looming over the housing transactions of friends and acquaintances like a carrion bird. "Joyce emailed me half a dozen wonderful possibilities," her mom went on. "We should get out and look at them right away before they're snatched up. How about I pick you up in an hour?"

"Mom, I can't. I have an obstetrician appointment at lunch time." Mentioning the word "lunch" made Melissa's stomach lurch. "Besides, I want to talk with Jeremy before I go looking at any houses."

"Melissa, he's going to have to grow up."

No, she hadn't imagined the disapproval. "What is that supposed to mean?"

"It means—" Beth's tone carried more than a hint of frost. "That if Jeremy doesn't have the ambition it takes to provide properly for you and the baby, then he's hardly in a position to object when—"

"You have no right to say he isn't ambitious!" Melissa protested, as if she hadn't thought the same thing countless times. "Jeremy's a brilliant teacher. He's doing something that matters." At least, until they suspended him. "Why can't you and Dad respect that?"

"Is he doing any writing these days?"

"I—" Her mother's question caught her off guard. "I'm not sure. I think so."

"Has he published one thing since you've been married?"

"Mom, it's not that easy to publish poetry these days."

"And god forbid he should work on something with commercial potential."

Why did she always have to play the referee between her husband and parents? "Mom, I don't want to talk about this now. I have to get ready for my appointment."

"Why don't I drive you there?" her mom asked. "Then we could go look at the houses."

Melissa groaned. "Mom, I told you—"

"All right. But I don't understand why your husband should think there's anything wrong with parents helping a young couple buy a house. I would think that—"

"Mom, I have to go. I'll call you after my appointment." Melissa hung up and groaned again. Pulling the covers up to her chin, she took a couple of deep breaths, letting the oxygen settle her stomach before sitting up and lowering her feet to the floor. Better. She'd make some toast, then shower and get ready for her obstetrician appointment. She reached for the robe she'd left on the floor beside the bed.

"Jeremy?" she called out, heading for the kitchenette. No answer, but on the small table she found a note. Went to work out. Love, J. Okay, exercise was good. If he'd do some writing, look for another job during the suspension, even better. Maybe she'd broach that later.

Melissa heated water and scrounged through the cabinet for a tea bag. Last one in the box. She'd try to remember to get more—ginger tea, perhaps. Good for nausea. She made a mental note to stop at the convenience store for tea and saltines. Melissa wasn't the type to make shopping lists. While the water heated, she slid two slices of whole wheat bread into the toaster.

Jeremy would become more excited about this baby. Ages, she thought, since they'd been truly enthusiastic about something, or looked forward to an event. Their relationship was like a wind-up toy that started at a gay, frenetic pace and gradually, almost imperceptibly, slowed.

They'd been so happy at first. Melissa smiled at a warm memory of the summer in the south of France, where they'd met. She and her two best friends had been doing Cannes in style, enjoying a week at the Ritz-Carlton, bankrolled by their parents—a last fling before Lori's upcoming wedding. Sun and wine had flowed in abundance. The three of them—carefree women in their mid-twenties, two still romantically uncommitted—had worked on their tans and shopped the boutiques by day, and combed the clubs by night. Idyllic. At least until Lori dropped the bombshell about Melissa's father.

The toaster popped and Melissa removed the browned slices. She banished the memory, as she'd done so often over the years. Better to recall meeting Jeremy later that week.

Everything about their romance so implausible. Absurd that Jeremy, fresh out of grad school and broke, should have been anywhere near the Ritz. But that summer, a small inheritance from his grandmother had allowed him a trip to Antibes. Jeremy's buddy Rick had managed to scratch up the airfare, too. They'd taken a jitney to Cannes for the day, treating themselves to the Ritz-Carlton's sumptuous brunch on the beach.

Rick, a hunky jock, more typically Melissa's kind of guy. Jeremy, slight of build and still pale enough that his sandy brown hair had looked darker than his skin. Cute, though. Melissa had come off a couple of relationships with bad boys, which elevated Jeremy's stock. She'd been primed to appreciate a gentle, clever schoolteacher who wrote poetry and nimbly worked his way around her defenses. Jeremy's bashful smile—half sexy, half little boy—stole her heart.

Their banter over brunch that first day had been playful, yet free of barbs. Their first kiss under the warm moonlight that night had surprised her with its heat. Melissa saw Jeremy every blissful day for the rest of that week. What were the odds of two New Jersey-ites from neighboring Union and Essex counties meeting and falling in love on the French Riviera? Clearly meant to be.

And so rich girl had married poor boy.

Melissa chewed and swallowed a mouthful of toast, waiting to see how it sat. When her stomach offered no protest, she went to the refrigerator for a jar of raspberry jelly. She'd endure morning sickness and more if this pregnancy rekindled the love they'd found on that golden beach. Rational or not, she wanted this new hope, clung to it. It scared her less and promised more than the prospect of grad school.

She'd stopped taking her birth control pills to make it happen.

The doorbell rang downstairs and Melissa frowned. Had her mother come over anyway? She pressed the intercom. "Yes?"

"I'm looking for Jeremy Barrett," said an unfamiliar voice. "My name is Leona Price, and I'm with Child Protection and Permanency."

Melissa's pulse raced. The investigation Jeremy talked about. "He's not here right now," she said into the intercom.

"I'm afraid this is quite important," the voice insisted. "May I come up and give you my card?"

"Uh, sure." Filled with foreboding, Melissa buzzed the woman into the building.

TWELVE

UNABLE TO REFUSE NIKKI Jordan, Jeremy sat in his car with her, two scant blocks from the Forrest School, staring into those glacier eyes like a lovesick fool. "Better go," he said. "You'll be late."

She massaged the back of his hand, a feather touch of her index finger, and Jeremy felt heat rise in his groin. "Nikki…" Almost a moan. Crazy to be here, he knew. "Go now," he urged.

She smiled. "Thanks for saving me from the cold. You're the best."

Jeremy pulled away, bereft, as Nikki trotted off. Where to now? Only 8:30 by the dashboard clock. He could have slept in instead of throwing on a pair of sweats, rushing out on a freezing morning and driving to the very place he was prohibited to be. Now Melissa would expect him to come home perspiring from a workout, but Jeremy's head ached, probably from all the wine last night, and the idea of the gym held no appeal.

Coffee, then. Breakfast at the diner. Already becoming a regular there, he thought.

A fried egg with rye toast and two cups of black coffee later, Jeremy felt sufficiently restored to consider going over to lift some weights after all. He tipped the waitress, paid the tab and walked outside. The sun had warmed things up a bit and he took heart. A workout would do him a world of good.

The call from Melissa caught him en route to the gym.

"Hey," he said. "How you doing? You were dead to the world. I didn't want to wake you."

"Jeremy…"

She sounded wide awake now. Serious. Scared. "What's wrong?" he asked.

"A woman from the state—from Child Protection—was here looking for you."

"Jesus." So soon?

"You have to talk with her," Melissa said, "and you absolutely need a lawyer." She drew a breath. "I called my parents."

"Yeah, and…?" Wary, unsure whether to be angry or grateful.

"It's all arranged. So please, don't give me any arguments, Jeremy. My father's attorney, Peter Winkelman, will meet us at my parents'. I already called the woman from Child Protection and told her to come there in half an hour."

Jeremy simmered. Everything orchestrated, just like that, and nobody consulting him. Yet, what choice did he have? "Why at your parents'?"

"Winkelman's idea. Their place makes..." Melissa hesitated. "A different statement than ours."

Hard to argue that, but it still pissed him off. "Mel..."

"Jeremy!" No mistaking the urgency in her voice. "Please, just go, will you?"

He gave up. "On my way."

Melissa's Escape pulled into the circular driveway fronting the Miltons' colonial as Jeremy got out of his Honda. She held out a card to him as they headed up the walkway.

"Here. Her business card. She'll be here any minute."

Jeremy glanced at the official looking card while Melissa opened her parents' massive front door. A short, rotund man in a navy blue suit, dark hair receding from his forehead, approached and held out a hand in greeting as they stepped inside.

"Attorney Peter Winkelman." He pumped Jeremy's hand and motioned toward the living room. "We'll be meeting in there. You can brief me before she gets here."

Jeremy followed him inside and stammered out a hasty summary of his situation. Winkelman listened intently, nodding from time to time, his questions few and to the point.

"Don't worry," he assured Jeremy. "I'll handle it."

"I—we may not be able to afford your fees," Jeremy said. The man's suit looked like it cost more than his monthly take-home pay.

Winkelman shook him off. "I do a lot of work for Howard. The arrangements are taken care of."

Yet again, Jeremy juggled the familiar blend of resentment and abject need that characterized his dealings with his father-in-law. Still processing all of it, he heard the front doorbell and felt the muscles in his neck tense.

Peter Winkelman flashed him a grin that radiated confidence. "We've got this," he said. "Just follow my lead."

THIRTEEN

Jeremy and his lawyer turned as Melissa entered the Miltons' living room, accompanied by a stout, middle-aged African-American woman.

"Is one of you Jeremy Barrett?" the woman asked.

Jeremy gave a nervous nod. "Yes."

"Leona Price. I'm an investigator with the Division of Child Protection and Permanency." She passed him her card. "May I speak with you…" She eyed Winkelman, then Melissa, "…in private?"

"Melissa," Winkelman said, "your parents are in the family room. Perhaps you'd like to join them."

A friendly tone, but it carried weight, Jeremy observed.

With a worried glance at Jeremy, Melissa left.

Winkelman stepped up to shake hands with Ms. Price. "Peter Winkelman." He gave her his card. "I'd like to sit in."

The investigator studied his card and frowned. "You're Mr. Barrett's attorney?"

"A friend of the family." He flashed her a disarming grin. "Please, have a seat." He motioned her toward an armchair, nudged Jeremy onto the sectional sofa, and sat down beside him.

Smooth, Jeremy thought.

As Ms. Price pulled a pen and legal pad out of her tote bag, his attorney reached into his jacket pocket. "Ms. Price, if you don't mind…?" Winkelman's lapis cuff link gleamed a soft blue as he displayed a small voice-activated recorder.

The guy came prepared.

The investigator frowned again. "Mr. Winkelman, you realize this is only an inquiry? No charges have been filed against Mr. Barrett."

The attorney smiled, teeth white and perfect. "Quite so. Jeremy is voluntarily assisting with your inquiry. And we appreciate your accommodating us by coming here." He held up the small recorder, waving it in the direction of her legal pad. "Unfortunately, my handwriting is indecipherable." A rueful chuckle. "My parents always wanted me to go to medical school. This is my way of taking a few notes of my own." He placed the device on the coffee table and switched it on.

Pursing her lips, the investigator gave a nod of assent.

Got her outgunned, Jeremy thought.

Speaking quickly into his recorder, Winkelman noted the date and names of the assembled parties. "For my records."

Leona Price cleared her throat, then glared at the recorder when it activated in response. She fixed her gaze on Jeremy, who felt a twinge of anxiety. "Mr. Barrett, the mother of one of your students has lodged a complaint with the Forrest School principal that you made sexual advances toward her daughter, Heather Lloyd." She turned to a fresh page in her legal pad. "I've conducted a preliminary interview with the student and I would like to hear your version of the situation."

"I never—" Jeremy began.

A discreet hand gesture from Winkelman cut him off. The lawyer turned to Ms. Price. "If I may…?"

She raised her eyebrows. "If you may what?"

"Perhaps you'll allow me to walk Jeremy through his account of the recent events. Then you can ask him your questions."

This must be the "follow my lead" part, Jeremy thought.

Leona Price pursed her lips, then waved a "whatever" assent.

"Jeremy," the lawyer asked, "are you acquainted with this Heather Lloyd?"

Jeremy nodded. Winkelman pointed at the recorder and he said, "Heather's a student in my Advanced Placement English class." He waited for his attorney's next cue.

"How would you assess her caliber as a student?" Winkelman asked.

Jeremy pondered the question. "Well, by definition, everyone in an AP class is good. I'd put Heather in the lower percentile, in terms of her written work."

Winkelman nodded slowly. "I see. Have you had any previous problems with Ms. Lloyd?"

"Problems?" Jeremy echoed. "Actually, yes." He and his lawyer were dancing, he realized. His own job, to follow and avoid stepping on any toes.

"What sort of problems?" Winkelman prodded.

Jeremy contemplated the Oriental rug, composing himself. His in-laws had exquisite taste, even if it wasn't his. "We were studying The Great Gatsby." He described the message he'd found in Heather's paper, and how he'd responded. "Then, yesterday Mr. Donnelly called me in and informed me of Mrs. Lloyd's complaint."

"I see." Winkelman shook his head, grimacing. "And what was your reaction, Jeremy?"

Step, two, three. His lawyer had deftly implied that the complaint was triggered by the incident with Heather's paper. And it was, wasn't it? "I was shocked," Jeremy replied. "Horrified."

The DCPP investigator made no comment, jotting notes on her legal pad.

"Did you at any time speak or act in a manner that might encourage this young woman's infatuation with you?" Winkelman asked.

"Absolutely not," Jeremy said. Sort of, he thought.

"Did you say anything to Ms. Lloyd of a sexual, romantic or suggestive nature—in or out of the classroom?" Winkelman arched his eyebrows, implying the absurdity of such a notion.

"Never." This might turn out all right.

"Did you make any physical contact at all with the young woman?"

"No, never." Jeremy shot a glance at the DCPP worker, still busy writing.

Winkelman gave him a quick nod and turned to Ms. Price. "Any questions?"

She perused her legal pad. "Mr. Barrett, were you in the habit of staring at Heather Lloyd during your class lectures?"

"Of course not." The back of Jeremy's neck prickled. He adjusted his shirt collar.

"So you didn't look at her?" The investigator raised her eyes to Jeremy's face.

"I make eye contact with my students." He forced his gaze to meet Ms. Price's. "You know, try to connect, engage them in discussion." He fidgeted in his seat, caught himself, sat still. "Possibly Heather was—impressionable." Jeremy caught a glimpse of his attorney's eyes narrowing in warning.

"And you never singled out Heather for any special attention—in or out of class?" Ms. Price asked.

Jeremy shook his head. "No."

She contemplated her notes. "Mr. Barrett, did you stroke the back of Ms. Lloyd's neck?"

"No!" Jeremy shouted, aghast.

"Did you pat her on the buttocks as she was walking out of the classroom?"

"What? Never! Did she say I did that?" Christ, he'd never done that to anyone in his whole life.

"Did you encourage Heather's romantic attention in any way?" the investigator asked.

"I did not," Jeremy said.

She lowered her pad and stared at him. "Why do you suppose she made such claims about you?"

"I don't know," he said. "Maybe because—"

"Mr. Barrett is not a psychiatrist, Ms. Price," Winkelman interrupted. "It would hardly be appropriate for him to speculate about the motives of a possibly unstable young woman."

Jeremy let out a breath. Wonderful thing to have a lawyer. He wondered if his father-in-law might let him keep the guy on permanent retainer.

"Now then, Ms. Price, do you require any further assistance from Mr. Barrett with your inquiry?" Winkelman asked.

She shook her head, closing her legal pad. "Not at this time."

Winkelman reached over and turned off the recorder.

The investigator stood. "Thank you Mr. Barrett." A cool nod at the attorney. "Mr. Winkelman."

"What happens now?" Jeremy asked her, drawing another warning look from his lawyer.

She shrugged. "The inquiry will continue."

"But what else will—?"

"Jeremy…" Winkelman cautioned.

Ms. Price chuckled. "You two are mighty smooth. But the fact is, this is an official investigation."

Jeremy's heart sank. It wasn't over yet.

FOURTEEN

"SO!" PETER WINKELMAN TURNED to Jeremy as the DCPP investigator took her leave. "Would you rather debrief with me privately, or shall we invite your family in to join us?"

Jeremy hesitated, debating. "Sure," he said, "bring them in." Nothing to hide. That was the way to go.

Winkelman grinned. "Atta boy! You sit. I'll go get them."

Bingo. Right answer, although Jeremy suspected the attorney merely wanted a bigger audience to hear his take on the meeting. Moments later, Winkelman returned to the living room with Melissa and her parents. Melissa took a seat next to Jeremy on the sectional, while her parents settled into two armchairs. Winkelman headed for the other end of the sofa and perched on the arm. They all looked up at him expectantly.

"Well?" Howard Milton demanded.

"I think you can all put your minds at ease," Winkelman declared. He turned to Jeremy, arching an eyebrow. "Unless you're expecting any surprise witnesses to come forth to corroborate the girl's allegations…?"

Jeremy shook his head. "Impossible."

"Well, then." Winkelman shrugged. "There's nothing to support her charges. Obviously the girl projected her romantic fantasies onto Jeremy, then lied to save face." He reached over to collect his tape recorder from the table and replaced it in his jacket pocket. "Who knows? Her mother may have egged her on. I've seen it happen. But now DCPP will conduct an intensive interview with the girl—without Mama present." The corners of his mouth curled. "You think the girl will stick to her story in the face of that?"

Melissa clutched Jeremy's hand. "Mr. Winkelman, do you think this will go to trial?"

"I highly doubt that." The attorney sniffed. "It takes a psychopathic liar to stand up under cross examination. Think your girl is ready for that, Jeremy?"

"No." Jeremy felt an unexpected wave of pity for Heather, picturing Winkelman grilling her on the stand.

"I'll tell you, Peter." Howard Milton leaned forward and spoke up in his usual tone of authority. "I'm wondering if we might have grounds for a slander suit."

Winkelman rubbed his chin thoughtfully. "Could be, Howard. I'll have one of my private investigators nose around. See if he can dig up anything on the Lloyds."

"Why would you do that?" Jeremy blurted out, unnerved by the notion of a private detective sniffing anywhere in his vicinity.

"Oh." The lawyer waved a hand dismissively. "You never know. Sometimes you find a pattern of allegations with people like this. You'd be surprised." He chuckled. "'Let he who is without sin,' huh?"

"Good point, Peter." Howard nodded.

"Please." Jeremy cringed. "Can we hold off on doing anything like that? I mean, you sounded like you thought things were under control, Mr. Winkelman."

"Peter," Winkelman corrected. "Might as well give it to the end of this week, see what happens."

"Well, I think this whole thing is simply too awful for words." Beth Milton shuddered. "The idea of my daughter having to go through this in her condition…"

"Mom!" Melissa broke in. "Please! It's a little early to start announcing it!"

Winkelman shot a quizzical glance at Howard.

Here it comes, Jeremy thought.

Howard beamed. "We're expecting our first grandchild."

"Well now!" Winkelman smacked his own thigh hard enough to make Jeremy wince. "Congratulations! Wonderful news." He bounded over to pump Howard's hand. "Don't worry. I won't let anyone spoil this happy time for you folks." Moving on to Beth Milton, the lawyer leaned down to kiss her cheek, then crossed over to buss Melissa. He completed his rounds by giving Jeremy's hand a hearty squeeze. "It'll be fine, son."

Did they all have to call him that? Jeremy nodded, carried out to sea by a huge wave of helplessness.

"Jeremy, Melissa," Beth said, "why don't you two stay for dinner?"

Even if Jeremy had any appetite, the prospect of a second dinner with his in-laws in as many days would have killed it. "Melissa and I should be getting home," he said. Catching sight of his father-in-law glowering, he realized how ungrateful he must sound. He walked over to Howard. "Sir, thank you for—for everything. And, uh—about last night…"

Howard clapped him on the shoulder, a bit too hard. "Don't mention it, son. You've had a lot thrown at you the past couple of days. But we'll get you back on track."

They shook hands, as if they'd just wrapped up a business deal.

"Melissa," Beth said, "why don't you ride home with Jeremy and leave your car here overnight? I'll pick you up in the morning and we can go see those houses. Then you can drive home from here."

"Houses?" Jeremy frowned. That again?

Melissa clutched his arm and pulled him toward the door. "We'll talk about it on the way home."

"Right," he said under his breath. He turned to the attorney. "Mr.—uh, Peter, I really appreciate…"

"Don't give it a thought, son." Winkelman smoothed his jacket and shot his cuffs.

As he walked out with Melissa, Jeremy heard Howard say, "Peter, stay and have a drink. There's something I'd like to discuss with you."

Later, he'd remember those words.

FIFTEEN

"DAMMIT, NO!" JEREMY POUNDED the steering wheel. "There's not gonna be any slander suit, Mel. Forget it."

"I don't understand!" she protested. "Why are you letting her get away with—"

"For crying out loud! Give it a rest. She's a mixed-up, hormonal kid."

"What about her mother?" Melissa demanded. "She at least should know better than—"

"I said, drop it!" The tires squealed as Jeremy braked hard for the traffic light at the bottom of the steep hill below their garden apartment complex. "I'm not suing anyone."

Melissa folded her arms and turned away.

The light turned green and he drove up the hill, taking a right into their development. He found a space, pulled in and turned off the engine. He looked over at Melissa, who stared ahead in sullen silence.

"Mel…" He broke off.

"What?"

"Nothing." Jeremy massaged his forehead, a headache starting.

"You know," Melissa said, "you haven't asked a single question about my obstetrician appointment. Not even when my due date is."

Her hectoring tone set Jeremy's teeth on edge. "So? When is it?"

"Do you actually give a fuck?"

"Christ, Mel!" Jeremy exploded. "I've had a few other things to deal with, in case you didn't notice." He took a breath. "Are you going to tell me the damned due date, or not?"

Melissa reached for the handle of her door. "Call the doctor and find out for yourself!"

"Melissa!"

She sprang from the car and stalked off toward their building.

Jeremy rubbed his forehead again and opened his door. Melissa had already entered the vestibule. He trotted up the walk and caught up with her mounting the stairs to their apartment. Hadn't they played out this stupid scenario only yesterday?

"Has it occurred to you," he said, following her up, "that I'm having the worst two days of my life?"

At the top of the stairs, Melissa pulled out her key and turned to him, sneering. "It's always about you."

"Wha-at?" He froze, halfway up the flight.

"My mother wanted to show me houses today. Houses they offered to buy for us, Jeremy! For us and our child!"

"Oh, hell!"

Melissa's voice got that put-upon tone he hated. "And I didn't let her. You know why? Because I was afraid you'd be upset!"

"I would have been."

"You, you, you!" she cried. "That's exactly what I'm talking about! Why do you have to make it such a big deal? Lots of parents buy their kids houses."

He let out a bitter laugh. "Yeah, but with yours there's always a catch. They fucking own us, Mel."

"That's not true!"

"Look," he said, "can we not argue about this on the stairs?"

"I don't want to talk to you at all!" Melissa fumbled with her key, agitation making her clumsy.

"Fine," Jeremy fumed. "Then don't. I'm going for a walk." He ran back down the stairs.

A blast of cold wind hit his face the moment he stepped outside, giving him second thoughts. He shivered. The temperature was dropping. Would winter never end?

Or this lousy week?

He pulled the car key from his jacket pocket. Better a drive than a walk in this cold. He got in the car, started it up, then sat, letting the engine idle.

Where was he going?

The gas gauge showed under a quarter tank. He'd go fuel up while he figured out his next move. He was drowning. Why didn't he have any say over the course of his own future? No one bothered to ask whether he'd like to be a father or a homeowner. Nobody would ask. Along for the ride, that's what he was.

As usual.

His thoughts drifted back to Nikki in his car that morning—her wide, blue eyes gazing into his. Why couldn't they have met when he was free to love her?

He pulled into the gas station and up to the pump. When he lowered the window, the attendant said, "Vrong zide," his accent so thick that he had to repeat it three times before Jeremy realized he'd parked with the gas cap facing away from the pump. With an abashed apology, he restarted the engine and maneuvered around to the other side of the pump. He passed the attendant his credit card and closed the window. On a day this cold, Jeremy appreciated New Jersey's ban on self service. Pumping your own gas might be a rite of manhood, but he preferred to stay warm.

Again he thought of Nikki.

She wouldn't have wanted him back then. None of the pretty girls ever had, Melissa the exception. He'd been so awkward, always self-conscious. Jeremy doubted Mel would have given him a second glance if they'd met under more mundane circumstances. A miracle she'd chosen him over Rick that summer in France.

They all chose his friend Rick.

Jeremy had been his wingman. Women only ever paid attention to Jeremy in hopes of getting next to his buddy. He grimaced, remembering a cruel case in point. What was her name? Catherine? Slender, long dark hair. The prototype of Nikki.

Bile choked his throat. Catherine, or whatever-her-name, had been all over him at that party. He'd crashed the event along with Rick—wouldn't have dared brazen his way in there except with Rick. Big house, nice furniture. Way better neighborhood than his own, or Rick's. In no time at all, girls had surrounded Rick, as if he emitted pheromones.

But that night, Catherine had clung to Jeremy's side. She'd allowed him to fetch beers for her, leaned into him, and laughed at his lame jokes. Touched him when she talked. He'd floated through that evening in a haze.

The spell was broken when she gave Jeremy her phone number as she left with her girlfriend. "Tell your pal to give me a call," she'd said, borrowing Jeremy's pen to scribble her number on the back of his hand.

He scrubbed it off in the bathroom as soon as she'd left, wishing he could wash away his humiliation along with the ink.

A rap on the car window snapped Jeremy back to the present. He lowered it and took his credit card and receipt from the attendant. He pulled out of the gas station, filled with gloom. Where the hell to now?

Home, he realized with a sinking heart. Nowhere else to go. He had no job, no income. His future rested in the hands of a lawyer paid for by his father-in-law. Jeremy had no choice, no vote.

Craving the balm of Nikki's voice, he pulled over and took out his cell phone, but settled for her voicemail. "It's me," he said. "Call me later. If you want, I mean," he added, as if that made it better.

SIXTEEN

"HEATHER!"

Her music blasting, Heather had missed her mother's perfunctory rap on the door. When her mom materialized at her bedside, Heather nearly jumped. Still that edgy.

She yanked out her ear buds. "What is it?" The look on mom's face told her something was up.

"I just got off the phone with that woman from Protective Services," her mother replied.

The pit of Heather's stomach chilled.

"We're going to have to talk with them again tomorrow."

Heather's gut emitted an ominous growl. "She's coming back here?"

Mom shook her head. "No, we have to go there. To the DCPP office."

"All the way to Trenton?" Heather had never even been down there, but knew that was where all the state offices were.

"No, the local office, in Cranford."

"Oh." Heather wrinkled her forehead. "Why do we have to go there?"

"I have no idea." Her mother rested a hand on the doorknob. "She said it's the usual procedure." She sniffed. "Whatever that means. Honestly, you'd think I answered enough of that woman's questions after you ran out of the room yesterday."

Heather caught the rebuke in that remark.

"Anyway," her mother added, "we have to be there at ten."

"But what about school?"

"You'll be excused. They'll give you an official note."

"Ohhh," Heather said. This sounded serious.

"Listen," her mother went on, "your father is going to be late tonight. You want to wait and have dinner at seven thirty, when he gets home? Or should I make you something earlier?"

"Seven thirty, I guess," Heather mumbled. All this going on and yet her father couldn't even bother catching an early train. "I'm not really hungry, Mom."

"Okay, then." Her mother started to close the door behind her, then turned back. "Oh, I almost forgot. That investigator said you'll have to be examined by their doctor."

"Huh?" Heather looked up, startled. "How come?"

Her mother shrugged. "Procedures. Who knows? Maybe they'll find some of that horrible man's DNA on you." She shut the door without waiting for a response.

Heather gulped. This whole thing kept getting worse. Desperate for moral support, she picked up her iPhone. "Hey!" she said when Nikki answered. "Want to come over? Crazy stuff going on."

"About time you called," Nikki replied. "Be there in ten."

As she ended the call, Nikki's phone chirped to announce a voicemail. She played back Jeremy's brief message and smiled. She'd call him later, after she got the scoop from Heather. She slipped on her shoes and headed out the door. Good thing Heather lived within walking distance, since Mom had taken her car keys.

Twenty minutes later she sat in Heather's bedroom, poking a finger at her pet guinea pig in greeting. "Cute. What's his name, again?"

"Pretzels," Heather said.

"That what you feed him?" Nikki made a clucking sound at the fluffy rodent, which sniffed her finger.

"Nah. He mostly eats lettuce."

Nikki eyed Heather's round midsection. "Guess you're the one who eats the pretzels, huh?"

Heather flushed. "Not so much."

"So what's the story?" Nikki demanded, cutting to the chase.

"It's—complicated." Perched on her bed, Heather drew up her knees to her chin, resembling a teenage fortress.

Sprawled beside her, Nikki stared with distaste at her friend's fuzzy, five-toed red socks. Such a dork. If not for her tech skills, Nikki wouldn't waste her time on Heather. "Look, you called me over here. Will you kindly tell me WTF is going on?"

Heather slumped forward, lowering her face to her knees. "It's embarrassing."

"All right, I get it!" Nikki snapped. "It's complicated and embarrassing. Want me to make it easier for you?" She sat up and stared Heather in the face. "It has something to do with Mr. B, right? And your paper." Nikki smirked as Heather's face turned red. "So how about you pick it up from there?"

Heather gulped. "I wrote some stuff on my Gatsby paper." She spoke without looking up from her knees. "And Mr. B gave me a crappy grade."

"What did you write?"

"Some stuff about him." Heather hesitated. "And me."

Nikki snorted. "Get out! Let me see."

Heather looked up, her eyes like saucers. "What? My paper?"

"Show me." Nikki stared at her, stone-faced.

A command from an alpha girl—the only one who'd ever deigned to notice her—and Heather had no business refusing. Biting her lip, she lowered her feet to the floor, and scooted over to her desk. Retrieving the paper, she returned and reluctantly passed it to Nikki.

Her blue eyes revealing only boredom, Nikki scanned Heather's essay until she hit pay dirt. A half-smile curled her lips. In a loud, melodramatic voice, she read, *"I'm waiting for your green light to shine for me, Mr. B."* She hooted. *"Not consistent with acceptable standards of scholarship."* Nikki chuckled. "Doesn't look like he was too impressed." She looked up at Heather, who averted her gaze. "Why'd you write this stuff?"

Heather shrugged. "I dunno. I thought…" Her voice trailed off.

Nikki rolled up the essay and bopped Heather on the head with it. "You thought what?"

"I thought he had a thing for me."

"A thing for you?" Nikki echoed. The nerve of this twit! "What gave you that idea?"

"It's —he looked over at me in class a lot. And I had this feeling…" Heather drew a breath. "Anyway, then my mother saw the paper."

"You let her see it?" Nikki drawled. The girl was positively feeble. "God, Heather! Why'd you do that?"

"She always looks at my grades."

Heather reached over for her paper and Nikki drew back her arm, keeping it out of her grasp. "So then what happened?"

Heather's empty hand dropped into her lap. "I had to tell her something. I explained about him looking at me, but she kept asking 'What else? What else?' So I sort of—added some stuff."

"About Mr. B? What kind of stuff?" Nikki demanded.

Heather mumbled a reply.

"What? What did you say he did, Heather?" Nikki leaned forward, practically in her face.

"I said he touched me."

Nikki stared at her in silence. Un-fucking-believable.

"And then my mom e-mailed the principal." When Nikki still didn't reply, Heather added, "So now there's this Protective Services investigation going on." Her eyes welled up. "And I have to go there tomorrow. They're even gonna have a doctor examine me. God, Nikki, I don't know what to do!" A sob broke from her throat.

Nikki shook her head. "You really screwed up, kiddo. Big time."

Heather cried, wiping snot from her face with her sleeve.

"You know, you got Mr. B into all kinds of trouble." Disdain filled Nikki's voice. "And he's a really popular teacher, too."

"I know," Heather mewled.

Nikki ruffled the pages of Heather's paper, letting her stew for a while. "Boy, I'd hate to be in your shoes if this stuff got out there—say, on Facebook." Heather's look of horror told Nikki she'd scored a direct hit.

"Facebook! Why would this get onto Facebook?"

Nikki's eyebrows rose in mock innocence. "Oh, you never know. But if people found out you made up stuff about Mr. B, and ruined his reputation..." She trailed off, letting Heather imagine the awful consequences. To make sure, she added, "People will think you were totally desperate for attention or something, Heather. You know, not everyone is as understanding as I am."

Now in for the kill.

"I can tell you this..." Nikki paused for effect. "None of the other girls would ever speak to you." I'll see they don't, she mentally added.

"Oh, god, Nikki!" Heather wailed. "What should I do?"

Nikki crumpled up Heather's paper and tossed it onto the bed, with a tsk! of disapproval. "I don't know, Heather. But if I were you?" She stared into Heather's wide, frightened eyes. "I'd think twice about what I told that investigator tomorrow."

SEVENTEEN

JEREMY PULLED INTO THE development, nearly dark now, and parked. He looked around for Melissa's Ford Escape. A gift from her parents for her last birthday, the sight of it never failed to annoy him. But now, unable to find it, Jeremy worried. Had she returned to her parents' house? Then he remembered: Melissa had left her car there.

Relief was instantly replaced by the thought that she'd called her father to come get her. That scenario posed more drama and grief than Jeremy knew what to do with. Anxious now, he hurried up to the second-level apartment.

He tried the door. Locked. Reached for his key. As he inserted it into the lock, the door jerked open. He stared into the swollen, tear-streaked face of his pregnant wife, whom he'd left alone while he'd gone off mooning after a teenage girl.

"Mel!" Flooded with a mix of guilt and relief, he reached for her. "Honey, I'm sorry I acted like such a jerk."

She buried her face against his shoulder, sniffling. "You frightened me—leaving like that." Her voice sounded high and strained, like a scared little girl's. He felt touched, even if her erratic hormones might be the cause.

"Shhh. I know." He stroked her thick brown hair, smoothing the messy waves. "I shouldn't have left you alone without your car." He nuzzled her ear, surprised by his feelings of tenderness. "Especially now."

"Oh, Jeremy!" Melissa turned her head, dampening his neck with fresh tears. "I'm sorry I was such a bitch. You've been going through hell and all I did was make it worse with my princess-y crap. I'm sorry. I got scared. If you're not with me on having this baby, then I can't—" She broke off. "I don't know what I'll do."

"Shhh." He drew her closer. She needed him. How long since that had happened? A twinge of arousal awoke in him. "I'm right here," he said, voice husky. "I'm in this with you, Mel."

She squeezed him, then pulled back from his embrace and gazed at him with red, puffy eyes. "I shouldn't have pressured you about those houses. This isn't the time to think about that, is it?"

He flashed her a grateful smile. "Not the ideal day."

"Okay." A smile. "Discussion tabled."

"Thanks." He exhaled. He felt lighter, almost giddy with relief and gratitude. And suddenly ravenously hungry. "Speaking of tables—is there anything to eat?"

"Huh!" Her grin widened and she rumpled his hair. "I'll see what I can do."

As she turned toward their tiny kitchen, sink piled high with dishes, a wave of desire swept through Jeremy. He caught Melissa's arm and drew her to him, his other hand already tugging at his jacket buttons. "If our baby wouldn't mind, maybe twenty minutes from now would be even better."

She giggled and yanked her sweater over her head. He took in the sight of her breasts, already fuller, rounder. Perhaps not small and perfect, as Nikki's might be, but Jeremy got hard looking at them. His jacket dropped to the floor beside Melissa's sweater.

Later, in the darkness, Melissa asleep beside him, Jeremy lay awake, uttering a silent prayer to the cosmos, since he didn't believe in a god. Please. Please make this thing with Heather go away. Spare me and I promise to be good.

His cellphone chirped on the night table beside him. Rather than disturb Melissa, Jeremy scooped up the phone and tiptoed into the bathroom. He closed the door and turned on the light.

A text from Nikki:

It'll be OK. Trust me.

A sign?

PART TWO

"She wasn't able to endure being at a disadvantage and, given this unwillingness, I suppose she had begun dealing in subterfuges when she was very young…"

—F. Scott Fitzgerald, *The Great Gatsby*

EIGHTEEN

HEATHER SAT BESIDE HER mother in the waiting area of the Division of Child Protection and Permanency office the next morning, playing out the options in her mind. None of them good. Admit she'd lied about Mr. B and face the wrath of her mother, DCPP, the Forrest School and maybe the law. Or keep lying and go viral as an untouchable among her peers.

She chewed a fingernail. Her mother glanced at her, then took hold of Heather's hand and pulled it away from her mouth. Mrs. Lloyd lowered her daughter's hand to her own lap and held it tightly. Until that moment, Heather hadn't realized her mother was nearly as nervous as she was. Had Mom guessed she'd lied?

The clatter of footsteps coming down the hall preceded the appearance of a woman—kind of old, but pretty cool-looking. Cropped gray hair framed a friendly, lined face. She wore large, turquoise earrings, a long black skirt and a print tunic top.

She approached and extended her hand, first to Mrs. Lloyd, then Heather. "I'm Sylvia Wolfe, a social worker here. Thank you both for coming this morning."

Like they'd had a choice.

Mrs. Wolfe smiled at her. "Please come inside."

Heather stood, her legs rubbery. Her mother got up, too.

"Oh, not you, Mrs. Lloyd," Mrs. Wolfe said. "I'm going to need to talk with Heather alone."

Alone? She hadn't expected that.

"I'd prefer to sit in while you talk with my daughter," Mrs. Lloyd declared.

Mrs. Wolfe regarded her coolly. "I'm afraid that's not possible."

"Why can't I?"

"I'm sorry," Mrs. Wolfe told her mother, "but that's the law in these situations. If you'll please have a seat, I'll talk with you afterwards, Mrs. Lloyd."

Her mother clenched her jaw and sat back down.

"This way, Heather." Mrs. Wolfe headed toward a door at the end of the hall and Heather followed, casting a helpless glance back over her shoulder at her mother. Mrs. Wolfe led her down a corridor lined with offices. When she stopped in front of an open door, Heather nearly crashed into her.

With a slight smile, she motioned Heather into the room. "Please take a seat."

This was it. A roaring sound filled Heather's ears as she entered the room, as if she were passing beneath a waterfall. Mrs. Wolfe followed her inside and closed the door behind them.

Heather's eyes darted around the office, taking in the minimal furnishings. A desk over by the window. A table in the center of the room, with two chairs. Pens and a notepad on the table, along with a carafe of water and a stack of plastic tumblers.

"Have a seat, Heather," Mrs. Wolfe repeated. "Would you like some water?"

Heather nodded, her throat too dry for speech. She pulled a the chair away from the table and sank into it. Mrs. Wolfe passed her a glass of water. Heather gulped down too much too fast and coughed.

"You okay?" The social worker looked at her as she sat down in the opposite chair.

"Uh huh." Heather inhaled, patting her chest. The spasm passed. She sipped more water, slowly this time. Mrs. Wolfe filled a second glass for herself.

"Um." Heather cleared her throat.. "I—uh—already told that other investigator everything yesterday."

"Yes, I spoke with her," Mrs. Wolfe said. "That was a preliminary interview. Today we'll need to cover some other things."

More stuff? Heather's pulse raced. What if they made her take a lie detector test, or something? She eyed the social worker. So far the woman had been friendly and nice, which made Heather feel bad about lying to her. Her mom always insisted she tell the truth. But mom wasn't here now, which meant Heather needed to think for herself. She had limited experience with that.

"All right." Mrs. Wolfe smiled at her. "I'm going to ask you some questions. Please answer as best you can."

"Uh huh," Heather mumbled. Her heart pounded really hard. Maybe she'd go into cardiac arrest or something. They'd have to stop the interview for that, wouldn't they? They'd have to get her mother. She took a breath, trying to calm down.

"Heather, can you tell me today's date?"

"Huh?" Didn't this woman have a phone, or calendar? Heather stammered out the date.

"Can you tell me where we are?"

What kind of retarded question was that? Maybe a trick? "We're at the DYFS office—oh!—I mean the Division of, uh, Child Protection." That must have been the trick, to see if she remembered the name change.

"Can you name the President of the United States?" Mrs. Wolfe asked.

Did the woman think *she* was retarded?

The social worker continued asking weird, dumb questions. Heather had to spell a word backwards and hoped she'd gotten it right. No, she didn't hear voices in her head. She began to wonder if one of them was crazy when Mrs. Wolfe shifted gears.

"Tell me about yourself," she said. "How do you like to spend your time?"

Heather shrugged. "I dunno. Doing stuff on the computer. You know, games, Facebook. Listening to music."

"Mmm hmm. Do you like school?" the social worker asked.

"It's okay, I guess."

"Tell me about your school."

Heather hesitated. "It's kind of hard. The classes, I mean. The school's pretty expensive, my parents said." She made a face. "It's supposed to help us get into a good college. Harvard, or something."

Mrs. Wolfe regarded her. "Is that what you want?"

"Sure. I guess."

The social worker asked her some more strange, pointless questions. Becoming more bored than scared, Heather jerked back to full attention when Mrs. Wolfe asked: "When did you begin to feel uncomfortable with Mr. Barrett's behavior toward you?"

Heather took another sip of water. "Umm, around the time we started studying The Great Gatsby in class, I guess."

"How long ago was that?"

"A few weeks." Heather thought for a moment. "Around the end of last month."

"What was it that made you uncomfortable?"

What should she say? "Like I told the other lady yesterday, Mr. B kept looking at me when he was talking to the class." He had, hadn't he? Heather wrung her hands in her lap. Her palms felt sweaty.

"When you say he looked at you, Heather, can you describe how? What was his expression?"

"I dunno." Heather reached for her water glass again. Empty. She spun the glass around on the table, wanting something to do with her clammy hands. "Like, I'd look up from the book, or my notes, and see him staring. Sometimes he'd be kind of smiling."

"Smiling at you?"

Heather looked away. "Yeah."

The social worker paused. "And what did you do?"

Heather shrugged. "Nothing, really."

"Did you smile back at him?"

Her face felt warm. Had she? "No. I don't remember."

"How did you feel when he did that?" Mrs. Wolfe sounded curious.

"I don't know. Weird."

"Weird, how, Heather?" The social worker looked at her intently, like she wanted to understand. People seldom looked at her that way.

"Embarrassed, I guess." No, more than that. She swallowed. "Kind of flattered."

"Flattered?" Mrs. Wolfe echoed.

"I mean..." Heather slumped in her chair. "There's lots of prettier girls in the class." She winced in embarrassment. "You know?"

"I understand how that is." Mrs. Wolfe's eyes softened. "So when Mr. Barrett looked at you, did it make you feel—special?"

"Kinda." That was true. No nice-looking guy had ever noticed her before. She'd been scared, but excited, too. And now it was all over. Everything was ruined. A wave of sadness washed over her.

"What is it, Heather?" Mrs. Wolfe asked in a soft voice.

Heather's lip trembled. "I—I thought he liked me."

The investigator nodded slowly. "So you wrote that note to him? On your paper?"

"Yeah." Heather wiped her eyes. So much longing, such hope when she'd written those words. She'd never done something that brave before. Tears blurred her vision. "But I was wrong," she whispered, dropping her gaze to the table. "I got it wrong." She sensed the social worker's eyes on her and looked up. The sympathy in the woman's face made her tears flow even harder. "I'm sorry," Heather murmured, covering her streaming eyes. "I'm really sorry."

Mrs. Wolfe's chair rasped against the carpet. A moment later she returned and placed a box of tissues on the table in front of her.

"Thanks." Heather pulled out a tissue and wiped her eyes, then took two more and blew her nose.

"Heather?"

"Yes, ma'am?" She wadded up the tissues in her hand.

"Did Mr. Barrett ever touch you?"

The social worker asked the question in a matter-of-fact way that made it somehow more powerful than all the drama from Heather's mother. She couldn't bear to meet the woman's eyes. "No." Enough lying. She sucked at it, anyway.

"Did he ask you to touch him?"

"No." Heather took a breath. Finally enough air reached her lungs.

"Did he ever ask you to meet him outside of class?"

"No," Heather admitted. "He never did any of that." At least, maybe Nikki and the other girls wouldn't be her enemies, now that she wasn't getting Mr. B into trouble.

"So you made up those things you told your mother about Mr. Barrett."

Her mother! Maybe the girls at school would spare her, but what would mom do? Heather lowered her eyes. "Am I going to be arrested?"

"No, Heather. What you did was seriously wrong," Mrs. Wolfe said. "I think you know that. The important thing is that you're telling the truth now. You got Mr. Barrett into terrible trouble."

"I'm sorry! I really am." Tears ran down her cheeks. "Honest, I never did anything like that before. I know it was wrong." She raised imploring eyes to Mrs. Wolfe. "I freaked out when my mom saw my paper. I—I told her all that stuff so she wouldn't get mad at me."

"What does she do when she gets mad at you, Heather?"

"Nothing, really." Heather squirmed in her chair.

"Does she punish you?"

"You mean, like hit me or something?" Heather shook her head. "Oh, no, never. Neither of my parents does anything like that."

"I'm glad to hear it," Mrs. Wolfe said. "Tell me, Heather, what's your father like? I haven't met him."

Heather shrugged. "Busy. He works really hard."

"I see," Mrs. Wolfe said. "So, what does your mother do when she's unhappy with you?"

Heather's hands rose to her temples. It hurt to think about the question. "If she's really mad?" She lowered her hands, shading her eyes. "She—um—makes me write her a letter."

Mrs. Wolfe frowned. "What do you mean?"

"I have to write an apology—by hand, no email or anything—and say exactly what I did wrong." Heather's face flushed. "And how come I did it." The rest of her words came out in a rush. "And if she doesn't like what I wrote? I have to do it over again." Shame burned her face. "She keeps all my letters in this binder."

The social worker remained silent. When Heather dared look up to meet her eyes, she saw sorrow in them. "I see," Mrs. Wolfe said.

Suddenly aware of all she'd revealed to the woman, Heather's eyes widened in dismay. "Oh, god," she exclaimed. "Are you going to tell my mom I said all that stuff?"

"No, Heather." Mrs. Wolfe smiled. "That won't be necessary. What I will do is see about getting you some help."

NINETEEN

THROUGH HER OPEN BEDROOM door, Heather heard her parents' raised voices coming from the kitchen. Arguing about her.

"They agreed to leave her in the class, but I actually think we should take her out of that school altogether!" Her mother's voice, shrill as a dentist's drill. "Those girls are a bad influence."

"What's the evidence of that?" Her father, as usual, the logical one.

"She's never done this kind of thing before! Lying? Writing love notes to teachers?"

Alone in her room, Heather burned with shame.

"She was never sixteen before."

She smiled a little, in spite of her distress. Nice of dad to say that.

"And I still don't trust that English teacher, either." Her mom's voice grated, nails on a blackboard. "We should change schools."

"Out of the question." Her father assumed his I'm-The-Breadwinner-Here tone. "She's in the best private school in this area. You want to jeopardize her college applications?"

"No, but—"

"Listen to me. You think the Forrest School is going to refund her tuition under these circumstances? You know how hard I worked for that money? She stays there, period. End of discussion."

Silence for a few moments, then her mother's voice. "We have to punish her."

Heather's spirits sank.

"Have you done anything yet?" Her father sounded tired.

"She's writing him a letter of apology."

"Another one of your letters." Getting annoyed, Heather thought. Probably hadn't had his drink yet. "Please," he said, "no major rewrites for a change."

Yay, Dad! He so rarely used his authority on her behalf.

"Do you want to be the one to check it over?" Mom demanded.

"Not really. But don't get into a big thing with her about it, okay?"

"Fine!" her mother snapped. "But no way is she getting a car for her birthday after this."

"All right," her father said. "Whatever."

So much for his sticking up for her. She should have known.

"And just so you know…" That was Mom, trying to get the last word. "You're going to have to pay for her to see a therapist."

"The insurance will cover it." A pause. "Does she really have to do that?"

"The woman at Protective Services said they wouldn't pursue charges if she does."

"All right. Find her a therapist, then."

"She said we should all go for family therapy, too." Her mother said it like an accusation. Maybe Heather wasn't the only one who wanted more of Dad's attention.

Her father sniffed. "Are you crazy? Someone around here needs to work for a living. You go, if you're so keen on the idea."

Heather hoped that wouldn't happen. Ice cubes clinked into a glass.

"Maybe a shrink can help her make some friends," her father said.

I wish.

"So, what's for dinner?" he asked.

Softly, so they wouldn't hear, Heather closed her bedroom door. Pretzels scurried around his cage, eager for her attention. She opened the cage and removed him, snuggling the soft guinea pig to her chest.

"You're my friend, right?" she crooned. "Even if I don't get a car." She stroked the animal's silken fur. "And you'll forgive me for what I did to Mr. B, won't you, Pretzels?"

TWENTY

FOUR DAYS INTO HIS suspension, Jeremy had taken to sleeping late, a consequence of restless nights and a way to kill off most of the morning. At first he'd put on a cheery façade, offering to whip up pancakes or omelets for brunch, until Melissa's ashen-faced refusals made it clear he'd be on his own for such fare. Jeremy cleaned the kitchen after he cooked, hoping that Mel might follow his example and straighten up the living room, strewn with her discarded clothing. By tacit agreement, they'd steered clear of such charged topics as houses, suspensions and lawsuits.

Without work to occupy him, images of Nikki suffused his mind. He'd been inspired to write a few lines about glaciers and fire, the first poetry Jeremy had written in ages. Today, with Melissa out grocery shopping, he opened the file in his laptop and reread the poem he'd been working on. Not half bad. He tinkered with it until Melissa's key turned in the door.

"Hon?" She opened the door, a brown bag filled with groceries cradled in one arm. "Can you get the other bags?"

"Uh, sure." Closing the file, Jeremy trotted downstairs and out into the cold, without a jacket. The Escape's trunk stood open, and he reached in for the two remaining bags. Shivering, he closed the trunk with an elbow.

His principal, Mr. Donnelly, stood on the sidewalk in front of him.

Startled, Jeremy lost his grip on one of the bags, which slid to the ground. He regained his hold, but not before a loaf of bread and a package of toilet paper slipped out.

Mr. Donnelly bent to pick them up. "Help you with that?" He reached for one of the bags.

"Huh? Yeah, thanks." What the hell was Donnelly doing on his doorstep? Jeremy handed him the bag, then relieved the principal of the bread and toilet paper, replacing them in the sack. "Uh—sir, what brings you here?"

"We need to talk." Donnelly angled his head toward the apartment building.

Too cold to argue. "It's upstairs," Jeremy said.

"Lead on!" The principal sounded jovial, like they were embarking on an adventure together.

Jeremy led the way upstairs. "Mel?" he called out, opening the door. "We have company!" He hoped she still had her clothes on. She tended to shed them and walk around half naked. Jeremy reached for the groceries Donnelly held. "Please, have a seat while I take these into the kitchen."

The principal passed him the bag and glanced over at the living room. Jeremy flushed with embarrassment. Melissa's clothing covered half the sofa and her sneakers lay in the middle of the floor. Magazines and dirty glasses littered the coffee table. She'd promised to clean up. Should he take the bags into the kitchen, or drop them and tidy up? Before he committed to either course, Melissa appeared from the kitchen—still clothed, thank god.

"Jeremy?" She stared at their uninvited guest. "Oh. Hello."

Holding the groceries, Jeremy gestured introductions with a tilt of his head: "My wife, Melissa. My principal, Mr. Donnelly."

"A pleasure, Mrs. Barrett." Donnelly shook Mel's hand.

"Here, Mel." Jeremy passed her the bags. "Why don't you put these away while we talk in here?"

Hoisting the heavy bags, she asked: "Can I get you something to drink, Mr. Donnelly? Some coffee, or water?"

"No, I'm fine, thanks."

As Melissa left the room, Jeremy scooped up her discarded clothing and dropped everything into a heap at the side of the sofa. He kicked her sneakers off to the side. No time to do anything about the coffee table.

"Would you like to sit down?" he asked the principal. "Can I take your coat?"

Donnelly held up a hand. "No need. I won't stay long." He lowered himself onto the sofa.

Jeremy removed some books from a chair, put them on the floor, and sat, waiting for the principal to explain why he'd come.

Mr. Donnelly leaned back, running a hand through his thinning hair. "Jeremy, I've had a call from the Protective Services people."

Jeremy caught his breath. God, what now?

"I wanted to come and tell you face-to-face," the principal continued. "Heather Lloyd has recanted her accusations against you. The investigation has been closed."

Jeremy sat, frozen, as if the news were a mirage that might vanish if he moved.

"I'm sure DCPP will get in touch with you directly," Mr. Donnelly went on. He pulled a handkerchief from his jacket pocket, removed his glasses and began cleaning them as he spoke. "It's quite sad, really. They wouldn't go into much detail, but I gather Heather's mother gave her some grief about that paper of hers and she made up a story to cover herself." He studied his glasses. Apparently satisfied, he put them back on and returned the handkerchief to his pocket.

"I see," Jeremy said, humbled by his good fortune. The cosmos had answered his prayer.

"Of course, the best thing about this is how quickly the whole matter's been resolved," Donnelly said. "By DCCP standards, at least." He smiled. "Jeremy, we want you back on the job."

The royal we.

"First thing tomorrow," Donnelly continued. "Unless..." He held out an open palm, as if extending an offering. "Unless you'd like another day or so to get your bearings. But I think the best thing all around is to get everyone back to normal, soon as possible. Wouldn't you agree, Jeremy?"

"I—uh, sure." Normal. He'd almost forgotten what that looked like.

"After all," Mr. Donnelly said, "The official line is that you're on leave, which can mean whatever you want it to."

How magnanimous. "But I cleared my things out of my office," Jeremy pointed out. "People probably noticed. And I was locked out of the computer system." A note of resentment crept into his voice.

"No worries," the principal assured him. "I have a proposal. We'll move you into a new office. A bigger one! That will explain your things being removed. You can say you were sick, or had a death in the family, or... is something wrong?"

Jeremy had been thinking of his father's recent passing. "Uh, no sir."

"Good. Now, there's a second part to my proposal," Donnelly said. "It's about Bob Jacobs." One of the teachers in the lower school. "He broke an ankle skiing last weekend."

"Too bad." Jeremy wondered what this had to do with him.

"It'll be a couple of weeks until he's up and around," Donnelly continued. "And I was hoping you would cover his English Comp class."

"The sixth graders?" Jeremy's voice rose with surprise.

"You taught that class when you first came to Forrest, right?" the principal reminded him.

"Well, yeah, but it's been a few years." Little kids?

"Bob's got his lesson plans in place. It'll be a breeze," Donnelly assured him. "It's the period right before your AP class, so you have it free."

So the big office came with a catch. The lower school classes were way over on the other side of the Forrest campus from the upper school. "Why not move Bob's students into my classroom, since it's empty that period?" he said.

Donnelly looked as if Jeremy had suggested airlifting the sixth graders by helicopter. "That wouldn't do. We want to keep them in familiar surroundings. Besides, the upper school girls wouldn't like the little ones parading around in their territory, would they?"

"I guess not." Jeremy resigned himself to a cross-campus dash between classes.

Donnelly gave him a light smack on the thigh. "Good, then. Settled."

"Sure," Jeremy muttered. Quite the politician, his principal. "Is there—uh, will there be a salary increase along with the extra teaching load?"

Donnelly's eyes narrowed. "For teaching one course for a few weeks? No, your compensation stays the same." He smiled. "But you keep the office." The principal's expression sobered. "Jeremy, we don't want any further unpleasantness, right? It's been a difficult few days for all of us. For the good of the school, we need to move on. Agreed?"

Jeremy stared at the principal, torn. He doubted that Donnelly had lain awake worrying at three AM all week, as he had. But he'd dodged a bullet. Been spared the unthinkable. He'd get his life back. And a bigger office.

He swallowed. "Yes, sir. I do."

"Excellent, son!"

Again, son? Jeremy pictured his father. What would he have thought of all this?

Donnelly kept talking. "This won't be forgotten at your next performance review, I assure you." He stood, and Jeremy rose as well. The principal shook his hand. "I'll have your things moved this afternoon to Cal Hardwick's old office. The one with the big window."

"I—thank you, sir." Jeremy walked him to the door, wanting the man out of there.

The principal beamed at him. "See you bright and early tomorrow." He turned back. "Jeremy, one more thing."

Now what?

"You won't mind if Heather stays in your AP class." A statement, not a question.

"I—uh, won't that be a bit awkward?" Disastrous, Jeremy wanted to say.

Donnelly passed a hand through his sparse hair. "Frankly, her mother is insisting on it."

"But—"

"And, when you think about it, there's less disruption that way, right?"

Jeremy's shoulders sagged. "I guess. Less disruption."

The principal clapped him on his drooping shoulder. "Good man!"

Jeremy let him out. When Donnelly's footsteps faded down the stairs, he closed the door and called out: "Mel?"

She'd already come into the living room, stood, glaring at him. "You idiot!" she exploded.

TWENTY ONE

"WHAT??" JEREMY STARED AT Melissa, stung.

"Your principal." She glared at him. "Why'd you let him off the hook like that?" Her dark eyes flashed with anger. "Why the hell are you letting everyone off so easy?"

"For crissakes, Mel!" Jeremy glowered back at her. "What are you talking about? I got my job back. What's the problem?"

"Duh!" She rolled her eyes. "Here you are, holding all the cards in this situation, and you let him push you around. Instead of suing that little bitch for slander, you're letting her back into your classroom."

"Mel—"

"And you even let him saddle you with an extra class. You had Donnelly in the palm of your hand. Why didn't you demanded a raise, a promotion? You had a chance to write your own ticket, Jeremy!" She waved him off. "And you kissed his ass."

"Wait a friggin' minute." Jeremy stepped toward her. "If you're going to eavesdrop on my conversations, at least get it right. The girl recanted. The principal came here to make good. I'll be back at school tomorrow. Nobody knows anything about Heather's accusations, or the suspension." Well, Nikki knew. "Don't you get it, Mel? No harm, no foul. Why start more trouble? A monster headache for us, and a disaster for the school. Who needs it?"

"We do," she said. "We need the money. We have a baby on the way, remember?"

"Oh, please," Jeremy said, grimacing. "Get a job, if you're so worried. Besides, even if her old man is a loser, at least our kid's got grandparents with deep pockets."

Melissa stalked off to the bedroom. The door slammed behind her, rattling the pictures on the wall.

Another fight. The same fight. And their crummy apartment too small to allow enough space when they argued. He grabbed his jacket, craving a drink. The grocery store for a six pack. Why the hell not? Even if Melissa didn't get it, he had something to celebrate. He had his job back.

And he'd see Nikki in the morning. All right, so he'd promised the cosmos he'd be good. Maybe it would be enough to be careful.

PROPPED AGAINST A PILE of pillows in bed, Nikki scrolled through the Facebook feed on her iPhone.

"Nikki?" Her brother burst through her bedroom door, a jar of peanut butter clutched in his chubby hands. "I can't get it opened. Do it for me?"

"I'm busy." And I'm not my brother's freaking keeper.

"But I'm hungry!"

"I said I'm busy!" she snapped. "Go run the jar under some hot water."

Pushing out his lower lip in a world-class pout, Brandon backed out of the room.

"And close that door!" Nikki barked.

He did.

Nothing very interesting on Facebook, Nikki decided. She phoned Heather. "About time," she said when her friend picked up. "Why haven't you returned my calls? It's been nearly a week. What happened with Protective Services?"

She waited out a long silence. "Nothing much," Heather said.

"What did you tell them? About Mr. B."

Heather mumbled something.

"Heather! Will you effing speak up? What did you say?"

"That he never did that stuff. That I made it up."

"Hah!" Nikki cackled. "Oh, wow. You must be in deep shit."

"Not so much," Heather said.

"What'd your folks do?"

"They're not gonna get me the car. And I have to write an apology to Mr. B."

"Too bad about the car," Nikki said. Like she cared? "But, you know, Mr. B might sue you or something, Heather."

"I guess."

"So DCPP didn't do anything to you?" Didn't those people even do their jobs?

"Well…" Heather paused. "I had to be examined by this doctor. And they told my mom I have to go for therapy."

"No shit?" Nikki said. A shrink, huh?

"Yeah. Listen, Nikki, I better get off now. I have to finish my letter to Mr. B. I'm going back to school tomorrow."

Nikki chuckled. "Yeah, sure. Listen, this time keep the mushy stuff out of it, if you know what's good for you."

"Uh huh. Bye, Nikki. See you tomorrow."

Nikki tossed her phone onto the bed. Unreal that Protective Services let

Heather off like that. Fucking therapy? On the other hand, maybe she could get some mileage out of that information. Heather hadn't been punished enough.

TWENTY TWO

THE MORNING LIGHT DISPLAYED Jeremy's new office to full advantage. The large window illuminated his New York skyline snow globe, perched on his new desk. His Casablanca poster hung on the wall and the Tom Seaver baseball rested atop a shiny dark wood bookcase, where Jeremy had installed the books he'd boxed last week. As if the events of the past few days had never happened. Taking his lecture notes and copy of Gatsby, Jeremy locked the door behind him and headed off to face the sixth graders.

Bob Jacobs's English Comp class went smoothly. Jeremy got a kick out of teaching the younger ones again. At the end of the period, he collected his things and power-walked across campus toward the upper school.

"Jeremy!"

He stopped to let his colleague, Marge Peterson, catch up with him.

"Are you okay?" she asked. They resumed walking, at a slower pace.

"Uh, sure." What to say? He still hadn't worked out a cover story for his absence.

"I mean, first you rushed out of here with a doctor's appointment, then you disappeared for a week. What's up?"

"Oh." Now he remembered their conversation last week. "I—uh—actually, Marge, it wasn't my doctor's appointment, it was Melissa's."

Her eyebrows shot up. "She okay?"

"Yeah. She's pregnant. The—uh, her doctor wanted her to stay off her feet." He swallowed. "So I took some time off." Sounded plausible. "She's fine now," he added.

His friend beamed. "Congratulations! That's great, Jeremy. When's she due?"

Oh, Christ. He'd never gotten that straight with Mel. He ran some rapid mental calculations. "Around the end of November, I think."

Marge cocked a finger at him, firing an imaginary pistol. "Tax deduction!"

Jeremy nodded, smiling.

A roomful of grinning girls and two objects atop his desk awaited Jeremy in his second period AP English class. He smiled at the girls, trying not to look at Nikki. Approaching his desk, he saw an envelope, his name handwritten on it, and a chocolate cupcake—adorned with a heart, in pink icing. Jeremy eyed them with unease.

"Morning Mr. B!" Tiffany, freckled and red-haired, the first to call out.

"Hey, Mr. B!" Samantha, owl-eyed behind round blue glasses.

"You feeling better?"

Jeremy nodded, canvassing the room, taking in the girlish grins. Heather sat way in back, face sickly pale. She darted a glance at his desk, lowered her eyes to the floor.

"Morning," he greeted them. Jeremy slid the envelope into a drawer. As he reached for the cupcake, his eyes met Nikki's, and Jeremy caught a trace of smile on lips as pink as the sugary icing. He looked away, shoving the cupcake into the drawer.

"Sorry I'm late," he said. "I'm covering a first-period class in the lower school for a couple of weeks. I'll get here as promptly as I can." He fixed them with a gaze of mock sternness. "I know I can count on finding you all in your seats." They smiled back at him. Good to see them again. "Now," he said, "let's get back to Gatsby, shall we?"

The period flew. Nikki's crystalline gaze lingered on Jeremy's as she walked out, last to leave. As soon as she was gone, he opened the desk drawer and took out the objects he'd put there. He tore open the envelope.

A brief handwritten letter:

> *Dear Mr. Barrett,*
> *I'm terribly sorry for the things I said. You are a great teacher and you deserve better. If you want me to write a make-up paper, I'll do it.*
> *Yours truly,*
> *Heather Lloyd*

He read the apology and regarded the cupcake with trepidation. No problem with Heather's letter—simple and sincere. But a cupcake with a pink heart on it? Wrong message. Who'd be that clueless? What to do about it—confront her with the dumb cupcake, or throw it away?

Nikki's voice interrupted his thoughts. "Like it?"

"Huh?" He looked up. She'd come back.

"I made it for you. Iced it, at least."

"Ohh." From Nikki then, not Heather. "It's—lovely," he stammered. "Thanks."

"What's that?" Nikki tilted her chin at the paper in Jeremy's hand. "A secret admirer, Mr. B?" She smiled. "Besides me?"

"Of course not." He stuffed the letter back into its envelope.

"I bet it's from Heather, right?"

He grinned. She always seemed to know things.

"Told you it would work out," Nikki said.

"Yes, you did," he replied. "What made you so certain?"

"Well…" Nikki cocked her head. "I had a little chat with Heather."

His eyes widened. "You did?"

"Uh huh." She reached to graze his hand. "I knew she'd listen to reason."

Jeremy pulled away his hand, glancing at the door. "Nikki, what did you do?"

Her lips made a tiny pout when Jeremy withdrew his hand. "Meet me later? And I'll tell you." Her blue eyes remained glued to his face.

His chance to draw the line. He'd promised. "Nikki—I don't think that's a good idea right now."

The pout deepened. "Don't you like me anymore?"

"Of course! Nikki, you know I do."

The blue eyes clouded with disappointment. "Please? I haven't seen you in so long. And my mom's been crazy all week." She lowered her gaze.

"Nikki, I…."

She looked back up at him. "Besides, don't you want to hear what I said to Heather?"

Jeremy's resolve melted. He'd been a heel to reject her after she'd gone to bat for him. "The park? Four o'clock."

She nodded, glacier eyes twinkling, then turned and slipped out the door, sleek as a Siamese cat.

This will be the last time, Jeremy vowed, watching her go. Only one last time.

TWENTY THREE

NIKKI WASTED NO TIME. How perfect that Heather's note and her own cupcake had turned up on Mr. B's desk at the same moment.

"Samantha!" Spotting a classmate from AP English in the hallway, Nikki rushed over and clutched her arm. "Did you catch that?" She leaned in to murmur in the girl's ear. "Heather left Mr. B a cupcake and a love note."

Samantha gaped through her oversized eyeglasses. "They were from her?"

By the end of the school day, Nikki's whispering campaign had gone viral. Did you know? She's been writing love letters to Mr. B. Have you heard? She left a cupcake with a heart on it right there on his desk. As each pair of lips spread the lie to each little ear, the tidbit grew juicier, its origin more remote. By the time classes ended, the story became Facebook fodder, no one recalling who'd started the rumors.

Which suited Nikki fine.

She read the posts on her iPhone, awaiting Mr. B on their usual park bench. Her deft thumb plunked away. We should all take it easy on poor Heather, she posted. She's in therapy. A nice touch, she reflected, imagining Heather reading it. See how I stuck up for you? The bimbo wouldn't know what hit her.

Nikki spied Jeremy's blue Honda pulling in across the street and closed her Facebook page. She leapt to her feet at his approach. As she reached to embrace him, he grasped her shoulders.

"C'mon," he said. "We can't stay here."

She grinned, game for whatever he had in mind.

Jeremy led her to his car, his eyes darting up and down the street. The afternoon was milder today. People might be out. But no, he decided, as they got into the Honda. The coast was clear. He pulled out.

They'd made it.

At the corner, braking for a stop sign, Jeremy spotted a beige Camry pulling out a block behind them. His hackles rose in foreboding. Probably nothing to worry about. Such a nondescript car. Still, the vehicle followed them, staying a block or so back as they wound through the local streets.

"Where are we going?"

Nikki's voice drew Jeremy's attention from the Camry. "Someplace special," he said. "A surprise."

"I love surprises!"

Jeremy smiled at her delight and glanced at his rearview mirror. No sign of the Camry. A false alarm. He followed the local streets to the Watchung Reservation, drove to the Seeley's Pond Picnic Area, and parked. A weekday and the lot was nearly empty, too early in the season for all but the hardiest hikers.

He turned to Nikki. "Ever been here?"

"Uh uh."

"Want to walk down to the pond?"

She smiled. "Sure."

They got out of the car and made their way toward Little Seeley's Pond. Nikki reached for Jeremy's hand, and he let her clasp it, more relaxed, alone here in this quiet, wooded place. So good to let go of all that stress. He stopped and turned to Nikki. God, she looked lovely, eyes bright, cheeks flushed with excitement. His poetry failed to do her justice.

Nikki let out a whoop of pure glee and threw her arms around his waist. "It's wonderful here!"

Jeremy didn't pull away. "Wait another month and it'll be glorious. Even better in the fall."

She tilted her face up toward his. "Bring me then?"

"Um, sure." A pang. He shouldn't promise this girl things. And he damned sure shouldn't kiss her, much as those perfect lips beckoned him.

Nikki flashed him a grin. "Show me the pond?"

He pulled back from her embrace, took her hand again. "Come on." They walked on in silence for a while. "So tell me," Jeremy asked, "what was it you said to Heather?"

Nikki leaned in, letting her shoulder bump against his as they strolled. "Nothing much. I suppose I appealed to her better judgment."

He stopped and turned to face her. "I owe you."

Nikki's arm snaked around his waist. "But you've already done so much for me, Mr. B."

Her words stung his conscience. What was he doing for this girl—to her? Melissa's accusation rang in his ears: "You, you, you! It's all about you." Maybe she was right—he was that selfish. The thought soured his happiness. He had to end this.

He gazed at Nikki. "You realize…" He brushed her cheek. "You're very special." My muse.

Nikki's lips curled into a smile.

"Look…" He hesitated. "We can't keep doing this."

Her smile wavered, and Jeremy's heart ached.

"Why not?"

She had to ask? "You mean, the fifty or so major reasons?"

She clucked her tongue. "You're not turning all Victorian on me, are you?"

He burst out laughing. "The ultimate English Lit major."

Nikki edged closer. "Let me read some of your poetry?"

Jeremy flushed. "The stuff's so old. I haven't written for a while." She'd hate it, he knew, find it corny.

As if reading his mind, Nikki pressed against him. "Maybe you'll write about me."

"Nikki!" He pulled away, hiding his red face. "We can't do this."

Her expression clouded. "You said you owe me."

He brushed a strand of raven hair from her face. "I owe you better than this."

She moved closer again. "But you want me, don't you?" Her voice low, insistent.

God, did he.

Loud barking made them look back the way they'd come. A golden retriever strained at its leash, rushing toward them with a panting middle-aged man in tow.

"Brandy, stay!" the man yelled. Ignoring him, the retriever surged forward, tail wagging deliriously. "I'm sorry." The owner yanked the leash to restrain his dog, already licking Nikki's outstretched hand. "She's undisciplined, but harmless."

"It's okay," Jeremy said. "Come on, Nikki." He grasped her arm. Crazy to bring her here. He'd counted on the reservation being deserted, wanted to remember her in this place.

"Do we have to go?" Nikki whined.

Maybe the guy will think she's my kid. "Yes. We do."

"Okaay." She gave Brandy a last ear scratch and followed Jeremy back to the parking lot. Silently, they got in the Honda.

"Mr. B?"

He faced her. Those pale blue eyes pierced him. He had to stop now, before he crossed any more lines.

"Are you going to stop seeing me?" Her voice quavered, like a hurt child.

And she was. Jeremy felt sick, knowing he would only hurt her more. But not yet. Not today.

He reached for her hand. "No, Nikki. I won't."

He pulled out. Glancing at the rearview mirror, Jeremy's blood ran cold as he sighted the Camry across the parking lot.

TWENTY FOUR

THE WHOLE DRIVE BACK from the Watchung Reservation, Jeremy watched in vain for the Camry. He half-listened to Nikki's chatter, responded in monosyllables, and, relieved, dropped her at their park. Driving on to the apartment, he continued to obsess. Should have gotten the Camry's license number. But then, do what with it? Not like he had an in with Motor Vehicle Bureau. One thing clear: No more rendezvous with Nikki. Had to stop. Had to.

"Mel?" Jeremy called, walking into the apartment.

Melissa emerged from the bedroom, cellphone to her ear. She met Jeremy's quizzical gaze with a frown and raised finger, signaling him to wait.

"When will we know for sure?" She grimaced.

"What's wrong?" Jeremy asked, alarmed.

Melissa held up a palm. "Okay. I understand. All right, I will."

"What is it?" Jeremy demanded when she ended the call.

She pointed at her laptop, sitting on the coffee table. "Google Pre-eclampsia."

They rushed to the sofa, Jeremy the first to reach the computer. "Two e's?" he asked. "A dash in between?"

"Who knows?" Melissa snapped.

"Wait," he said. "Here it is." They both leaned in to peruse the Wikipedia entry. "Jesus!" Jeremy read aloud: *A medical condition producing dangerously high blood pressure during pregnancy and potentially serious risks to mother and child.* "Seizures?" he exclaimed. "Did the doctor say you have this, Mel?" He eyed her as if she might fall to the floor twitching any moment.

"The condition doesn't develop until later in the pregnancy," she said. "There's a blood test they can do in a few weeks."

Jeremy scrolled down the page, skipping past a bunch of technical stuff. "Then...?"

"Here!" Melissa grabbed for the cursor. "This is what he was talking about. My PP13 level, from the blood work they did."

Jeremy scanned the section on early methods of diagnosis. A low level of Placental Protein 13, considered a possible indicator of Pre-eclampsia developing later.

"So he's not saying you have the condition, right?" He blew out a breath. "According to this, they'll have to check your Placental Growth Factor levels at the end of the first trimester."

"But what if I do have it?" Melissa insisted. "Jeremy, I'm scared."

"Come on, Mel." He closed the Wikipedia page and leaned back on the sofa. "You're getting way ahead of yourself."

"But it could—"

"Fucking tests," Jeremy muttered. "Just give you more useless shit to worry about."

"We were so happy about the baby," Melissa said.

She believed that? He looked away, uncomfortable.

"How will we get through the next few weeks?" Her eyes implored him.

"Mel, I—"

"Jeremy! What should we do?"

He shook his head. "I don't know." Nature offering a way out? "If you're so worried," he ventured, "I mean, if your health is at stake, maybe we should think about, you know...uh, terminating?" Her look of horror told him he'd made a big mistake.

"An abortion?"

"Well, it's not like this is our last chance to have a baby, right?"

"Jeremy!"

"I mean, wouldn't it be better if we tried to build up some savings before—"

"I can't believe you're saying this!" Melissa wailed. "The other day you promised you were with me."

"Yeah, and yesterday you called me an idiot," he shot back. Another mistake.

Melissa got up from the couch. "You said I could count on you."

"You can, Mel! I only meant—" Jeremy stood and reached out, but she pulled away.

All at once she turned ashen. Her hand rose to her mouth. "Oh shit, I'm gonna puke." She rushed for the bathroom.

Jeremy sank back onto the sofa. He leaned forward, his head drooping to rest in his open hands. Again, that sensation of things closing in—the Camry, the baby, Nikki. He, too, wanted to throw up.

IN HER ROOM, HEATHER read post after humiliating post on Facebook, heartsick. She'd become a joke. Way worse than all of them ignoring her, like before. No one was supposed to know what had happened with Mr. B. Her note, the false accusations—all of that was confidential. The Protective Services lady had promised her. The principal, too. Yet here she was, a public laughing stock. Who'd told?

She hated to think Nikki had. But who else knew? She reread Nikki's post. Supposedly defending her, but Nikki went and blabbed about Heather going for therapy. That was private, personal.

Heather turned off her laptop and looked over at Pretzels in his cage. "Think I should call her?" she asked the guinea pig. And say—what?

A tap on her door and her mom walked into the bedroom. "I made an appointment for you with a therapist," she announced. "Tomorrow at four."

"Oh," Heather said. So soon. "Who? Where?"

"She's right in town. A psychologist. Dr. Gold." Her mother frowned. "Or was it Golden? Something like that."

"Oh," Heather repeated. "How'd you find her?"

"Through the insurance. She's in network."

"Uh huh." Heather nodded. Not much else to say about it.

"Did you give him the letter?" her mom asked.

"Huh? Oh, you mean, Mr. B?"

"Who else would I be talking about?" her mother snapped. "What did he say?"

"Umm, nothing. I mean, not yet, anyway."

"Didn't you give it to him?" Mom demanded.

Heather hesitated. "I left it on his desk."

"Heather! Why didn't you hand it to him personally?"

Was she serious? "I—I didn't want to make a whole big scene out of it, Mom."

"But did he read it?"

"I guess. He—uh—picked it up and put it in his desk," Heather said. "He must have read it after class."

"Well, check with him tomorrow, Heather. You make sure he read that apology." Another frown. "If I'd realized you weren't going to hand deliver it, I'd have sent it by certified mail." Her forehead crinkled. "We should have. Then we'd have proof of receipt."

"Mom!" Heather groaned. "It'll be okay, honest."

"Make sure you check with him tomorrow, you hear me?"

"Yes, ma'am," Heather mumbled.

"All right, then. Dinner in half an hour." Her mother walked out without waiting for a response.

So, a therapist appointment tomorrow afternoon.

"At least it's a woman, huh Pretzels?" That lady at Child Protection had been nice, listened to her. Heather went over to the cage, poked in a finger to pet the guinea pig. "Think she can help me handle Nikki?" She stroked the animal's brown and white fur. "Better be some therapist, Pretzels," she muttered.

TWENTY FIVE

JEREMY LEANED OVER THE bed to kiss Melissa goodbye. "Want me to pick up anything on my way home from school?"

She gave him a sleepy smile. "More saltines?"

"You got it." He patted her dark, rumpled hair. Thank god they'd worked out a truce. He hoped it would last this time. "I'm off," he told her.

He drove to the Forrest School, still worrying about the Camry.

Parking in the faculty lot, he pushed aside his fears to focus on a roomful of sixth graders. The class went smoothly enough and Jeremy trotted across the campus to AP English.

He walked in and saw it. An apple on his desk—the biggest, reddest, most in-your-face specimen he'd ever seen. He did a classic double take—a cursory glance at his desk, followed by a head jerk back to the enormous piece of fruit. A few giggles erupted from his students.

Of all things, Jeremy blushed.

C'mon, get it together, Barrett. What are you, a greenhorn student teacher? His eyes darted to Nikki, sealing his doom. His face turned red as the Honeycrisp on his desk.

"Uh…" Buying time, he went to his desk and picked up the fruit, making a show of examining it while his heartbeat returned to normal. He looked around the room. "This must be the Big Apple," he quipped. Laughter and a few groans, but no longer at his expense.

Jeremy held up the apple. "So, who left this for me?" Go bold or go home. "Perhaps Eve?" He wiggled his eyebrows, milking it. "Or the serpent?" More giggles and a few sidelong glances at Heather, who stared down at her desk.

Enough. He still didn't get the joke, but he'd regained control. "Anyway, thanks, whoever you are." He gave the juicy piece of fruit a last appraising look. He considered taking a bite, for effect. But, who knew? Might be a sharp object hidden inside. "I'll save it for later," he said. He put the apple back on his desk. "Now, let's get back to Jay Gatsby's obsession with Daisy."

Obsessions. Jeremy had become an expert on that subject.

His preoccupation with Nikki might end up as badly as Jay Gatsby's. At least Gatsby pursued a woman his own age. He had to end this thing. He was going to be a father, even if the idea terrified him. Again, he promised: No more contact with Nikki outside of school. No meetings, no texts. This time he meant it. Jeremy got through the class on autopilot, keeping his eyes anywhere but on Nikki.

At the end of the period, she would be the last to leave. She'd stay behind to confess she'd left the apple, as she'd acknowledged the cupcake yesterday.

But she didn't.

As she walked out with the others, Nikki met his inquiring gaze with a blue-eyed expression of pure sweetness and innocence. Baffled, he watched her go.

"Mr. B?"

Heather stood at his desk, books clutched to her chest like a bulletproof vest.

"Yes, Heather?" Keeping his tone neutral. Not crazy about being alone in the classroom with her. "What is it?"

"I—um." Her cheeks flushed. "I wanted to…"

"Yes?"

"Did you get the letter I left you?"

"I did." What to say? Thank her for it?

"Was it—okay?"

Her face pinched and drawn with misery, Heather looked forty, rather than sixteen. Jeremy pitied her. Who was he to judge her? "It was fine, Heather. Apology accepted."

She looked up at him, her face going slack with relief and gratitude. "Thank you," she whispered, and rushed to the door.

"Heather?"

She turned, eyebrows shooting upward.

"That apple—did you…?"

She shook her head. "Not me. I swear it, Mr. B."

She hurried off, leaving Jeremy with yet another mystery on his hands.

TWENTY SIX

HEATHER STOLE A GLANCE at the clock in Dr. Goldman's office. Only ten minutes left. Her first session, and she wished it were longer. So much she wanted to tell the doctor.

"Those girls are up to something else now." Heather's finger traced a nervous circle along the armrest of her chair.

"What are they doing?" Dr. Goldman asked.

"Someone left this apple on Mr. B's desk." She darted a glance at the psychologist's face, then looked away. "And the girls acted like it was me who did it."

"That must have been very uncomfortable. What did you do, Heather?"

A shrug. "Nothing. Ignored them. Sort of."

Dr. Goldman nodded. "Okay."

"But I wish—"

"What? What do you wish?"

"That I could stand up to them." Heather lowered her gaze.

"I see." Her therapist paused. "If you want, I can show you some techniques that might help."

"Like what?" Heather's eyes shot up to meet the doctor's.

"Hmmm." Dr. Goldman thought for a moment. "How to speak up. Talk to those girls in a calm and confident way."

Heather slumped in her chair. Ask me to swim the Hudson, why don't you? "I don't feel calm and confident." Dr. Goldman, on the other hand, looked relaxed and poised. This woman might teach her something.

"Sometimes, Heather, if you act as if you feel a certain way, the feelings follow."

"Yeah?"

Dr. Goldman smiled. "We call it fake it till you make it."

Heather laughed. "Cool."

"Want to try something before we end the session?"

Heather grinned. "Sure."

"Good. We'll start with centering in your body. As you sit there in your chair, Heather, imagine you're a mountain."

Weird, but they worked on it for the rest of the session and Heather liked it. When Dr. Goldman suggested she practice at home, Heather agreed. Being a mountain was way better homework than they gave at school.

The first test of her therapist's training came all too soon.

Heather walked into AP English the next morning to find a cluster of girls around Mr. B's desk, giggling. As she passed them, she concentrated on her breathing, like Dr. Goldman had showed her. But then she saw what they were all laughing about. A box of tiny heart-shaped candies, the kind with corny messages on them, there on the desk. Heather scurried to her seat, breathing faster.

Moments later, Mr. B came in. He frowned at the smirking girls around his desk.

"Take your seats, ladies." As they retreated, he stepped over and examined the offering on his desk. He picked up the box of candies, hefting it. "Didn't know they still made these." He handed the box to a girl in the first row. "Pass 'em around. Looks like there's enough for everyone." Then he launched into the lesson.

Pretty cool, the way he handled that. Still, Heather wished he hadn't sent those candies into circulation. The box of miniature hearts made its way back, coming closer to her seat. Murmurs and chuckles followed along the way.

You're a mountain.

The candies approached, only a row away. One of the girls, Tiffany, read the inscription on a little heart, in a loud whisper.

"I love you." A few titters.

"Let's settle down," Mr. B warned.

"Be mine," another girl read. Giggles, now.

"Mr. B," someone added. Not a whisper that time. Heather caught a sidelong glimpse of Nikki, smirking.

"Love, Heather!" A chortle, then a muffled guffaw.

"Ladies!" Mr. B called out.

But the laughter had its own momentum now.

All eyes on her, Heather had nowhere safe to look. Breathe! Nice and slow. But the more she inhaled and exhaled, the more Heather grew light-headed, scared she'd hyperventilate. If she passed out, at least she wouldn't have to sit there, all those eyes boring into her, hearing that laughter.

Be a mountain.

But Heather didn't want to be a mountain now. She wanted to be invisible.

"Stop it!" she exploded. "Leave me alone!"

"Enough!" Mr. B shouted, the first time Heather ever heard him yell. "Heather, all of you, stop it right now." He charged to the back of the room, snatched up the nearly empty box of candy hearts and hurled them into the waste basket beside his desk.

"Shouldn't waste food." Somebody—Samantha?—a stage whisper.

Mr. B turned and scanned the room, eyes flashing with anger. "Let's get back on track." He resumed the lesson.

Not the end of it. Not hardly. Heather knew she'd get plenty more chances to apply her therapist's training. Fake it till you make it—yeah, right. Would she ever?

She'd practice. A lot. Maybe Mom would let her see Dr. Goldman twice a week.

TWENTY SEVEN

END OF THE SCHOOL day found Jeremy eager to leave. He'd handled the apple, but those candy hearts? They'd spooked him. And this time he'd lost control of his class. Bizarre, this stuff on his desk. Like starring in a remake of The Blair Witch Project, checking for dead animals and bones planted outside his tent each morning.

And the witch? Heather, maybe? Gathering up books and papers in his new office, Jeremy considered the idea and rejected it. She'd need Meryl Streep's acting chops to pull off the stunt of sneaking in those gifts while looking so freaked out by them. Besides, Heather had taken plenty of ridicule this morning.

Nikki, then? He'd barely said a word to her on the way back from their disastrous trip to the Watchung Reservation yesterday. Punishing him, maybe?

No. Not Nikki. What a rat to even think it. Chalk it up to fraying nerves.

Those nerves took yet another shock when Jeremy walked out of his office and saw Nikki waiting for him in the hallway. Late for her to be hanging around.

"Hey," he said. "Let's walk." Better than being caught loitering with her.

She fell into step beside him. "That was way weird in class today, huh?"

"Pretty surreal." From the corner of his eye, Jeremy watched her. "Nikki...?"

"What, Mr. B?" Glacier eyes came around and locked onto his.

"Did—uh, you leave those candies on my desk?"

She flinched, like he'd struck her.

"Sorry," Jeremy muttered. What a bastard, even to ask! But who, then? "You think it was Heather?"

Her blue eyes clouded. "The other girls say so."

"Do you believe them?" Cruel putting Nikki on the spot, but who else could he turn to? No way he'd bring this mess to Donnelly and have him digging around.

Nikki hesitated. "I don't think it's fair to make any accusations, Mr. B." Solemn and big-eyed as an owlet. "Do you?"

"No. Of course not." He forced a smile. "Hey, getting late. We'd better go."

Nikki flashed him a radiant grin. "Where to?"

Shit, that came out wrong. "No, I mean I've got to be getting home. See you tomorrow, Nikki." Jeremy hurried off.

TOMORROW?

Nikki seethed, watching Mr. B hustle down the hallway. Not her imagination, then. Blowing her off. After all the trouble she took to find those candy hearts.

Not that she regretted that. Quite a number they'd worked on Heather, all right. But they'd only ruffled Mr. B's feathers. The next gift needed to be something even more special.

More—personal.

Perhaps a return to the color motif she'd introduced with that apple. Red for embarrassment—Heather's, of course. Caught red-handed—unless he behaved—the threat for Mr. B. And that gave Nikki a totally brilliant idea of what to sneak onto his desk next. Wait a couple of days, let the suspense build. Anticipation heightens torture.

Irresistible. Heather such a perfect target—gullible, weak, dim-witted. And she had it coming. The gall, imagining for one second that Mr. B could possibly be attracted to her! As if. Protective Services let her off too lightly. Her punishment fell to Nikki. Good thing their classmates were no Einsteins, either. An occasional hint that Heather was the anonymous gifter and they glommed onto the drama like a reality TV series.

Quite the bonus that Mr. B came late to class now. A breeze for Nikki to plant stuff on his desk. In her first period study hall, guess who had the job of dropping off the attendance sheet at the office? That came with the privilege of leaving early enough to stop by Mr. B's empty classroom.

Nikki trotted down the corridor. Skipped! She had a mission now. A very special purchase to make.

TWENTY EIGHT

TO JEREMY'S RELIEF, A couple of days passed without any new gifts on his desk. But this morning, he walked in on a cluster of girls huddled around his desk, giggling.

"Take your seats, please," he snapped. They scooted off, and he approached his desk. What now? He saw the object of their mirth and his jaw dropped. It might have come fresh from the Victoria's Secret catalogue.

A lacy, red garter.

"All right, who does this belong to?" Jeremy lifted the garter with two fingers, as if it were radioactive.

Whoops of laughter erupted, along with a loud "Whoo-hoo!" One of the girls called out: "Is that yours, Heather?" Another round of glee ensued.

"No!" Heather shouted, her face red as the garter.

"Quiet!" Jeremy yelled.

Another voice: "Think it fits her?"

"Try it on, Heather!"

"Yeah, try it on."

"Enough!" Jeremy barked. "This stops right now." He'd laughed off the other gifts, a regular Mr. Nice Guy, but this had gone too far. Worse, he'd lost his cool, had to get things under control. Always something with Heather. He shouldn't have accepted her back in his classroom.

Jeremy shoved the garter into his pants pocket. "If someone wants to claim it after class, see me. Otherwise—" He glared at them. "The whole class can expect an exam tomorrow." His eyes circled the room, seeing their grins dissolve.

The rest of the period passed without incident. As the girls filed out, looking chastened, Jeremy shuffled his papers, avoiding their faces. Let the guilty one come to him. But which one? The last of them left the room, leaving him with little hope of a confession and already regretting his threat. Not his style to punish the whole class for one person's transgression. Hardly the Marines here, and they were good kids, generally wanting to please him. Now his hold over his favorite class had slipped. What the hell was going on?

He pulled the garter from his pocket and studied it, as if it held an answer.

Maybe he should show it to Donnelly, but then what? A lot of questions Jeremy had no answers for, and not likely to get any answers from the principal. None he'd like, for sure. What then, have a crime lab test the garter for DNA samples?

Hell, not even a crime here. Yet Jeremy sure felt like a victim.

"Mr. B?" Nikki stood in the doorway.

The garter still in his hand, Jeremy blushed and thrust it back in his pocket. "Nikki—" She looked the picture of wide-eyed innocence. "It's not yours, is it?" Bad question. Jeremy forced away an image of Nikki wearing the lacy, red thing.

"You know I wouldn't do that to you." She sidled up to his desk.

Bad idea, being alone in the room with her. "I'm sorry, Nikki. I don't understand what's going on."

"Don't worry." Her slender hand settled on Jeremy's arm, made his pulse race. "I'll find out." She grinned. "You know me." With a wink, Nikki left.

The situation ate at Jeremy. He ruminated, still chewing on it when he came home. He'd tell Donnelly tomorrow. No, only make things worse. Maybe the joke had played itself out. Give it a few more days.

At dinner, his moodiness drew a complaint from Melissa. "You've been so distant since you went back to school. What's wrong?"

"Nothing." Jeremy pushed a morsel of chicken around his plate.

"Any more trouble with that girl?"

"Not at all," he lied.

"The baby, then? Is that what's worrying you?" she pressed.

With a pang of guilt, Jeremy realized he'd barely thought about the baby for days. "Nothing's worrying me," he repeated. "Why, are you worried about it?"

"Well, the PP13 thing, yeah," Melissa said.

Jeremy frowned. "The pee pee…?" He caught his mistake as soon as she scowled at him. "Oh, the protein. No point in worrying about it, Mel. We just have to wait until they do the next test."

"Thanks for the brilliant advice."

The meal continued in silence.

He kept his distance from Melissa afterwards, working on lesson plans at his laptop, accomplishing little. When Melissa announced she was going to bed, he considered working on his poem. Then his cellphone bleeped—a text from Nikki.

Got the 411. See you tomorrow. Park @ 4?

He'd promised not to meet her outside of school. But if Nikki knew something… He texted his assent.

More optimistic now, Jeremy headed for the bedroom, pulling off his sweater as he went. He tossed it onto the chair opposite the bed, where it landed on top of a pile of Melissa's clothes.

Propped against the pillows, Melissa looked up from her Kindle. "You okay?"

"Fine." Jeremy emptied his pockets, putting coins and keys on the dresser. When he pulled out his wallet, something lacy and red fluttered to the floor.

Melissa sat up. "What's that?"

"Huh?" Jeremy followed her gaze to the floor. The garter lay at his feet. He knelt to retrieve it, but Melissa leapt out of bed and reached for the garter. He snatched it up before she got hold of it.

"Jeremy! What is that?" She grabbed, snagging one end of the garter. It stretched taut between them as he pulled it away. "Give me that!" Melissa demanded.

He released his hold and the garter snapped into Melissa's grasp.

TWENTY NINE

JEREMY STARED AT THE red garter dangling from Melissa's finger.

"What are you doing with this?" she demanded.

For an awful, deer-in-the-headlights moment, he drew a blank. If he told her about the stuff going on in his class, she'd get back on his case about suing Heather, standing up to Donnelly, or god knew what else. "It's—it's for you," he stammered, improvising.

Melissa's dark eyes bored into him. "Don't treat me like an idiot." She twirled the garter around her finger. "What's the deal here, Jeremy?"

"The deal?" He arched an eyebrow, had an idea. He edged closer to her. "I'll show you the deal."

"Jeremy!" Caught off guard, Melissa backed away.

He pulled the garter off her finger and slipped it onto his wrist. Taking hold of Melissa's shoulders, he steered her backwards toward the bed.

"Jeremy? What the fuck —?" Her eyes widened.

He swiveled, pulling her down on top of him on the bed. "I want to see it on you," he said huskily.

"That's such bullshit," she protested.

He kissed her before she said anymore and rolled her onto her back. He pulled up the oversized tee shirt Melissa wore to bed, exposing her torso. His fingers crept up under the shirt and caressed her swollen nipples.

"Oh my god. Jeremy." Her back arched with pleasure.

He kissed a slow path across Melissa's rounding belly. He'd get away with this. Her breaths were coming rapidly now and Jeremy yanked her panties down to her knees, then pulled them off, tossing them to the floor. He slipped the garter off his wrist.

"I knew red would be good on you." He slid the garter over her ankle and inched it up her calf, over her knee, securing it midway up Melissa's thigh. "Oh, yeah," he breathed. "Yeah, that's good."

Lying back on the bed, Melissa craned her neck for a look. Jeremy eased her legs apart and lowered his face to her crotch.

"You bastard." Her head sank back onto the pillow.

It worked out even better than he'd hoped.

BY THE TIME MELISSA dragged herself out of bed the next morning, Jeremy had gone. A bout of queasiness—mixed morning sickness and dread—gripped her as she bent to retrieve the red garter from the floor beside the bed. The sex had been surprisingly good—grumpy and distant as Jeremy had been of late. But she didn't buy the seduction routine he'd pulled. Since when was Jeremy the type to buy her lingerie?

She opened a dresser drawer and tossed the garter inside, then went to the kitchen. Something going on with him. Melissa heated a kettle of water for her tea. Maybe more to the whole business with that girl than he'd admitted?

The kettle whistled and Melissa's cellphone rang. She picked up the phone and held it against her ear while she poured hot water over the tea bag in her cup.

"Hi, Mom."

"How are you, darling? Any updates on your condition?"

"I'm good," Melissa said. "No new developments. I see the doctor again next week." She carried her tea into the living room. Finding the coffee table in its usual state, she balanced the cup on a stack of books.

Beth Milton touted the latest properties she'd found for Melissa and Jeremy. "Why don't you come and look at them this afternoon?" she urged. "You don't want to wait until you're too far along to handle the move, do you?"

These days, Melissa found it hard enough to move herself, much less a household, thanks to relentless morning sickness. "Mom? I think we should hold off on the house-hunting."

"But, darling—"

"I mean, if you think about it—" Melissa stifled a burp. "It'll be easier to care for a baby in the apartment. We won't need the extra space for at least the first year."

"But the market, Melissa! Prices will only go up."

"Besides, Mom, I've got enough on my hands keeping this place clean, let alone a house." Melissa surveyed the disarray. True enough.

"It's Jeremy, isn't it?" Her mother's tone soured. "He's giving you a hard time about buying a house, right?"

No, Melissa thought, not since she'd stopped raising the subject. "It's both of us, Mom. We think it would be better to wait."

Her mother sighed. "I hate seeing you live like that, dear. Especially since you don't have to."

"I know, Mom." Melissa kneaded the furrow between her eyebrows and fought down her rising gorge. "Honestly, I'm fine. Call you later." She made a kissy sound into the phone and hung up before her mother pressed her any further.

But she wasn't fine. Instead of bringing them closer, her pregnancy had widened the chasm between Jeremy and her. She took a sip of her tea, already growing cold, wishing she knew what was really going on.

THIRTY

JEREMY ARRIVED AT THE park shortly before four. No sign of Nikki, so he sat on the bench to wait. After a few minutes nervous energy drove him to his feet and he paced back and forth like an expectant father—which, in fact, he was. Melissa deserved better of him. What a shit, being here, after her passionate response to his seduction last night. How long since he'd initiated anything like that?

The ten minutes he waited for Nikki dragged by like an hour. At last she appeared, a little breathless, in a rush. Despite his misgivings, Jeremy's throat caught at the sight of her. Her cheeks shone against porcelain skin, her dark hair and blue eyes glowed in the afternoon sunlight. How had he stayed away from her?

"I missed you," Nikki said. "I was afraid you'd stopped liking me."

"Never," Jeremy whispered. So lovely. A yearning arose within him, a drunk handed a shot of golden whiskey after a vain attempt at sobriety.

An approaching voice jolted Jeremy back to his senses—a woman, talking on a cellphone. "We'd better not stay out here," he told Nikki. "Come on. My car's over there."

She followed him to the Honda.

"I can't stay long." Nikki closed the passenger door. "I promised my mother I'd do the laundry and clean the bathrooms before she gets home."

Both? When she had homework? Jeremy held his tongue. Much as he wanted to be her protector, he had another agenda today. Nikki's text last night said she'd learned something about the anonymous gifts. He glanced out the window at the deserted street. Might be safe to talk there in his car.

"What did you find out?" he asked.

"Well…" Nikki fidgeted with a lock of shiny black hair. "I didn't want to be too obvious, you know? Asking a lot of questions?"

"Uh huh." He peered out the window again. "But…?"

"I heard two of the girls talking. One said she saw Heather leave the stuff on your desk."

"Who?" Jeremy pressed. "Which girl?"

Nikki looked away. "Please, do I have to say? I hate to rat on other people."

"Sure, I understand." Jeremy bit down his frustration. "What else did you hear?"

She hesitated. "The other one saw Heather drawing stuff in her notebook during math class."

"Stuff?"

"Romantic stuff." Nikki made a face. "Hearts with your initials and hers." She bit her lip. "And some sexual things."

Jeremy grimaced. "Like what?"

Nikki shook her head. "I don't know. I'm sorry. They walked away. I didn't want to follow them."

Jeremy swallowed his disappointment. He'd already pushed too much. "No, of course not."

Nikki leaned back in the passenger seat. "I'm kind of worried about her, Mr. B."

"So am I." He had more to worry about. Heather sounded pretty wacko. What might she pull next?

"They made her see a shrink," Nikki added.

"Sounds like a good idea." Jeremy hesitated. "Nikki, has Heather talked to you about any of this?"

"Not really." Her gaze dropped to the floor.

A prickle of apprehension ran down Jeremy's neck. "Nikki? Is there something you're not telling me?"

"I—no, I've told you everything I know, Mr. B." Her eyes flickered up to meet his, skittered away. She reached for the door handle. "I'd better go."

"Wait!" Jeremy reached for her arm, but she was already getting out of the car. Now he'd done it—injured this sweet, innocent girl. He leapt out the driver's side door and caught up with her. "Nikki, wait! Don't go." Abandoning his earlier caution, he pulled her into his arms. "I'm sorry. I shouldn't have put you on the spot like that."

Nikki flung her arms around his waist. Her lips were warm against his, and Jeremy didn't pull away. When he finally let her go, he caught a glimpse of a beige Camry down the street, driving away.

THIRTY ONE

NIKKI CAST A DISDAINFUL glance at the pile of dirty laundry on her bedroom floor. Tough shit. Let it wait. Coming home from the rendezvous with Mr. B, she'd hatched a brilliant plan. One that would convince him of Heather's guilt.

To set things in motion, she phoned Heather. And right away, hit a snag.

"What do you mean, you're not going on the DC trip?" Nikki demanded. "You absolutely can't skip that, Heather. It's, like, a tradition. It'll be awesome."

The spring class trip to the Capitol—a chance to sightsee, smell cherry blossoms, and sneak alcohol and drugs into the hotel. What sane kid would pass up the opportunity? Only Heather, which said a lot about her mental health.

"What's the deal? Your mom making you stay home?" Nikki goaded her.

"Nuh uh." Heather mumbled. "I'm just not that into it."

"Oh, come on," Nikki urged. "It's gonna be way cool. I thought we'd share a hotel room." Like she'd be caught dead rooming with Heather.

"I don't know."

Nikki heard the hesitation. Determined, she pushed on. "Look, girlfriend." She mimed sticking two fingers down her throat when she called Heather that. "I get it that things haven't been so great lately. All that shit on Facebook and everything." In fact, Nikki counted that particular shit as a major public relations coup on her part.

"Yeah." Heather sounded like a whipped puppy.

"Think about it for a minute. Here's your chance to get back into the groove. You know? And if you stay away? It'll only make things worse."

"Well…"

"I bet your shrink would tell you that, right?" Nikki coaxed.

"All right," Heather relented. "I'll think about it."

"No! Don't think. Go for it," Nikki pressed. "The sign-up sheet will be posted at school tomorrow. Don't wait, or all the slots will be taken. We have to go sign up first thing in the morning. Meet you at eight thirty. Okay? Heather?"

"I guess so. Yeah."

"Way to go!" Nikki crowed. "You and me in DC. Let's be the first to sign that sheet." She hung up, hoisted her cellphone in triumph and snapped a grinning selfie. Portrait of the girl genius. Too perfect.

It proved easy as stealing coins from her dumb little brother's piggy bank.

Nikki and Heather got to the DC sign-up sheet on the bulletin board early enough that only two other girls beat them to it. They printed their names and added their signatures next to them, exchanged high fives, and headed off to class. Halfway there, Nikki "remembered" she'd left a book she needed in her locker and dashed back down the hall, telling Heather to go ahead without her. No point in both of them being late, right?

As it turned out, Nikki arrived only a few minutes late to class. She'd had a brief wait until the coast was clear, then snatched the sign-up sheet from the board. Checking to make sure nobody was there to see, she'd given the sheet a satisfied once-over, folded it, and stashed it in her bag. About a half dozen of her classmates had already signed up for the trip. Tough luck. They'd have to do it over again after people discovered the sheet had vanished. No biggie. If Nikki didn't mind signing up again, why should the other girls?

And now she had Heather's signature. All she needed was some tracing paper.

THIRTY TWO

DEAD TIRED, JEREMY RUSHED into AP English, again playing Beat the Clock in his race from the other end of the Forrest School. He'd slept poorly once again. Although his desk had been free of offerings the past two days, anticipation kept him on edge.

And today—lo and behold—a large, perfect, bright yellow banana awaited him, atop a folded sheet of paper.

Fruit again. Phallic symbol fruit this time. He blinked, hoping it might disappear. Then he noticed the paper. Pushing aside the banana, Jeremy unfolded the sheet and read. He gasped—that obscene. The typed note bore a name at the bottom, signed in ink.

Heather.

He recognized her signature, same as on the apology she'd written him.

Jeremy's head jerked up, his eyes shooting to the back of the classroom. Heather stared into space, expression blank, despite the murmurs and titters breaking out around the room. Then her eyes met his.

"Out." The word rasped from his lips. A pulse drummed in his ears.

Heather gaped at him, turning pale.

"You heard me. Go!" Jeremy's voice rose. Silence fell over the room.

Heather's mouth opened, but no words came out. She sat, frozen in her chair.

Jeremy took a step forward, pointed at the door. "You go to Mr. Donnelly's office, Heather. Now! I'll be there shortly." Hands icy, his fingertips tingled with an urge to throttle her. So Nikki had been right. "Go!" he thundered.

Heather tottered to her feet. She made her way to the front of the room, avoiding the eyes that followed her. Meanwhile, Jeremy used the classroom phone to summon a sub to sit in for him. When he hung up, Heather stood at the door, staring at him, her face drawn and ashen.

"It wasn't me." Voice high, but firm. She left.

Jeremy's turned to face the silent classroom. The laughter had died, his students cowed by his display of anger. The sight of their wide-eyed, frightened faces abruptly transformed his fury into acute embarrassment. He'd lost it and they'd all seen. Nikki, too. Shame kept his gaze from her.

He took a steadying breath and swallowed. Had to get out of there. "I want you to write an essay while I'm gone." Time for the test he'd spared them the other day. "Gatsby, Chapter Two. What is the significance of the valley of ashes? Five hundred words by the end of the period." He'd like to make it a thousand, but they'd never manage that.

They stared back at him. A tentative hand went up. "Mr. B? Is this an open book assignment?"

"No questions," Jeremy snapped. "Start writing." He snatched the offending note from his desk, crumpled it and thrust it into his pants pocket.

"Mr. Barrett?" One of the clerical staff stood in the doorway.

"They have an assignment," Jeremy told her. "Please monitor them for me. I'll be in Mr. Donnelly's office." He walked out without waiting for her reply.

In the hall, he stopped, struggling for composure. He ran a jittery hand through his hair, doing more harm than good.

"Jeremy?" Marge Peterson came up beside him. "You okay?"

He grimaced.

"I—ah—saw Heather coming out of your classroom, looking upset," Marge said. "I asked her what was going on, and she told me you'd sent her to Mr. Donnelly's office."

"Uh huh."

"I asked her why." Marge cocked her head. "Know what she said?"

Jeremy looked at her, waiting.

"That it was a mistake."

"Mistake!" He pulled the wadded-up note from his pocket, smoothed it open and handed it to Marge. "Does this look like a mistake to you? It came with a banana."

She read the message, shaking her head. "Good lord! But it doesn't make sense. Why would Heather sign her name to something like this?"

"Damned if I know what goes on in her head."

"But are you sure it's her signature?" Marge persisted.

"Absolutely." Jeremy took the paper from her. "Look, Marge, I know you mean well, but I've got a situation going on. I need to get down to Donnelly's office."

"Jeremy, wait." She took hold of his elbow before he walked away. "Do you know what they're doing to her? On Facebook?"

He froze. "What are you talking about?"

"You know I'm on the prevention team this semester. About bullying?" All schools in the state were now required to designate faculty to troubleshoot any instances of peer abuse among students.

"Yeah. So?"

"So you know I monitor their social media posts."

"Oh." Jeremy hadn't realized that. "And…?"

"And lately the herd has been preying on Heather."

"What do you mean, 'preying on her'?" A pinprick of dread arose in his gut.

"She's the butt of their ridicule. The other girls make fun of her, pretty much every day. They're saying she's in love with you, leaves you presents and love notes in class."

A fucking circus. "Jeez, Marge, why didn't you say something?"

"I intended to tell you about it today. I'd hoped it would blow over."

"Well, I'd say it's blown up." Jeremy's hand went to his head, raking his hair into even more unruly spikes. "Look, I'm going to Donnelly's office. If you want to come along and put your two cents in, I don't mind. But let's get moving."

THIRTY THREE

WITH MARGE IN TOW, Jeremy entered the principal's office to find Heather waiting in the reception area. The girl sat hunched in her chair, arms folded. She didn't look up when they walked in.

"Go ahead," Mrs. Marvin, the principal's assistant, told Jeremy. "He's waiting for you." She looked at Marge, eyebrows raised.

"She's coming in with me," Jeremy said.

Heather studied the floor in silence as they walked into Donnelly's inner sanctum.

As always, the array of his degrees and certificates on the opposite wall commanded Jeremy's attention. Seated at his desk below the display, Donnelly looked up, face furrowing. "What's going on, Jeremy? All I got out of Heather is that you sent her here." The furrows deepened. "And why are you here, Marge?"

"I came in my capacity as bullying troubleshooter," she said.

"I see." Angry folds stood out on the principal's forehead. "All right, then, what's this all about?"

Jeremy passed the wrinkled note to Donnelly. "I found that on my desk this morning."

Donnelly examined the note and looked back at him.

"It had a banana on top of it," Jeremy explained.

"Oh." The principal pursed his lips and dropped the paper onto his desk. "I see. Another of Ms. Lloyd's little love notes?" He frowned at the sheet of paper, then nodded toward the sofa, table and chairs that served as his conversational area. "Better sit down and give me the full story."

When they were settled, Jeremy cleared his throat. "It seems someone's been leaving things on my desk in AP English class lately."

"Things?" Mr. Donnelly leaned back on the sofa.

Jeremy fidgeted in his chair. "Candy, fruit."

"Candy?" the principal repeated.

"Uh—little candy hearts."

"And now a signed note?" Donnelly shook his head. "So Heather's still at it."

"Mr. Donnelly." Marge craned forward in her chair. "I think you should be aware that Heather's being bullied on Facebook."

"Bullied? How?"

"The other girls make fun of her," Marge said. "They joke about her being in love with Jeremy and wooing him with gifts."

Jeremy's face grew warm.

"So?" the principal said. "Apparently that's what she's been up to. How does it qualify as bullying, if it's true?"

"But what if it isn't?" Marge protested. "They've been taunting her relentlessly. Why would Heather set herself up for that? More likely someone else staged all this at her expense."

Donnelly squinted. "That strikes me as a needlessly baroque explanation, Marge." He stood, went to his desk and retrieved the note. "Look." He held out the paper to her. "The girl's signature is on it." He thrust the paper at Jeremy's face. "Is it her writing? Do you recognize it?"

"Definitely." Jeremy nodded. "That's Heather's signature." He turned to Marge. "I hear what you're saying, but Heather's developed some sort of—" He hesitated. "Uh, fixation on me."

"But suppose somebody forged her signature?" Marge persisted. "If one of the other girls did that, it most certainly would be bullying. And the school would have a responsibility to intervene."

"Ms. Peterson." Donnelly removed his glasses and massaged the bridge of his nose. "Perhaps you're taking this troubleshooting business a bit too far. You seem to be looking for trouble, rather than shooting it." He sniffed.

His condescending tone irritated Jeremy. Donnelly didn't give a shit what was going on. The principal wanted the whole thing to go away. As he had.

"I'm trying to do my job, sir," Marge said. "I recommend you look into it. At least read those Facebook posts. We could have Heather log onto her page right here, and—"

Donnelly waved her off. "We're not doing that. And it doesn't matter. This business has Heather's name written all over it." He flourished the note. "Literally. I'd say it's time we invited the author in to join us." He motioned toward the office door. "Marge, would you bring Heather in here, please?"

"I still think—"

"Now please," Donnelly snapped.

Marge set her jaw and walked out.

Jeremy's throat went dry. He wanted to get this over with, too, maybe even more than Donnelly. Marge's warnings disturbed him. But hadn't Heather brought this on herself?

Marge returned with the girl, Heather's expression steely.

Jeremy had never seen that look on Heather's face before.

"Sit down, Heather," the principal ordered. He handed her the note. "Is this your signature?"

Heather perused the page, cheeks flushing. "I didn't write this."

"Is that or is it not your handwriting?" the principal pressed.

"I didn't write it, and I didn't sign it," Heather repeated, emphatic. "I've never even seen it before."

A pretty tough customer, standing up to Donnelly like that. Jeremy felt a grudging admiration. Either Heather had become a world-class liar, or Marge was right. The more he considered it, the more unsettling the idea became.

"Heather, Mr. Barrett tells me you've been leaving him little gifts in class." Jeremy winced at the principal's mocking tone.

"True?" Donnelly thrust his face at Heather's.

"No." Heather hesitated. "Just the apology I wrote him." She licked her lips. "About my paper. Nothing else."

"Well, missy, I hear otherwise."

Heather opened her mouth, then closed it again.

"Furthermore," the principal said, "I'd say you chose a peculiar way to express remorse over that episode with your paper, young lady." He gave Heather a withering look.

Hate to be in her shoes. Jeremy gripped the arms of his chair.

"Mr. Donnelly…" Marge interjected.

"Not now."

Jeremy wiped a clammy hand across his forehead. This sucked. Should have kept Donnelly out of it.

"The last time you lied, we gave you a great deal of consideration, Heather," Donnelly continued. "But now, I'm afraid you've used up your supply of good will and second chances."

Heather looked down at the piece of paper in her hand. She crumpled it and tossed it to the floor. "I didn't do anything."

"That's it!" Donnelly clapped once, a sharp sound like a gunshot report. "Heather, I am suspending you, immediately and until further notice, for repeated lying and disrespect. You go have a seat outside with Mrs. Marvin, while I phone your mother."

Tight-lipped, Heather stood and walked out. Marge followed her.

Jeremy stood, eager to get out of there.

"Just a minute, Jeremy."

Donnelly's abrupt tone yanked him back into his chair.

"I don't know what's been going on in that classroom of yours." The principal's tone implied that Jeremy ran a brothel or crack house. "But there's been more than enough trouble coming out of there for one semester."

"Mr. Donnelly!" Jeremy protested. "That's hardly my fault."

"See that you get things under control," he snapped. "Or there will be consequences. Understood?"

"I understand." Jeremy hurried out of the office.

He understood the principal, all too well, but not the shenanigans going on in his classroom. He thought he'd solved the problem. Now he wondered whether all he'd accomplished was to drive the final nail into Heather's coffin.

PART THREE

"No amount of fire or freshness can challenge what a man can store up in his ghostly heart."

— F. Scott Fitzgerald, *The Great Gatsby*

THIRTY FOUR

LETTING OUT A LONG breath, Jeremy closed the principal's office door behind him, only to spot Heather waiting in the reception area. Their eyes met and her look of reproach seared through him. Jeremy averted his gaze and hurried out, lacking words to answer that silent accusation.

Marge accosted him in the corridor. Behind her glasses, her eyes flashed with excitement and her broad face wore a ruddy flush.

"My god, Jeremy, wasn't that awful? Donnelly didn't even give her a chance. I can't believe he just blew off the cyber-bullying like that. Can you?"

In his distraught state, Jeremy found her outrage over the top. "Marge…"

"Jeremy." She peered at him through her glasses. "What did Donnelly mean in there? About that being another one of Heather's love notes?"

She'd caught that. Little point in concealing it, Jeremy decided. "A few weeks ago, I assigned them a paper on Gatsby. Heather's included a personal mash note to me."

Marge's mouth formed an O. "What did you do?"

He described his response, Heather's subsequent accusations, his suspension. A relief to get it off his chest.

"My god!" Marge's face tightened with concern. "What an ordeal for you. Oh!" Her eyes widened with sudden comprehension. "That day I saw you rushing out of school so early…"

"Yeah." Jeremy nodded. "Anyway, then she recanted and I came back." A bitter chuckle. "And so did Heather. That's when all this other stuff started—the candy, the fruit." He winced. "And the rest of it."

"I see." Marge adjusted her glasses, which had slipped down the bridge of her nose. "Jeremy, who else knows about all this?"

He shrugged. "No one. I mean, my family and my lawyer. But nobody here at school except Donnelly."

"None of the other girls?"

"I certainly didn't tell them, Marge."

"Did Heather?" she persisted.

Jeremy shook his head. "I don't know. Why would she?"

"Think about it, Jeremy. If one of the other girls set her up, she must have known about Heather's accusations. Any idea who might have done it? Another girl in your AP class? Someone who saw Heather as a rival for your attention?"

"No. There's nothing like that going on." Yet Jeremy heard the warning bell sound, deep in his brain. *Do you have a secret admirer, Mr. B? Besides me?*

"I'm not going to drop this," Marge said.

"But—what can you do?"

"Write up a report, send it to the district. Or Protective Services."

Jeremy's gut twisted. Not DCPP again. "Marge, don't challenge Donnelly. You'll be risking your job." And mine.

But Marge looked stoked, a bull dog ready to spring. "Someone has to stand up for that poor kid."

"But—"

"I've gotta go, Jeremy. Better get back to your class. Period's almost over."

"Yeah," he muttered. There'd be no stopping her.

HEATHER SLOUCHED IN THE passenger seat of her mother's car, leaning against the window. She stared out as if she were watching the passing scenery, when, in truth, she hardly noticed where they were. Mom had gone on and on, the whole way home from school. It gave Heather a headache.

"I don't understand you. Are you trying to destroy all your chances to get into a good college?"

"I didn't do anything," Heather insisted.

"Your principal showed me the note with your signature on it."

Heather replied through clenched teeth. "I didn't write it."

Mom clucked her tongue. "What in the world is that woman doing with you, for the money we pay her?"

Heather turned from the window and stared daggers at her mother's profile. "Who? Dr. Goldman?"

"Whatever her name is."

"She's good." Heather looked back out her window. "I like her."

"And that teacher!" her mother fumed. "Are you covering up for him? I never trusted him. We should never have let you back in his class."

Your idea, Heather thought, but refrained from saying. "Mr. B is okay." Used to be, anyway.

"Heather!" Her mother sounded exasperated now. "You tell me the truth about that note!"

"I did. It wasn't me who wrote it."

"Then—what? You're saying someone forged it?"

Her mother didn't believe her, made the whole idea sound crazy. But it had to be true. "I guess, yeah."

"But why?" her mother demanded. "Who would do such a thing?"

"I don't know, Mom." But by now Heather had a pretty good idea who. Even if she still had no clue why.

MORNING FADED INTO AFTERNOON, shadows dimming the corners of his office. Slumped at his desk, Jeremy couldn't shake that image of Heather, her look of sorrow. No, not sorrow. He slowly gathered up books and papers. Disillusion. She'd seen right through him. But how? Heather didn't know about Nikki.

Jeremy crammed the books and papers into his briefcase, turned off the light and left, locking his office door behind him. He imagined Heather's eyes following him through the hall, down the stairs.

Instead, he discovered Nikki waiting by his car in the teachers' parking lot. She came up behind him, reaching for his elbow.

"It was her, right, Mr. B?"

Startled, Jeremy turned and stared, searching Nikki's perfect face. Did he catch a flicker of triumph there? Or had Marge's talk about rivalry made him paranoid?

"I—I really can't discuss it."

Nikki's eyes widened a fraction. "Not even with me?"

Normally that look and appeal from her would have moved him. Now he hesitated, reluctant to risk giving her any more ammo. Sickening to see her that way, his muse. And yet. Better be the adult now. "I'm sorry, Nikki."

Her face fell.

"I can't." He turned to go, heartsick.

"I was only trying to help you, Mr. B."

Such wistfulness in her voice. He stopped, didn't turn around. "I know, Nikki. I have to go now." He got into the Honda, pulled away without looking back.

Look where you're going. Keep your eyes on the road ahead. You've been driving blind. Like his father's voice inside Jeremy's head. God, how he missed Mike Barrett, needed him now.

THIRTY FIVE

JEREMY PULLED UP AT the apartment shortly after four. He turned off the engine and lingered in the driver's seat. He saw Melissa's car, knew she'd be upstairs. He seized a few more moments to sit with his disquiet. A neighbor walked by and waved. Jeremy raised a hand in a return greeting, blinked to clear his head, and got out of the car.

Melissa must have heard his footsteps, because the apartment door swung open as Jeremy reached the second floor. "We have company." She angled her head toward the living room.

Jeremy raised his eyebrows, and a familiar voice called out: "Hey, Baby Daddy! Get in here, man."

"Rick?" Jeremy walked in, gaping at his old friend, who rose from the sofa. "Holy shit! What are you doing here, bro?" He rushed into a bear hug. Since Rick's move to California, Jeremy rarely saw him.

"Business trip, last minute. Thought I'd surprise you guys." Rick pulled back from their embrace and regarded Jeremy with a roguish grin. "And here, you're the ones surprising me. Melissa told me the news. Congratulations, dude! Imagine you being Papa Jeremy." Rick gave his shoulder a playful punch.

"I can't believe this." Jeremy stared at his friend's suntanned face, the handsome features, always impossible to compete with. "How you been? How're your folks? You see them yet?" Rick's parents still lived nearby in Livingston.

"Yeah, I'm staying with them for a couple days. They're great. Talking about moving down to Florida, can you believe that?" Rick chuckled. "They can hang out with your Mom. How's she doing?"

"Good," Jeremy replied. "Well, pretty good, considering."

Rick's smile faded. "Must be tough for her since your Dad's gone."

"Yeah, kinda." Weird. He'd just been thinking of his father. "But, you know, she's coming along. She's got plenty of friends."

"And a grandchild on the way!" Rick's lopsided grin returned. "I hear that's worth major points in the Florida grandparent circuit. Must be perking her up."

"Yeah." Jeremy gestured toward the sofa. "C'mon, sit. Get you a beer?"

"Absolutely." Rick settled onto the couch.

"I'll get it." Melissa headed for the kitchen. "You guys chill and catch up. Rick, you'll stay for dinner, right?"

"On one condition," he replied. "We go out and celebrate, and I buy."

"Deal," Jeremy said.

NIKKI STARED INTO THE barren refrigerator, cursing under her breath. Mom hadn't picked up groceries before she left for work. Probably didn't get up in time. Sleeping off the contents of that empty vodka bottle sitting on top of the recycling, she guessed. Fuck that. Let Mom put out the can for tomorrow's pickup. Damned if she'd do it.

Having eaten only a candy bar for lunch, Nikki was ravenous. She contemplated a half-full jar of chunky peanut butter, the staple of her brother Brandon's diet, but it didn't appeal to her. She wanted some fresh fruit, maybe a yogurt. Disgusted, she slammed the refrigerator door and stalked to the pantry closet for the saltines.

The bitch. What were the chances she'd hit the supermarket on her way home from her shift at Macy's? Slim to none. *Do you know what it's like to be on your feet all day?* Nikki imagined the whine in her mother's voice. *And your father late with his child support again.*

Fuck, she'd leave too.

She hoped Mom would pick up a pizza on the way home. Nikki opened the package of crackers and stuffed one into her mouth. Stale. She grabbed a couple more from the pack anyway and walked off, leaving the pantry door open.

Things used to be better. When her father still...

No. Nikki pushed aside that thought before it claimed any more real estate in her head. No use dwelling on shit like that. Better to savor the coup she'd pulled off on Heather today. What a mastermind! She could be a freaking Hollywood director, right? Freaking Sofia Coppola.

Nikki swallowed the last of her cracker and thrust another into her mouth. So hungry. Hungry for so much. The nerve of Mr. B, putting her off like that today. Again! Her Special Older Guy, and he treats her like that?

UnFucking Acceptable.

Rejection and abandonment? Not for Nikki Jordan. No more. Mr. B had a choice—shape up or suffer the consequences.

Starting tomorrow.

THIRTY SIX

ALTHOUGH RICK INSISTED HIS expense account would cover a four-star restaurant of their choice, Jeremy held out for their favorite local BYOB Italian place and brought along a decent Cabernet they had on hand. One day it might be the Barretts' turn to reciprocate Rick's hospitality, and Jeremy preferred not to set the bar too high. The food did not disappoint.

Over appetizers of Mussels Fra Diavlo, Stuffed Mushrooms, and Asparagus and Prosciutto drizzled with Truffle Oil—which the three of them shared, family-style—Rick announced that he'd put a down payment on a place in Newport Beach.

"A small cottage," he said.

"But in Newport Beach!" Melissa marveled. "Near the water?"

Rick shrugged. "A block away."

Jeremy shook his head. Talk about the rich getting richer.

"Aah." Rick waved his hand dismissively. "It's not that big a deal."

"We've been talking about house hunting," Melissa said.

Jeremy shot her a warning glance, as he reached to dip his bread in the last of the Fra Diavlo sauce.

"Makes sense, with the baby coming," Rick said. "Where you looking?"

"Basking Ridge, maybe," Melissa said.

"Nowhere yet," Jeremy said at the same instant.

"Okaaay." Rick looked from husband to wife with a wry smile. "So, Jeremy, how's your writing coming along?"

Jeremy realized his buddy meant to toss him a life preserver, not a curve ball. But his writing? Not a topic Jeremy wanted to discuss. "Uh, haven't had much time for it lately," he stammered, hoping he wasn't blushing.

Melissa pursed her lips.

Jeremy pulled his shirt collar away from his neck. More than wine making him sweat.

"Too bad, man," Rick said. "Your stuff is awesome." He raised the wine bottle in Melissa's direction, but she shook her head and covered her empty glass with her hand. Rick nodded. "Right, Mama." He poured more wine into his own glass and topped off Jeremy's. "You know, Mel, he showed me some of those poems he wrote after that summer in France. No wonder you fell for this guy."

Jeremy caught her eye roll and gulped more wine. The waiter appeared and cleared their appetizer dishes.

"He still the soulful romantic?" Rick teased.

Jeremy gritted his teeth.

"Oh, sure." Melissa aligned her silverware. "He's into red lace garters these days."

"Woo hoo!" Rick lifted his glass to salute Jeremy. "Do tell!"

Jeremy yanked his napkin from his lap and dropped it onto the table. "Melissa will tell it better. I'll be right back." He ignored Rick's puzzled look and headed for the men's room.

At the sink, Jeremy splashed cold water on his flushed face and dried off with a paper towel. The reflection staring back at him from the mirror looked utterly defeated. He'd always run a distant second to Rick, but now he'd fallen so far behind that catching up was out of the question. His friend, who'd started out a jock with mediocre grades, now enjoyed money and success. What did he have? Supposedly the smart one, Jeremy didn't make enough to afford a house, assuming he'd even keep his job. No wonder his wife considered him a loser. Nice going, Barrett.

Add to his stellar portfolio one blind infatuation with a sixteen-year-old girl.

Jeremy lowered his eyes, too disgusted to look at his reflection. Measuring himself against Rick tonight made everything clear. He'd latched onto Nikki as a desperate fantasy of a second chance—as a writer and a man—instead of going out and staking his claim, like Rick. A stupid, half-assed risk of what little he had. Adding to his shame, Jeremy knew he'd played a part in hurting Heather. Everything he touched turned to shit. He left the men's room before he did any further damage, like smashing his fist through the mirror, and returned to their table.

The entrees had been served during Jeremy's retreat to the men's room, but Melissa and Rick had waited for him, rather than dig into their meals. They looked downright cozy, Melissa laughing and leaning in toward Rick, her hand resting on his arm. They looked up at him—their expressions all amusement and no guilt—as Jeremy took his seat. Maybe Melissa had regaled Rick with an account of the red garter incident. He hoped not.

"Go ahead," Jeremy urged, picking up his fork. "Don't let it get cold."

"Great food," Rick said, savoring his Osso Bucco. "Glad you picked this place."

"Yeah." Jeremy sliced off a piece of Veal Francais and slid it into his mouth. He didn't deserve to eat anything this good.

"So." Rick looked from Melissa to Jeremy. "You guys hoping for a boy or a girl?"

Melissa shook her head, swallowing a mouthful of fish. "Please! Too early. It's probably bad luck to even think about that yet."

"Nah." Rick speared his veal shank with a marrow fork. "Gotta think about names, right?"

Jeremy pushed around the veal on his plate. "Plenty of time for that."

"Hey." Rick sat back in his chair. "Why not name the baby after your old man, Jeremy? Michael—or even Michaela, if it's a girl." He shook his head. "Your dad was the best. Too bad he can't be around to meet his first grandchild."

A wave of sadness killed the rest of Jeremy's appetite. He didn't want to hear any more about his father tonight.

Rick went on. "Remember when you kicked that football through your neighbor's window? What were we—ten, twelve years old?"

"Twelve." Jeremy remembered, all right. He'd been aiming that kick about sixty degrees in the other direction.

"You broke a neighbor's window?" Melissa snickered.

"Shattered the fucker." Rick chuckled. "Made some racket, too. So the guy comes storming out of the house..." He paused, laughing in earnest now.

"Oh, boy," Melissa said.

Jeremy gulped his wine.

"And Jeremy's dad comes out of the Barretts' at the same time."

"What happened?" Melissa looked at Jeremy.

"Nothing, really." Jeremy shrugged. "I had to pay for the new window, from my allowance and by doing yard work for the neighbor."

"Yeah," Rick said, "but the point is how your dad stayed totally calm. He defused the whole thing."

Jeremy nodded, his throat tight. For the second time that night, he heard his father's voice. *Accidents happen. But we have to pay for the damage we do.*

If only Mike Barrett was here to take charge again, help Jeremy out of the mess he'd made. But maybe better that he wasn't around to see his worst fear confirmed—that he had a failure for a son. Aimless, whether it came to a football, a career or a real commitment to his marriage. Jeremy stared down in misery at his half-eaten dinner.

"Aren't you going to finish your veal?" Melissa asked.

"No." Jeremy put down his fork. "I've had enough."

THIRTY SEVEN

JEREMY DID HIS BEST to stay engaged for the rest of the meal. Melissa and Rick laughed and chatted through dessert, but he had no appetite. Finally Rick paid the check and to Jeremy's relief, declined his half-hearted invitation to come up for an after-dinner brandy, pleading an early sales call. After Rick drove off in his rented Lexus, Jeremy and Melissa trudged upstairs to their apartment.

"You okay?" She peered at his face. "You hardly touched your dinner. And you were so quiet."

"I'm fine," Jeremy assured her, unbuttoning his shirt.

"Rick seems well," Melissa ventured.

"I'll say." He remembered the easy laughter between his wife and friend. "Little cottage by the ocean, and all."

"Hey." Melissa's fingers grazed Jeremy's bare chest as he pulled off his shirt. "Is that what's bothering you?"

Letting the shirt drop to the floor, Jeremy put an arm around Melissa and kissed the top of her head. He smelled a trace of coconut and wondered if she'd used a new shampoo. "No." He sighed. "Well, maybe a little." His gaze traveled around the cramped apartment, with its cheap furniture, piles of clothing and books. "We're a long fucking way from Newport Beach."

Melissa pressed her lips to his neck. "And he's a long way from married with a baby on the way. It's okay. Really." She stared up into his eyes. "As long as we're together in this."

Jeremy felt a knot inside him loosen. Did she mean that? Could Melissa still love him, in spite of all the ways he'd fallen short? "Of course we are," he murmured, drawing her into an embrace. He pulled back and searched her face for signs of doubt or disappointment. But she was smiling, her eyes soft.

Suddenly he wanted nothing more than to make it right between them, to become once again the shy, romantic boy who wrote poetry for her. "Mel?" he said. "I know I've been distant lately. I'm sorry. I've been scared of being a father, afraid I'll screw up. Distracted by all that stuff at school." He placed a finger over her lips before she replied. "Sweetheart, I promise I'll do better. I'm with you. I'm here for our child." He meant it.

She threw her arms around him. "I love you."

No more, Jeremy vowed. Done with Nikki once and for all. Before he came in to bed, he opened the file with his half-written poem, read it one last time. "Goodbye," he whispered, and deleted it.

ALL THROUGH AP CLASS the next morning, Jeremy felt Nikki's eyes on him. He avoided her gaze, but those blue lasers blazed through him. Whenever their eyes did meet, he felt exposed, as if she were reading x-rays of his mind and soul, seeing the sickness there.

Does she know it's over? Or did he need to say the words and remove any shreds of doubt from both their minds?

Nikki lingered at her desk at the end of the period, gathering her things, the last to leave the classroom. Her eyebrows arched into a silent question as she approached his desk.

Jeremy stared back at her, torn.

"Meet me later?" she asked.

A fluttering arose in his chest. Yes, he'd have to spell it out. But not here. "The park at four."

She nodded, her lips curving in a smile, and left.

Jeremy exhaled, drew the first full breath he'd taken all period. He waited a few beats to make sure Nikki had walked off before he stepped into the hallway.

"Jeremy!"

He turned. Marge Peterson hurried up to him, a look of excitement on her round face.

Not a good sign. "What's up?" he asked.

She glanced around the corridor, still crowded with students heading to their classes. "In here." Marge drew Jeremy into his classroom and closed the door.

He eyed her quizzically. "What is it?"

"Do you believe in coincidence?" She gave him a conspiratorial look.

"Marge, what are you talking about?"

"Yesterday morning they posted the sign-up sheet for the DC trip." She paused.

"So?"

"And yesterday afternoon, it was gone."

Jeremy frowned. "What do you mean, 'gone'?"

"Missing," Marge announced, with a triumphant grin. "Removed from the bulletin board. Gone!"

"Marge…" Jeremy's face knotted with impatience.

"So I started to wonder." Marge tapped an index finger against her forehead. "Because I, for one, don't believe in coincidence."

Who was she, Sherlock fucking Holmes? "What are you talking about?"

"I'm talking about the fact that Heather Lloyd signed that sheet yesterday morning. Signed," she added, "as in signature."

"But—how do you know?"

"Because I called Heather this morning to check it out."

"Called Heather?" he echoed in bewilderment. "Why?"

"Jeremy!" She might as well have said duh! in front of his name. "Don't you see? Someone took that sheet to get Heather's signature."

"That's...that's pretty far-fetched, don't you think?"

Marge's eyes narrowed behind her glasses. "Far-fetched? What's far-fetched is the notion that Heather set herself up for ridicule and suspension. I told you yesterday that her signature on that note was a forgery. Jeremy, this can't be a coincidence."

A rushing sensation filled his ears, like sinking into cold water. A long line of people awaited his restitution. Melissa. Heather. Nikki. Too many. He'd never make it right.

"What?" he croaked, "do you propose to do about it?"

"Talk to Donnelly, of course."

Of course. Marge would never sit by for an injustice. And what about him? Jeremy quailed at the prospect of facing Donnelly after the principal's warning.

"Come with me?" Marge asked.

Do it. Step up. But to what end? His presence was bound to trigger Donnelly, maybe make things worse for Heather. Marge would do a better job of it without him. And he had Nikki to deal with. One crisis at a time.

Jeremy shook his head. "No, you go ahead. There's nothing for me to add to the discussion."

Marge stared at him for a silent moment and walked out.

THIRTY EIGHT

MELISSA RAN THE VACUUM cleaner back and forth across the living room carpet, frowning. The bag needed changing, and she didn't have another. Rick's surprise visit the previous day had prodded her into a burst of tidying. He'd hinted he'd drop over to say goodbye on his way to the airport, and she wanted to make a better impression this time. Despite her reassurances to Jeremy last night, Melissa realized how their cramped quarters must look to the owner of a house in Newport Beach. She hoped that tossing out a stack of old magazines and picking up piles of dirty clothes might make the place more presentable.

As she turned off the vacuum cleaner, Melissa's phone bleated out a text from her father.

Call me.

She did. "What's up, Dad?"

"Are you at home?"

"Ye—es." His somber tone unnerved her.

"Alone?"

"Yes. Daddy, what's—?"

"I'll be right there."

Melissa unplugged the vacuum cleaner and stashed it on the floor of the coat closet. She glanced around the living room, which looked a little better. Fluffing a throw pillow, she heard the downstairs doorbell and buzzed her father into the building. His heavy tread mounting the stairs made her uneasy. She opened the door, reading trouble in the pinched lines of his face and grim set of his jaw.

"Dad? What is it?"

"Sit down." He steered her to the couch.

"What's happened?" They sat. "Is Mom all right?"

"She's fine." Her father pulled an envelope from his breast pocket. He started to place it on the coffee table, then drew back his hand, holding the envelope in his lap. "Sweetheart…"

"Dad?" The tiny hairs on the back of Melissa's neck prickled.

"You know that your mother and I love you," he said. "And anything we do is out of concern for your well-being." His gaze bored into her. "And now, the baby's."

"For god's sake, Dad! What's going on?"

"I'm sorry." He passed her the envelope.

THE DAY SPED BY for Jeremy, dreading his confrontation with Nikki. His last period had now ended. Another hour and it would be time to drive to the park. Should he even go? Why meet her, only to say he wouldn't meet her anymore? And suppose he lost his nerve, couldn't bring himself to tell her? He'd be tempting fate to keep this rendezvous.

But he had to go.

He needed to say the words of farewell, needed the finality of that. And Nikki needed to hear them. He owed her an explanation for no more golden afternoons, no more secret glances exchanged in the halls.

No more dreams, at least not for him. Nikki had a lifetime of dreams ahead of her. But at least he'd spare her from wondering or doubting herself. He owed her that.

Owed Melissa so much more.

Jeremy headed for his office, resolved. He'd go. He'd end it. Begin to make things right.

THE FIRST PHOTO MADE Melissa gasp. Her hands shook as she leafed through the rest, the images blurring as tears flooded her eyes.

"I don't understand. Who took these?" Her voice broke. "Who is that girl?"

Her father's hand squeezed her shoulder, and she smelled the familiar scent of his aftershave as he leaned toward her. Cried harder.

"They were shot by a private investigator who works for Peter Winkelman."

"That—lawyer?"

"His investigator submitted a report." Her father's voice so calm as he blew her world to smithereens. "The girl is one of Jeremy's students. Her name is—"

"I don't want to know her name!" Melissa sobbed, raising her hands to her tear-drenched eyes. "I don't understand. Why did Winkelman put a detective on Jeremy?"

"Because I told him to." Her father's tone was matter-of-fact. "Where there's smoke, there's fire. When that girl accused him, I said to myself—"

"Her?" Melissa lowered her hands, eyes darting from her father to the photos, and back again. "But—she recanted. Are you telling me—?"

"Honey." Howard brushed aside a damp tendril of Melissa's dark hair. "It's a different girl."

Melissa squinted, trying to work it out. A different girl? There were two?

"He's been meeting her after school." Her father reached for the stack of photos, leafed through them and passed some back to her. "These were taken at the reservation."

Melissa forced herself to look at the snapshots, taking in more of the details this time. The grin on Jeremy's face. The girl's shiny black hair. She felt sick.

Her father passed her more of the photos. "They only went there that one time. Usually they meet at this park, a few blocks from the school. Around four in the afternoon."

Without wanting to, Melissa tried to recall what she usually did at four, used to do when her world was still intact.

"Melissa." Her father's voice gentle, yet carrying its inevitable authority. "Why don't you pack a bag now and come home with me? We'll arrange to get the rest of your things later."

"Home?" She blinked at him.

"Back to the house. You don't need to stay in this crappy apartment now."

Melissa shook herself, as if breaking free of cobwebs. Where was home? Where did she belong? She lowered her gaze to the threadbare carpet, to her father's well-polished shoes.

"You did this." Her eyes rose to meet Howard's. "You did all this without asking me." She glared at him. "You and that lousy lawyer." Her voice rose. "You had no right."

"Melissa." Like he was reasoning with an unruly child. "You're upset. When you've had a chance to think, you'll see that it's best for you and the child if—"

"But you had no right!" Her voice shrill now, edged with hysteria.

Her father scowled. "Be realistic. He was never good enough."

On her feet now, Melissa's hands clenched into fists. "Get out!"

Howard Milton stood, reaching toward his daughter. "Sweetheart—"

She shook him off. "Get Out Of My HOUSE!!"

He took a step back, hands raised in surrender. "All right, all right. Look, I'll send your mother over. Promise me you won't do anything rash, Melissa. He isn't worth it."

"GO!" she screamed so loudly that her throat hurt.

He went.

In her newly vacuumed, unusually neat living room, Melissa wept, her wet fingers groping the terrible photos. Usually they meet at this park. Around four.

Around now.

She scooped up the pictures and stuffed them back into the envelope, on her way there.

THIRTY NINE

JEREMY GOT OUT OF the car and walked slowly into the park, head lowered.

The last time.

He raised his eyes to look around for other visitors, saw none. His gaze traveled from the patchy grass up to the bare tree branches. A few more weeks and buds would appear there. Green shoots would spring from the ground. He might have shared that with Nikki.

He swallowed his sorrow, determined to go through with this.

And there was Nikki, waiting at their regular bench. He drank in the look of her—the slender frame, that dark, glossy hair. He stopped to savor the sight of her sitting there, waiting for him. That exquisite creature, waiting for him! And once she turned and saw him, the beginning of the end.

She did turn, smiled. Jeremy's heart ached. He wouldn't see that smile anymore.

MELISSA DROVE WILDLY.

She sped through a traffic light, ignoring the angry blasts of horns around her, hands cold and clammy on the steering wheel. So shaky she feared they'd slip off. She tightened her grip.

Where? Where was this park?

Near the Forrest School, she knew. Melissa drove on, far too upset to consider stopping, asking someone. Did this park have a name? No matter. If it was near the school, she'd find it, drive around until she did.

Her foot pressed down on the accelerator.

NIKKI RUSHED INTO HIS arms and Jeremy tensed, determined not to return her embrace.

She edged back, scanning his face. "What's wrong?"

He offered up an awkward smile, but her narrowed eyes told him she didn't buy it. "Nothing," he said. "It's just—we have to talk."

"Ok-aay." Her expression brightened. "Why don't we go back to that neat place at the Watchung reservation and talk there?"

Why not? One last time. Tell her there. But, no. Too foolhardy. "It's better if we talk here." He led her to the bench.

"Mr. B?" Nikki sounded wary. "Has something happened?"

"No. Well, yes."

"What—?"

"Sit down." Jeremy sank onto the bench.

She sat beside him, eying him anxiously. A small furrow formed on her forehead, between those crystal blue eyes.

"I—Nikki, we can't do this anymore." He barely got out the words through the tightness in his throat.

"What do you mean?"

"We can't meet like this—outside of school."

Nikki stared at him, open-mouthed. "But—why? I count on you so much. Don't you care about me anymore?"

Jeremy reached toward her, then dropped his hand to his lap. "It's not that, Nikki. You'll always be—special—to me." How special, she'd never know. He remembered his foolish attempt to capture her in poetry, deleted now. All over.

"Then why won't you see me?"

"Because my wife is having a baby." He hadn't planned to say that. Hadn't a clue what to tell her.

Nikki stared, as if he'd grown horns. "What does that have to do with us?"

Jeremy gaped. He'd assumed she'd give up. It dawned on him that this might prove even harder than he'd anticipated. "Nikki…"

"It's not like I expected to get married, or anything." A note of petulance crept into her voice. "So you're having a kid. So, congratulations."

"You don't understand. My wife, Melissa—" He swallowed. "She needs me."

Nikki got up from the bench and glared down at him. "What if I need you, too?"

UP AND DOWN THE streets Melissa drove, in a widening circuit from the Forrest School. No students around. The school day had ended and they'd gone—to expensive homes, or the mall, or wherever kids went in this affluent suburb.

Except the one in that park with her husband.

Where?

Near the school, her father had said. She turned the wrong way onto a one-way street, braked hard. The envelope of photos flew off the passenger seat, onto the floor of the car. Cursing, Melissa barreled ahead and made the next right turn.

And there was Jeremy's car. On the street, next to a wooded area.

The park.

She pulled in behind the Honda, killed the engine. With trembling hands, Melissa undid her seatbelt, bent over to collect the photographs from the floor. A few had fallen out of the envelope and she shoved them back in. A full deck.

She got out of her car.

A path led between the trees and Melissa followed it. She heard voices as she approached. Jeremy's voice:

"I'll always care for you, Nikki."

FORTY

"I'LL ALWAYS CARE FOR you, Nikki. But be realistic." Jeremy kept his tone light to cover his growing anxiety. Much as he'd dreaded ending it with Nikki, it never occurred to him she might have other ideas. "You'll have plenty of boy-friends, believe me," he assured her. "You don't need a decrepit old guy like me."

Nikki's blue eyes glittered with amusement.

It wasn't all that funny. Why look at him that way? Again, a joke Jeremy didn't get.

"You're not so—" Nikki's gaze suddenly skittered off over Jeremy's shoulder.

He turned to see what had diverted her.

"You bastard!"

"Melissa!" A wave of vertigo swept over him, as if he were on deck in a hurricane. "Wha—what are you doing here?" His eyes dropped from her furious face to the envelope clutched in her hands.

"Catching you red-handed, you shit!" Melissa glanced over at Nikki, glared at Jeremy again.

"Don't be ridiculous." He mentally replayed his exchange with Nikki, trying to reconstruct what Melissa had overheard. "I was just—"

"Liar! I know what you've been doing." Melissa pulled a handful of photos from the envelope and threw them at his face.

"Oww!" Jeremy lurched backwards as the sharp edge of a snapshot clipped him square in the eye. The photographs scattered at his feet. Holding a hand over his streaming eye, he squinted down at them. "Oh, shit." The Camry!

"Damn you!" Melissa sobbed. "You said you'd be here for me and the baby!"

Nikki tittered. "Congratulations."

Melissa gasped as if she'd been punched. She and Jeremy both whirled and stared at Nikki, who grinned like a Cheshire cat.

"You must be very happy," Nikki said.

A low growl from Melissa made Jeremy turn back to her. All the color had leached out of her face.

"You little bitch!" Snarling, she lunged at Nikki.

"No!" Jeremy threw his arms around his wife. "Nikki!" he shouted. "For god's sake, get out of here!"

He heard her tinkling laughter, her retreating footsteps.

"You, you—!" Melissa strained toward Nikki, struggling against Jeremy's hold.

"Please," he begged. "Let's go home and talk about this."

Melissa went limp, sagging in his arms and weeping like a lost child. "How could you?"

"I didn't! I swear. Nothing happened. Anyway, it's over." Too late, Jeremy realized how incriminating that sounded.

"You miserable fuck!" Melissa wrenched free of his grasp and shoved him away. "We're finished! I'm going home and changing the locks. Go get a room at the Meadowview Inn, or sleep in your goddamned car, or—or go stay with your little tramp!" A stinging slap to Jeremy's cheek, right below his bruised eye, punctuated her last word.

"Oww!" he bleated. "Melissa, wait!"

She ran out of the park.

"Please!" He sped after her.

FROM HER VANTAGE POINT behind a tree, Nikki smiled as they rushed past. Marital breakup as spectator sport. She ambled along after them, far enough to observe Melissa get into a Ford Escape parked in front of Jeremy's Honda and slam the door, narrowly missing his fingers.

"Ouch." She clucked her tongue. "Looks like Mr. B is having a tough day."

Shaking her head, Nikki strolled back to the bench and knelt to collect the photos strewn on the ground. She sifted through them, nodding in appreciation.

Nice. Especially this one.

She slid the trophy into her jacket pocket, moments before Jeremy returned. Smiling, Nikki held out the stack of photographs to him. "Thought you might want these."

He took the pictures, nodded mutely, then turned and headed back toward his car, head down, shoulders hunched.

Like a decrepit old guy.

"See you, Mr. B," Nikki crowed.

FORTY ONE

IN HOT PURSUIT, JEREMY made it to the apartment in time to see Melissa go inside. He jumped out of the Honda and tore up the stairs, reaching the top as she slammed the door. The chain rattled inside and he muttered a curse.

"Melissa!" He pounded on the door.

"Go away!"

"Come on," he pleaded. "Can't we talk about it like adults?"

"Adults?"

Bad word choice. Jeremy rested his forehead against the closed door. "Melissa, I know I fucked up."

"Go to hell!"

He sighed. "All right. Look, I'll go to the motel, okay? Can I at least come in for ten minutes to pack a bag? I need a change of clothes for work."

Silence, followed by the sound of the chain sliding free.

Cautiously, Jeremy opened the door, checking to make sure Melissa wasn't poised to whack him in the face with a cast iron skillet.

She sat on the sofa, arms folded, face a mask of fury.

"Thank you," he said. "I'll go throw some things in a bag."

No reply.

In the bedroom, Jeremy considered the luggage collection on the top shelf of the closet and pulled down an overnight bag. Filling a larger suitcase signaled surrender. As he stuffed in socks and underwear, Melissa's feet rustled across the carpet. He looked up, hopeful.

She glared from the doorway. "So how long have you been a pedophile?" Her voice dripped with disgust.

"What? I'm not! I didn't do anything with her. And even if I had, I'm still no pedophile," he added indignantly. "For your information, sixteen is the age of consent in this state."

Melissa snorted. "Oh yeah? Even for fucking her teacher?"

"I didn't have sex with her!" Christ, he sounded like Bill Clinton. "Honest to god, Mel, all I did was counsel her and—and write some, uh, poetry about her, okay?" The truth might help.

"Poetry?" Melissa sneered. "Oh, that I've got to see." She wriggled her fingers. "Come on, show me."

"I—I deleted it."

"You're a liar. A liar and an asshole."

"Look, I'm an idiot, I'll grant you that," he conceded. "But I swear I didn't sleep with her. Whoever took those damned pictures for you got it all, Mel. Nothing happened. Nothing." He pondered. "If something had, wouldn't your photographer have captured the moment?"

"My photographer?" Her eyes opened wide.

"Well, didn't you? Hire someone to follow me, I mean."

"You bastard!" Melissa yelled. "How dare you try to make me the bad guy here?"

"Hey, spying on your partner isn't exactly the moral high ground." Another mistake.

"Pack your shit and get out of here, you—you pervert!" Melissa stormed out, slamming the bedroom door.

Shit. He kept making things worse. He resumed his packing, adding a pair of jeans and khakis to the bag, then a sweater, two shirts and some tees. He hoped he wouldn't need more than that.

Would he?

He sank onto the bed as it dawned on him that his marriage might be over. As he absorbed the idea, muffled voices came through the closed bedroom door.

Now what? Had Melissa called the police?

Fumbling with the catch, Jeremy hastily closed the overnight bag. He threw it over his shoulder and opened the bedroom door. Now he made out the sound of Melissa crying and the voice of his mother-in-law, soothing her. He took a steadying breath and stepped into the living room.

FORTY TWO

IN THE LIVING ROOM, Jeremy found Melissa weeping onto her mother's shoulder. Beth Milton shot him an outraged glare. "You animal! Ungrateful monster!"

Ungrateful?

Jeremy meant to offer an attempt at peacemaking, but Beth's words brought him up short. Of course. He was supposed to be grateful, eternally in debt to his in-laws for their largesse. Their tolerance of his unworthiness.

Well, fuck that.

"I'll be at the Meadowview Inn," he snapped at Melissa, ignoring his mother-in-law. "In case you want to arrange for any additional surveillance."

Leaving the door open, Jeremy walked out. His wife's sobs and her mother's hectoring followed him downstairs.

He drove to the Meadowview Inn and checked in. An old-style motor court, outdoor stairways connected its two floors. Jeremy toted his overnight bag up to the second floor, tossed it onto the king-sized bed and sank down beside the bag. He surveyed his temporary quarters. The wallpaper looked faded. No sofa, just a desk and swivel chair. But the place appeared clean.

Jeremy's indignation over his mother-in-law's affront had subsided from a boil to a simmer. The image of Melissa sobbing on Beth's shoulder gnawed at him now, and he pulled out his cellphone. His call went straight to Melissa's voicemail, so he texted a peace feeler. Awaiting her response, Jeremy picked up the remote, studying the plastic sheet that listed available cable channels. Not bad. HBO and Showtime, plus a lot of sports. He'd survive a night or two.

But the price of the room worried him, given the anemic funds available on his Visa card. Suppose Melissa went on a revenge spending spree? They'd go right over their limit. Then what? Would they throw him out? Maybe he'd find a cheaper motel over on Route 22, but it wouldn't be as convenient for work.

He glanced at his phone. Still no reply from Mel.

Bravado kicked in. What the hell? If Melissa didn't come around in a day or two, he'd move then. Meanwhile, he'd enjoy what little comfort he could squeeze out of this lousy situation.

The thought of creature comforts made Jeremy aware of his empty stomach. Prone to emotional eating, despite his slim build, he'd skipped lunch. Dinnertime approached and he pulled his wallet from his pants pocket to take stock of his liquid assets. Enough for a pizza and a six pack.

Still no word from Melissa.

He scrolled through his contacts and called his regular takeout place for a large pie with sausage and mushrooms. Before hanging up, he changed his mind and switched the sausage to pepperoni. Melissa hated pepperoni, so here was an opportunity to treat himself. He scooped his car keys from the bureau and headed out to pick up some beer on the way to the pizzeria.

The expedition took about twenty minutes, all consumed with worry. His wife, job and future—the immanent risk of losing them all. Jeremy returned to the motel with a heavy heart, a hot pizza, cold beer and a growling stomach.

He juggled his armload of supplies, trying to slide the key card into his room door. The light flashed red and he muttered a curse. He was never any good with these damned entry cards, even with both hands free. He withdrew the card to try again.

"If I get that for you, can I have a slice of pizza?"

Jeremy spun around, nearly losing the pie. The key card slipped from his hand and fell to the ground.

"Nikki! What are you doing here?"

She knelt, retrieved the card, and slid it expertly into the slot. "Back in the park, I heard your wife tell you to come here." The light flashed green and she opened the door. "I told the guy at the desk you were my dad." She giggled and walked into his room.

"Nikki, wait," Jeremy pleaded. "You can't come in here. We could get into serious trouble." He would. He shuddered, picturing zoom lenses zeroing in on the motel room.

Hands on hips, Nikki smirked. "Well, we definitely will be screwed if you stand out there making a scene." Eyes narrowed, she looked menacing. "Or I make one, in here."

Jeremy gulped. With a glance to either side of the door, he stepped into the room.

At once, Nikki closed the door behind him. "Gotcha!" she chortled, advancing a step toward him.

"Nikki—" He backed away, holding the pizza box between them.

She reached out and lifted the lid, peering inside. "Great. Pepperoni. Let's eat first."

"First?" Jeremy repeated, his voice nearly a squeak. "No! Nikki, you have to go."

"I wanna beer." She yanked the six pack from under his arm and pulled off a can, dumping the rest onto the desk.

"You're too young to drink!" Jeremy stared in dismay as she broke off the tab and took a generous swig from the open can.

"Mmm." Nikki wiped a drop of beer from her chin. "How about some pizza? I'm starving."

Keeping his eyes on her, Jeremy warily lowered the pizza box to the desk next to the beer. His own appetite had vanished. "Just one slice, then you have to leave."

Helping herself to the pizza, Nikki flashed him a kittenish smile. "But why? You're separated now, aren't you?"

To Jeremy's horror, she carried the slice and beer over to the bed and perched on it. She crossed her legs, contentedly chewing pizza. She washed it down with another swallow from the can, and winked.

"Come on over. Plenty of room."

Often as he'd fantasized this scenario, all Jeremy felt now was terror. A nightmare. Any minute now he'd wake up home in his own bed, preparing to go teach English Lit to a roomful of sweet, innocent kids.

"Mr. Beee-eee..." Nikki crooned, holding the beer can between her knees. She patted the bedspread beside her.

Jeremy snatched up a can of beer, tore off the tab and downed half in a single glug. He found his voice. "It's—it's been a long, difficult day, Nikki. I'm sure you can understand that I'd like some privacy right now."

"Awww." Pink lips curled in a pout. "Don't you love me anymore?" She took another glug of beer.

Oh god. She must be drunk. Here he was, in a motel room with a sixteen-year-old student who might pass out on his bed any minute. Or worse, wouldn't. His wife's freelance photographer, the guy in the Camry, might be outside right now, filming them through the window. Any moment, the police would pound on the door, and—

The window!

Jeremy's eyes shot to the open curtains. He'd neglected to close them. A sitting duck. He rushed over to pull the drapes together and spied his friend Rick, standing outside, poised to knock.

"Oh, Mr. Beee-eee!" Nikki sang out again from the bed.

Catching sight of Jeremy at the window, Rick waved and pointed to the door.

FORTY THREE

HEART THUDDING, JEREMY GAVE Rick a sickly grin through the motel window. What the hell? Did somebody post a neon sign in the lobby with directions to his room? He held up a finger, signaling his friend to wait, and closed the drapes.

"What's going on?" Nikki called out from the bed.

"Shhh!" He turned from the window. "My friend is out there."

"What??"

"Please!" Jeremy approached the bed. "He wants to come in. I don't want him to see you here."

Nikki grinned and took another swallow of beer. "Not into sharing me, huh?"

Insistent rapping on the door kicked Jeremy's heart rate into the tachycardia zone. He pointed a shaky finger toward the bathroom.

"In there. Quick!"

When Nikki didn't budge, he rushed over and grabbed her arm, pulling her off the bed.

"Hey!" she protested, sloshing beer onto the bedspread.

"Jeremy?" Rick's voice came from outside the door, accompanied by even louder knocking. "What's going on in there?"

"One sec!" Jeremy propelled Nikki into the bathroom, still clutching her beer and half-eaten slice of pizza. He pointed at the toilet. "Flush!" Closed the bathroom door.

"Be right there!" he yelled in the direction of the door. The toilet flushed and he breathed a silent thanks to Nikki. "Coming!" he called out with more conviction, undoing the button on his fly as he raced to the door. He made a show of buttoning up his pants as he let Rick into the room.

"Fuck, man!" A scowl creased Rick's strong features. "What's going on?"

"Sorry. Upset stomach." He wiped his sweaty palms on his pants, as if he'd washed his hands.

Rick nodded, still frowning. "I'm not surprised." His eyes traveled to the pizza box and cans of beer. "Think that's the best thing for your digestion?"

"Huh?" Jeremy followed his friend's gaze. "Oh, no. Not really."

"Pizza still hot?" Rick went over to the table and opened the box. "Pepperoni, huh?" He helped himself to a slice and settled into the empty chair.

No! Don't get comfortable. Jeremy's stomach lurched. Any moment now he really might have to run for the bathroom. Except Nikki was in there.

"Wha—what are you doing here?"

"Aah, man." Rick shook his head, chewing. "I stopped by the apartment to say goodbye on my way to the airport. Found your mother-in-law there, scraping Melissa off the walls. What the hell have you done, Jeremy?"

"Nothing, really. Not so much." He sighed. "What did she tell you?"

"That she saw photos of you with some girl. One of your students, for crying out loud. Jeez, Jeremy! Are you crazy?"

"Yeah, maybe." Jeremy's eyes welled. Rick's mention of the pictures reminded him he still had them. He'd taken them from Nikki and shoved them in his jacket pocket at the park, barely looking at them. He should burn the wretched things. But to what end? There'd be other copies, a digital file. They'd go viral. Ruined, and he'd brought it all on himself.

"Hey, are you listening to me?"

"Huh?" Jeremy looked up, realizing that Rick had been talking to him.

"I said, how could you do that to Melissa at a time like this?"

"I—you don't understand, Rick. The girl, she's a student of mine. She's been going through a bad time. Family stuff. I—I just tried to be there for her. I guess things got a little out of hand." Jeremy wondered how his disclaimer might go over with Nikki, there in the bathroom. "But there was no sex, I swear it."

"Yeah, well, Melissa's the one you need to convince." Rick looked at his watch. "I'd better go, or I'll miss my flight."

"Right!" Sounding too eager. "I mean, yeah. Hey, thanks for stopping by, Rick. Appreciate it, man."

Rick stood and drew Jeremy into a hug. "You'll sort it out. Call me."

Jeremy clung to his friend, moved that Rick had come to check on him. "I will."

Rick pulled free of the embrace, nodded at Jeremy and left. The moment the door closed, Jeremy heard the shower running in the bathroom.

Oh, god no. She wouldn't.

"Nikki?"

No reply but the sound of water. Jeremy swallowed, trying to calm down. Maybe a shower would help her sober up. He reached for his half empty beer and took a gulp. At least Nikki had waited until Rick left. It would be all right. He'd manage this.

Loud banging on the door killed his optimism.

"Jeremy?"

Rick! A frisson of pure, naked terror raced up and down Jeremy's spine. Hide! Under the bed! screamed his reptile brain.

"Jeremy, damn it! Let me in. There's something I forgot to tell you."

Jeremy stood, frozen.

"C'mon! I'm gonna miss my plane. It's important."

Breathless with fear, Jeremy went to the door, opened it a crack and peered out at Rick. "I—I was about to get in the shower."

Rick pushed the door open. "It'll only take a minute." He walked past Jeremy into the room, eying him. "You always start the shower before you take your clothes off?"

"Umm." Jeremy's mind went blank. "Umm, what did you need to tell me?"

"It's about Melissa," Rick said. "She wanted you to know she's not the one who put the photographer onto you."

"Oh. Uh, thank you." Before Jeremy came up with anything more to say, the sound of running water in the bathroom abruptly ceased.

FORTY FOUR

THE TWO MEN STARED at each other in the silent motel room, the moment surreal.

Rick broke the silence. His head jerked toward the bathroom, and he glowered. "You bastard. She's in there, isn't she? She's been here the whole time. You played me for a sucker."

"Rick, I—"

"Mr. Beee-eee!" Nikki warbled from the bathroom. "Ready or not, here I come."

"No!" Jeremy shouted. "Nikki—"

The bathroom door flew open. Nikki emerged, a towel wrapped around her damp, nude body. A skimpy towel.

"Oops!" Her hand stifled a giggle. "Didn't know we had company."

Rick sneered. "So this is how you're helping her with family problems, huh?"

"No," Jeremy protested, "it's not like that."

Nikki giggled. "Is too."

"And to think I stuck up for you." Rick shook his head, lip curling. "I actually told Melissa to give you another chance. Bastard."

"Rick, wait! I can explain." Jeremy took a step toward him.

"Forget it. I'm out of here." Rick turned to go. "Hasta la vista, pal."

"Bye, bye!" Nikki waggled her fingers at Rick.

Jeremy shot her an angry glance and grabbed Rick's left arm. "No, Rick. Don't go like this."

"Let go of me, asshole!" Rick struggled to break Jeremy's hold. "I've got a plane to catch."

Jeremy clung to his arm, determined. "Not until you let me—"

"I said, let GO!" Rick's right arm drew back. His fist smashed into Jeremy's nose.

The moment of impact exploded across Jeremy's senses. The sound of cracking bone mingled with Nikki's piercing scream. Blinding white light, searing pain, a sharp metallic smell. The raw-meat tang of blood flooding his mouth.

With an animal groan, Jeremy sank to his knees, tears pouring from his eyes and blood gushing from his broken nose.

"Shit." Rick rubbed his swelling hand.

"You creep!" Nikki shrieked. "What have you done to him?"

"Shh-shhh." From the floor, Jeremy tried to quiet her before her cries drew outside attention. But he could scarcely breathe, much less talk. He fought down the bile rising in his throat. The pain of vomiting would be unbearable.

"I'm going to call the police!" Nikki cried.

"Yeah." Rick flexed his bruised knuckles. "You do that, sweetheart." He looked down at Jeremy, his handsome face twisted in disdain. "See ya, pal."

He walked out, slamming the door.

"That louse!" Nikki knelt beside Jeremy. "God, Mr. B. I think he broke your nose. Should I call an ambulance?"

"Nuh." A bloody post-nasal drip made it hard to enunciate. "Nuh, don."

"Poor Mr. B."

Nikki's hand brushed back his hair. Jeremy cupped his dripping nose.

"Here, better take this." Standing, she bent over and pressed a towel into his hands.

Gratefully, Jeremy held it to his throbbing face. A moment later, he realized where that terrycloth had come from. Drawing a sharp breath that sent new waves of agony coursing through his nose, Jeremy looked up at Nikki—her slender, naked body porcelain-pale, except for petal-pink nipples, a lush shock of dark pubic hair. Beads of water from her shower still evaporated on silken skin, luminous in the lamp-lit room.

She leered at him, breaking the spell.

With a moan, Jeremy dragged himself across the carpet, inching a few feet away from her. Feeling faint, he leaned back against the foot of the bed and took in the sight of Nikki through half-closed eyelids. Exquisite. Heaven and hell, meeting here in this room.

"Mr. B." Nikki came toward him. "Jeremy…" Her voice a teenage caricature of sultry.

"Nuh!" His hand shot up to stop her approach.

She'd never called him by his first name before. That recognition struck him with a peculiar poignancy. He realized how much he'd liked being 'Mr. B' to a beautiful, admiring girl. Gazing at Nikki's lithe form, he saw her for what she was—a girl. Not so innocent, except in the manner of a ravenous lion cub. But a youth, to be sure.

No, not a youth. Youth incarnate. She was immortality. Redemption. A fabulous dream, and now Jeremy had come to painful awakening. Even had he not been lying on the floor, choking on his own blood, he'd never have violated this nymph, even if she begged. What he'd craved was to be her hero.

Instead he'd been her chump. And now his foolishness would cost him everything—now, when he'd finally begun to value what he had. Blind, stupid fool.

"Nikki?"

"Yes?" She rushed over, sank to the floor beside him.

A scent of roses. Must be his imagination. How could he smell anything through the fractured mess of his nose?

"Would you—?" Jeremy swallowed, trying to clear the mucus from his throat. "Please, would you get dressed and go find me some ice?"

"Sure."

To his immense relief, she threw on her clothes and grabbed the ice bucket.

As soon as Nikki was out the door, Jeremy tottered to his feet, reeling at a wave of vertigo. The blood-soaked towel slipped from his hand. But the bleeding seemed to be subsiding.

Ice would help. He'd get some later.

He lurched to the door, doubled locked it and fastened the chain. "Sorry, Nikki," he whispered. He leaned against the closed door, exhausted and queasy. Shortly, he heard her knock.

"Mr. B? You okay?" A pause, then more banging. "Hey! Open up."

"Nikki—I'm okay, but you have to go."

"But—why?"

"Because nothing is going to happen between us." Jeremy's voice now firm, adult. "What's happened was my mistake, and I'm sorry. But it ends here."

"But nothing happened!" Disappointment in her voice.

"And nothing will."

"Don't you even want the ice I brought you?"

"Thanks. If you'd leave it outside the door, I'd be grateful."

"This is your mistake, Mr. B," Nikki warned. "What you're doing right now." An ominous pause. "I can bring you down, you know." Venom in that voice.

Jeremy sighed. "No, Nikki. I already did that to myself."

"Your wife, then." A malevolent laugh. "Wait and see."

The sudden crash of ice cubes cascading against the door made Jeremy recoil. He heard the rattle of the bucket dropping to the floor, the pounding of Nikki's footsteps, trailing away.

FORTY FIVE

A HOWL ROSE IN Nikki's chest, demanding release, as she jogged to her car in the motel parking lot. Car keys became her weapon. She slashed at random vehicles, gouging paint, picturing Mr. B's face. You had your chance and blew it. Nobody got away with dumping Nikki Jordan.

He'd find out.

She reached her car, got in. Sat and drummed restless fingers against the steering wheel. Growing dark and she wasn't supposed to drive at night with her provisional license. Nikki's VW Beetle had been a gift from her father before he took off. He paid her insurance premiums, but she depended on her mother for gas money. If she got a ticket, Mom would jump at the excuse to ground her. Sure, Nikki could make it home before dark. But that was the last place she cared to be right now. She pulled out her phone and called Heather.

"Something's happened," Nikki said. "Come and meet me."

"Kinda late," Heather hedged. "We have school tomorrow."

"We?" Nikki echoed. "Thought you got suspended."

"Mr. Donnelly unsuspended me."

The hint of satisfaction in Heather's voice stoked Nikki's anger.

"He called a little while ago," Heather added. "He said I could come back."

Nikki's jaw muscles clenched, hard enough to crack walnuts. Couldn't anything go right for her today? "How come?"

"He said there was some doubt about the—uh," Heather stumbled over the words, "the authen-ticity of my signature on that note to Mr. B. My mom thinks we should sue the school. But my dad doesn't want to."

"Really?" Nikki's voice could have curdled milk. "Listen, I need to see you, Heather. Now. I'm in real trouble."

"What's—?"

"It's about Mr. B."

"Oh." Heather hesitated. "I don't think—"

"I'll be at Starbucks. Hurry." She hung up.

"YOU OKAY MISTER?" The burly cashier at the pharmacy winced in sympathy as Jeremy handed him a bottle of ibuprofen to ring up. "You don't look so hot."

"I'll be fine." Jeremy avoided eye contact with the man, whose narrow, pockmarked face attested to an acne-prone adolescence. Spying a rack of disposable lighters, Jeremy selected one and placed it on the counter. "Oh, and this."

He'd burn those damned snapshots of Nikki and him back at the motel. Who the hell put that detective on him, anyway? Not Melissa, according to Rick. Whoever did must have copies, or a digital file.

Fuck, burn them anyway. If only for the satisfaction of reducing them to ashes. But first take the painkillers, and finish off the beers he'd left chilling in the ice bucket. Put some more of the ice on his nose.

Send Melissa another message.

The cashier rang up Jeremy's purchase, clucking his tongue at the lighter. "Shouldn't be smoking with an injury like that, sir."

"No." Jeremy tossed down some bills. "I won't."

"All right, then." The man handed over his change. "You take it easy, huh?"

"Yeah. Thanks."

Night had fallen when Jeremy pulled into the motel parking lot. As he got out of the Honda and closed the door, he heard the slam of another car door, like an echo. He turned in the direction of the sound, his pulse racing. Please, god, not Nikki. In the dim light, he recognized the figure walking toward him.

"You!" He frowned at Rick's approach. "You come back to finish me off? Break my legs, or something?"

Rick halted, beyond Jeremy's reach, and regarded him sheepishly. "Sorry. I shouldn't have gone off on you like that. I got halfway to the airport, but couldn't leave things this way." He drew a few paces closer and studied Jeremy's swollen face. "Aw shit, did I break it?"

Jeremy shrugged. "Doesn't matter." The idea that anyone gave a shit about him tonight made him magnanimous.

"No, it looks bad," Rick insisted. "Let me drive you over to the ER to get it x-rayed."

"What, so we can sit around for hours in a crowded waiting room, with buzzing fluorescent lights and a blaring TV?" Jeremy shook his head. "No, thanks."

"But—"

"Really, it'll be okay."

Rick took another step toward him. "All right, then." He spread his arms wide and closed his eyes. "Go ahead."

Jeremy stared at him in confusion. "What?"

Eyes still screwed shut, Rick stuck out his chin. "Hit me, man."

Jeremy snorted with laughter, and immediately clutched his nose. "Oww!"

Rick opened his eyes. "Ahh shit," he groaned, as Jeremy covered his face.

"It's okay." Jeremy held up the plastic drug store bag. "I got some ibuprofen and there's two beers left up in the room. Hey." He gave Rick a tentative smile. "Wanna join me?"

Rick returned his grin. "For the beer? Yeah. I'll pass on the ibuprofen."

"I don't suppose you have anything stronger?" Jeremy asked hopefully. "Percocet or something?"

"I've got some Valium in my bag. For the flight, you know? I'll get it." Rick went to open the trunk of his rental car.

"Great." Jeremy followed him. "Any chance you have a bottle of scotch in there, too?"

Rick's grin widened. "No, but I can get one. Back in five."

"Awesome," Jeremy said. "Meet me upstairs."

FORTY SIX

RECLINING ON THE BED, every pillow in the room propped behind him, Jeremy dumped four ibuprofen tablets from the container into the palm of his hand. He washed them down with a glug of scotch, leaned over and passed the bottle to Rick, who occupied the motel room's only chair.

"That's a lot of pills." Rick frowned. "You sure you don't want to go to the ER?" The bottle poised en route to his mouth. "I'm still sober enough to drive."

Jeremy waved him off. He doubted either of them were sober enough to make it there.

Rick shrugged and took a generous swallow.

"Thanks for these." Jeremy picked up the prescription vial of Valium from the night table. "They oughta knock me out for the night."

"Go easy," Rick cautioned. "That stuff is potent, especially mixed with booze. Take one when you're ready to sleep. They work fast." He passed the bottle back to Jeremy, then leaned back in his chair, one denim-clad leg crossed over the other.

Jeremy sipped the whiskey, feeling its heat rise to his sore face. "Why the fuck did you slug me, anyway?"

"Cause you had it coming. Cheating on Mel like that."

"Who're you? Sir Fucking Lancelot?" Piqued, Jeremy recalled how cozy Rick and Melissa had looked at the restaurant. "Who appointed you to be her goddamned champion?"

"Hey, she deserves one," Rick shot back. "You know, it really pisses me off that you lied to her. And me." He leaned over for the bottle, took a swig and returned it to Jeremy. "Don't get me wrong," he said, "I know guys who do that stuff all the time." Glassy eyes reproached Jeremy. "But not you."

"Yeah." Jeremy stared at the label on the half-empty scotch bottle, rather than meet Rick's gaze. "There was no sex, Rick, I swear. God knows how she tracked me here." He picked at the label. "I dropped my key and she grabbed it, let herself into the room." Jeremy peeled off a strip from the label and flicked it to the floor. "She threatened to make a scene. I had to let her stay."

Abandoning the ragged label, Jeremy drank more scotch. "B'lieve me, I know what a jerk I've been. The whole thing was a half-assed fantasy. An early mid-life crisis, maybe." He passed the bottle back to Rick.

"But why?" Resting the bottle on his leg, Rick stared at Jeremy with a bleary gaze.

How to answer that? Jeremy reached for the vial of Valium, rolled it in his hands, as if absorbing its tranquilizing effects through his palms. "You wouldn't know how it feels to be a failure."

"Wha?" Rick demanded.

"No!" Jeremy cut him off, the scotch loosening his tongue. "You gotta career anna beach house, and—and always bein' the one who gets the hot women. How would you unnerstand what makes a loser like Jeremy Barrett need to feel like somebody, for a change?" He groped for the bottle, but Rick held onto it, staring at him.

Jeremy lowered his hand. "I know, I know. I messed up my whole fucking life, an' I have no one to blame but myself." He lunged at the bottle. "Will you gimme that thing, already?"

Rick passed it over, shaking his head. "You don't get it, do ya, pal?"

Jeremy drank in silence.

"Y' know." Rick gave a harsh laugh. "I'm a medi—medi-ocre jock who got some lucky breaks. But you—you've always been smart, and—and good. I mean it," he insisted, as Jeremy made a face at him. "I've looked up to you since we were kids."

"Then you're an even bigger moron than I am." Jeremy swallowed more scotch, his face growing warmer. Despite his cynical rejoinder, Rick's admiration touched him.

"No," Rick insisted. "You were my best friend. An A student. And then you married this great girl, who was crazy about you."

"Was," Jeremy repeated bitterly.

"No, man, she loves you." Rick reclaimed the nearly empty bottle. "Iss that damned family of hers."

"Well, yeah." Jeremy sank back into the pillows. His friend had made an excellent point.

"But, ssee…" Rick slurred, "tha's something I respect about you, buddy. You din let the Miltons buy you. You did your own thing, teaching and all."

"Yeah. So?" Jeremy burped. "What've I got to show for it?" Were the lights dimming? He thought about the scotch, but let his head sink back into the pillows instead. "Ev'ryone knows what a loser I am. My dad, he always knew."

Dropping the empty bottle, Rick lurched from his chair. He wobbled over and leaned on the bed near Jeremy's feet.

"Hey!" He pushed on the mattress to rouse Jeremy, who slowly opened one swollen, bruised eye. "Hey!" Rick shook Jeremy's foot. "Listen'a me."

Jeremy opened the other eye and gazed at him woozily.

"Your ole man loved you," Rick insisted. "An'e wuz proud'a you. B'lieve me, I know." He sank onto the bed. "Way he talked about you."

"Jez sayin' that," Jeremy murmured, fading.

"Nuh uh." Rick dragged himself up along the mattress, curling into a fetal position alongside Jeremy. "Mike loved ya. He'uz juss afraid you'd think 'e waz'n smart enough." He yawned noisily. "To 'preciate your poetry, 'n all."

"Yeah? That so?" Jeremy wanted to smile, but his lips felt too rubbery.

"Abs'lutly," Rick said, with a last burst of energy. He added, more faintly, "'Kay if I take a li'l nap 'fore I go?"

"Sure." Jeremy drifted off, hoping he'd remember Rick's reassuring words in the morning. His final thought as sleep enfolded him was that he'd forgotten to take any of the Valium.

FORTY SEVEN

FLUSHED AND BREATHLESS, HEATHER slid into a seat across from Nikki at Starbucks. "I—I can only stay a few minutes. I told my mom I was walking over to the library before they closed."

"You walked here?" Nikki stared as if Heather had told her she swam the English Channel.

"It's only half a mile." Heather took Nikki's napkin and blotted her sweaty forehead. "I couldn't exactly ask for my mom's car when it's already dark, could I? With my provisional license?"

Nikki suppressed an eye roll. Personally? She'd have taken the freaking car without asking. What a wuss. But Nikki didn't need a confederate who possessed initiative—that was her department.

"What's going on?" Heather asked. "You said you were in trouble."

"I am." Nikki fingered the straw protruding from her half-finished smoothie, avoiding Heather's curious gaze.

"And it's about Mr. B?"

Nikki nodded. "It's bad." She bit her lip.

"Nikki—tell me!"

"He tried to rape me."

Her revelation had the desired impact. Heather gasped. "What? When?"

"Just now."

"But—where?" Heather cast a nervous glance around the coffee shop, as if rapists might lurk at the tables.

"At the Meadowview Inn. He's staying there because his wife kicked him out."

Heather shook her head, perplexed. "But—what were you doing there?"

Nikki's hand shot out, gripped Heather's wrist. Hard. She fixed a steely gaze on the girl. "You swear not to tell?"

"Oww! You're hurting me." Heather yanked her hand free. "Tell what?"

Nikki's blue eyes darted around the Starbucks before zeroing back in on Heather's. "We've been seeing each other."

Heather stared, bug-eyed. "You and Mr. B? No way!"

"Way. We've been meeting after school. He took me to the Watchung

Reservation."

"Get out!" Heather's eyes narrowed in disbelief.

Nikki reached into her jacket pocket. "Here, see for yourself." She passed the photo she'd snatched at the park.

"Wow!" Heather gawked at the snapshot. "But—that's illegal! He's your teacher. Nikki, you have to tell."

Nikki took back the photo, her eyes boring into Heather's. "Tell?" she echoed. "How much good did that do you?"

Heather flinched. "But—that was different. I—I made it up." She swallowed and looked at Nikki. "So, what happened? At the motel, I mean?"

Nikki leaned back and drew a breath, going over the story she'd crafted for Heather's benefit. "Mr. B called me from the motel. I think he was actually crying."

"No shit!" Heather exclaimed, impressed.

"He told me he had to see me. He was devastated. Of course, I said I couldn't," Nikki added hastily. "But then he begged."

"God."

"So I drove over there. It wasn't dark yet." She fiddled with her straw, doing her best to convey embarrassment, an emotion entirely alien to her.

"What happened?" Heather prodded.

Nikki paused as if it pained her to go on. "As soon as I came into his room, he put the Do Not Disturb Sign onto the door and locked us in. He even put on the security chain."

"Omigod! Didn't you try to run?"

"Yeah! But—" She hesitated. "But then he grabbed me. He said he was in love with me and couldn't wait anymore. Then he—" Nikki put a convincing catch into her voice. "He tried to get my clothes off."

"Nikki! Did you scream?"

"I did better." A brave smile. "I slugged him."

"You hit a teacher?" Heather looked at her, in awe.

"Uh huh. He'd left a can of beer on the desk and I grabbed it. Socked him right in the nose with it."

"Wow! You actually hit him."

"I had to. Self defense. When I think what might have happened..." Nikki shuddered. "Anyway, he went down, his nose all bloody and everything, and I got the hell out of there." She blew out a breath. "And then I called you."

"Oh, Nikki. This is unbelievable. Awful." Heather shook her head. "We should go to the police, right now. He shouldn't be allowed to get away with it."

A slow smile spread across Nikki's face. "Maybe he won't."

FORTY EIGHT

THE MOMENT JEREMY'S EYES opened, he knew he would puke. He sat up, ready to bolt for the bathroom, and looked around, bewildered. Not his bedroom. Too sick to sort that out, he spied a waste basket on the floor, lurched out of bed and lunged for it. Half awake, he vomited, tasting scotch.

That much accomplished, Jeremy surveyed the surroundings from his vantage point on the carpet. A motel room. The sound of a shower running. But if he wasn't at home, not Melissa in the bathroom. Then, who...?

A jolt of panic roused him to full wakefulness. He started to get up, and a dull ache radiated from the middle of his face, bringing a vague memory of Rick punching him. But when? And why? Sketchy images surfaced in Jeremy's mind. He recognized the room. The Meadowview Inn.

Oh god, was that Nikki in the shower? But I locked her out. Did she get the manager to let her back in? Had she spent the night?

The shower stopped.

Jeremy forced himself to his feet, preparing for a quick escape. The bathroom door opened and he was startled—then relieved—when Rick emerged, one towel around his waist, another scrubbing his wet hair.

"Hey, you're up."

"What are you doing here?" Jeremy stared.

Rick chuckled. "Yeah, I know. Looks like we polished off that whole bottle of scotch last night. I can barely remember what time zone I'm in." He cocked his head, appraising Jeremy's bruises. "Jeez, you look like you went a few rounds with Mike Tyson. How're you feeling?"

Jeremy took stock. His nose hurt, but not with the throbbing agony of last night. A headache, too, either from the punch or the scotch.

"Not too bad."

"Good." Rick nodded. "Still, you should see a doctor today, get an x-ray. Maybe your nose needs fixing." He made a rueful face. "Anything your insurance doesn't cover, send me the bills."

"Sure, thanks. But I think I'm okay." The prospect of anyone touching his sore nose, even for therapeutic purposes, made Jeremy queasy again. "What time is it?" And what day? Tuesday, he remembered.

"Nearly eight. I'm heading over to the airport."

"Eight?" Jeremy's first class started in an hour. He'd be late, had to get moving. He rushed forward—too fast—and reeled.

"Hey!" Rick reached out to steady him. "Easy, now. Better lie down and get some more rest."

Jeremy took a deep breath, felt steadier. "Nah. I've got to get to class."

Rick frowned. "You're going in?"

Jeremy stared at him. It hadn't occurred to him not to show up. But Rick had a point. What awaited him there? And how would he explain…?

Anxiously, Jeremy hurried to the bathroom and checked his reflection in the mirror. Holy shit. His heart sank at the sight of his heavily bruised eyes and swollen nose. Maybe he'd say he'd been mugged.

Then it dawned on him. Suppose Nikki told the real story. What then?

"Hey, Jeremy?" Rick called out. "I'm gonna check out the lobby, see if they've got some coffee down there. Want me to bring you a cup?"

"Yeah, great." Coffee sounded almost like salvation.

"Back in a jif."

Jeremy went to the toilet to pee, relieved to find at least one of his bodily functions operating normally. He considered the shower—could he stand under the spray without letting it hit his face? Worth a try. Shaving? Out of the question. Before he lost his nerve, Jeremy turned on the shower, adjusted the temperature and eased his way under the water.

Not bad. The hot spray relaxed the knotted muscles of his shoulders and back. He sighed, soaping himself. Take this a step at a time. Get clean, get dressed, drink some coffee.

Decide whether to become a fugitive from justice.

By the time Jeremy finished his shower, Rick had returned with their coffee. Jeremy sat on the side of the bed and took a sip, feeling the caffeine begin to clear out his remaining mental cobwebs. As his brain focused, he thought of Melissa and grabbed for his cellphone.

Still no word.

As he texted her another apology, pleading to see her, Rick asked: "So what did you decide to do about work?"

"Just a sec." Jeremy sent the text and looked up at his friend, shrugging a jacket over his turtleneck. He considered Rick's question. A million reasons not to show up at school today. Every instinct warned him to stay away.

Then again, he'd allowed his instincts to lead him around by his nose—or maybe, his dick—for weeks. And look where that had brought him. It might be time to listen to his head, for a change.

"I really should go."

Rick frowned. "Not to be negative here, but do you think you're in any shape to face what might happen?"

"Maybe not." Jeremy stood, reached for his overnight bag and pulled out clean clothes. "But I'm not sure that matters."

Rick's eyes narrowed. "What's that supposed to mean?"

"I don't know. Just—I've screwed up so many things already. I think it's time I started cleaning up the mess I've made."

Rick nodded. "Good luck, pal."

FORTY NINE

JEREMY PULLED INTO THE faculty lot. He'd barely make his first class on time, yet he sat for a moment, preparing himself. All the way to the school, he'd debated: go straight to the principal's office and confess everything to Donnelly? The angel on one shoulder whispered into Jeremy's ear: Do the honorable thing. Face the consequences. At least you'll regain your self-respect and peace of mind.

From his other shoulder, the devil hissed: Are you fucking crazy? Wait and see if you get away with it. Jeremy hadn't decided. He longed to talk with Melissa. If he didn't have to face this alone, he might be able to deal with it.

As he approached the entrance to the school, his cellphone played Melissa's ringtone. Eagerly, he pulled it from his pocket.

"Mel! Thank god!" The words spilled from his lips. "Sweetheart, I'm sorry, so very sorry for everything. Please let me come and talk to you."

"Where are you?" The urgency in her voice made him hopeful. She wanted to see him! "I'm walking into the school." Jeremy pushed open the entrance door. "But I could come home right after—"

"Jeremy! The police were here looking for you."

Jeremy caught sight of Mr. Donnelly, planted in front of him like a sentry, and froze.

Scowling, arms folded, the principal stood, flanked by two uniformed policemen. They took a step toward Jeremy, and Donnelly shot him a smug grin. One of the cops produced a set of handcuffs.

"Oh no," Jeremy murmured.

"Jeremy?" Through the phone, Melissa's voice rose with alarm. "Are you there? What's going on?"

"Jeremy Barrett?"

"That's him," the principal said.

The policeman with the handcuffs came forward as his partner announced: "We have a warrant for your arrest. You have the right to remain silent…"

"Jeremy!" Melissa shouted. "What's happening?"

"I—I have to hang up. They're here. Mel, I'm gonna need a lawyer."

"...you have the right to an attorney," the cop droned, right on cue. While he recited the Miranda rights, his partner took the cellphone from Jeremy's hand and thrust it back into his jacket pocket, then spun him around, cuffing Jeremy's hands behind his back.

A few students stood by, gaping.

What a show.

"Look, it's Mr. B," one of them said.

"My god, what happened to his face?"

Amid the sea of student and faculty faces, all staring at him in horror, Jeremy spotted his friend Marge Peterson. The look of disappointment on her face struck him like a blow.

I'm sorry, Marge.

Donnelly's voice behind him: "Barrett, you degenerate, you're finished. You'll never step inside a classroom again."

No, probably not.

The cops led him away. The last familiar face his eyes beheld on the way out the door was Nikki's, her expression stony and inscrutable as the Sphinx.

Part Four

"So we beat on, boats against the current, borne back ceaselessly into the past."

— F. Scott Fitzgerald, *The Great Gatsby*

FIFTY

NIKKI WATCHED, STUNNED, AS the police led Mr. B away in handcuffs. She'd overslept and skipped breakfast after a restless night spent plotting his fate, And now this. Two minutes later, and she'd have missed the whole thing. When she caught Mr. B's eye on the way out the door, Nikki stared at him, gnashing her teeth.

Robbed.

Nikki, patient spider, had painstakingly woven her perfect web. Caught and captive in her silk, Mr. B had been hers for the tasting. She'd expended such care—such love, such relentless appetite—and it had worked! Maybe he thought he'd escaped last night, but that photo of the two of them she'd swiped ensured Mr. B had to do whatever she wanted—until she finished with him. Look how the snapshot worked on Heather. The stupid girl would have swallowed any story Nikki wove.

Snared. And now some dumbfuck cops had stolen him away.

Nikki fumed. She'd find a way to get back at that parasite, the scum who'd betrayed her. Heather. Hadn't she warned that little bitch? Made her swear not to tell? But she'd gone and done it anyway, before Nikki had a chance to savor her triumph.

She'd pay.

Furious, Nikki headed down the corridor, in search of Heather.

"Nikki." Out of nowhere, the principal appeared. "I need you to come to my office."

"Now?" Nikki didn't bother to hide her indignation. Effing thwarted at every turn.

"Yes." Mr. Donnelly took her by the elbow. "There are some people waiting to talk with you."

More alarmed than angry now, Nikki had no choice. She accompanied him down the hall to his office, conscious of classmates' eyes following them. That little bitch, Heather!

They passed through the reception area to the inner sanctum of Mr. Donnelly's office. Three people—two men and a woman—already sat there.

Three sets of eyes bored in on Nikki as she entered.

"This is Nikki Jordan. Nikki." The principal turned to her. "Let me introduce these people." He gestured toward a dark-haired man in a crisply pressed blue suit. "This is Mr. DellaRocca from the Prosecutor's Office."

The man stood. Unfolded. Nikki had to look up. At least six four. Nodding at her, he had cold eyes, a blank expression. A lizard. He shook her hand with a firm grip, making it clear who was in charge here. He gave Nikki the creeps.

"And this is Mrs. Wolfe, from Protective Services," the principal said.

The woman had gray hair and wore a long skirt. She gave Nikki a phony, friendly smile. The good cop. Well, fuck that.

"And Detective Burns." Mr. Donnelly indicated a middle-aged man with a shiny, bald, chocolate-brown head. The real cop. Nikki swallowed.

The detective smiled. "Good morning, Nikki."

"Now then." Mr. Donnelly clapped his hands, like he did when he called assembly to order. "Sit down, Nikki. These people have some questions."

Nikki remained on her feet, her gaze taking in the room. Four on one. Cornered. How to play this? She turned to the principal. "Shouldn't my mom be here?"

Donnelly indicated an empty chair. "It's all right, Nikki. I already called her. They're short-handed at the store and she can't leave."

Right. Mom of the Year comes through again. Not.

"She gave consent for you to be interviewed, as long as I'm present," the principal added.

Nikki shot him a baleful look. Like he was gonna protect her?

"Sit," the principal repeated, more insistently.

Resigned, she sank into the chair.

The DCPP woman gave Nikki another of her fake sympathetic smiles. "Would you prefer your mother to be here?"

Like she's gonna protect me? Nikki shrugged. "Nah, I guess not."

"All right then," Mr. Donnelly said. "Nikki, tell these people all about what happened between you and Mr. Barrett."

FIFTY ONE

"JEREMY!" FRANTIC, MELISSA PRESSED redial.

Voicemail.

The police were there, he'd said. Arresting him. Her throat constricted. She could hardly swallow or breathe.

I'm going to need a lawyer, he'd told her.

Her legs wobbly, Melissa sank into a chair at the kitchen table. A part of her seemed to be looking on, observing her own distress and panic. What did she owe him? He'd cheated.

Maybe.

She didn't know anything, anymore. Leaning over the table, Melissa lowered her head into her hands. The tears came. Pregnant, alone and scared. How was she supposed to deal with all this?

She picked up her phone, speed-dialed her father. Howard Milton, the rock, the keystone. He always knew what to do.

"Dad?" Mel's voice quavered. "Oh, Daddy, I think Jeremy's been arrested. He needs a lawyer. He needs—"

"Sweetheart!"

Her father's voice enveloped her like a balm.

"He's not your problem anymore."

His words a gut punch. "What are you saying?"

"It's time you came home, Melissa. I'll take care of you and the baby. Pack a bag and I'll be there in—"

She caught her breath. "You! You did this. You took those pictures and turned him in. Didn't you?"

"Melissa…"

"Didn't you?" Her voice rose. "You had no right! No right to mess up my life."

"Melissa," Howard said in an oh-so-patient voice, "Jeremy is the one who's messing up your life. Who's always messed up your life."

"But he's my husband. We're having a child."

"You don't need him, sweetheart. Think about it. What's he ever given you?"

A lacy red garter, the first thought that popped into her head. And a baby.

"Mel?" Her father sounded testy. "Answer me."

"Poetry. He used to write me poetry." A pang of sadness swept through her.

"Ha!" Her father laughed, derisive. "Like that ever paid the rent. Sweetheart, face the facts. You have a child coming. You'll both need to be provided for. I'm the one who can do that. You know that, don't you?"

Yes, Melissa knew what her father could do. It sickened her to remember some of those things. She'd spent years trying to forget. Her spine straightened and her shoulders shifted back from their slouch. The muscles of her chest expanded. Her body knew what she and her baby needed.

"Tell me," he demanded. "What can that loser possibly offer you that I can't?" Crowding her, smothering. Like he always had.

"Some fucking room to breathe," she shouted. For the first time in her life, Melissa hung up on her father.

FIFTY TWO

"STEP UP TO THE desk!"

Jeremy had no choice. The cop at his side grasped his handcuffed arm and pushed him forward.

"State your name."

Stammering a reply, Jeremy heard a click behind him and found his hands suddenly freed from their restraints. Relief flooded him. He flexed stiffened fingers. The ride to Criminal Court in Elizabeth had taken a half hour, long enough for the cuffs to chafe Jeremy's wrists and make his arms feel like they were being slowly drawn from their sockets. Even more distressing, he'd been unable to protect his fractured nose. Not that anyone had threatened to hurt it. But the constant anticipation of a fist or a fall, along with his utter helplessness, kept Jeremy breathless with fear the entire trip.

The arresting cop passed some papers across the desk to the booking officer, a tall, uniformed policeman with close-cropped, salt-and-pepper hair. He scanned the document, looking bored, then glanced at Jeremy.

"This is a warrant for your arrest on a charge of assault."

"Assault? But I never—"

"Remove all jewelry and empty your pockets," he ordered.

"Yes, sir." Good manners might count in his favor.

The other cop snickered. "Looks more like someone assaulted him." The booking officer ignored him.

Reluctantly, Jeremy unfastened his watch and placed it on the booking desk. He tugged at his wedding ring, snug on his finger. It finally came off and he felt a twinge, wondering when or if he'd put it on again. He emptied his pockets: wallet, coins, keys, cellphone. Reaching into his jacket, a stiff edge pricked his fingertip.

Oh, shit no.

The snapshots of him with Nikki. He'd meant to burn them last night, but forgot all about it after he and Rick started on the scotch. Now they'd incriminate him. But what choice did he have? Jeremy pulled out the photos and placed them on the booking desk. Catching a glimpse of the snapshot on top, he winced. The camera had captured the one and only time Nikki had kissed him. Who'd done this? Who'd set him up?

The cop at his side peered at the photos and guffawed. "Well, looky here. Guess he's starting a scrapbook, huh?" He winked at the booking officer, who ignored the remark as he bagged the pictures and added them to his itemized list of Jeremy's scant belongings.

Maybe he'd seen worse. "Um, officer," Jeremy ventured, "do I get to call a lawyer?"

The cop behind the desk silently passed Jeremy a folded orange garment and a pair of rubber sandals. "Remove all clothing."

"All...?" Jeremy looked around in alarm. "Here?"

The booking officer cocked his head toward a door off to the side.

"Cavity search on this one?" asked the policeman at Jeremy's side.

Jeremy caught his breath.

The booking officer shook his head and waved him off. Jeremy could have hugged the man in gratitude.

"Let's go, buddy." The cop reached for Jeremy's elbow again.

The booking process might have been worse. Jeremy felt mortified stripping under the gaze of his arresting officer, but he'd been spared the dreaded cavity search. He held up a number to his chest while they photographed him, an experience he'd never expected to endure in his lifetime. He hoped he'd never see those on Facebook. But who the hell would recognize the bruised, swollen face in those mug shots as Jeremy Barrett, anyway? As for the fingerprinting, Jeremy, as a teacher, had been through the process before. Digital these days, not the inky mess they showed in cop movies.

When he'd made it through all that, Jeremy summoned his courage. "Can I make my phone call now?"

His keeper, as Jeremy had come to think of the cop who'd shepherded him through the booking process, grunted and handed him a telephone.

"Thank you." Now, who to call? For the past hour, Jeremy had brooded on that question, and kept coming back to the same answer. His call went to Melissa's voicemail.

"Please, Mel, you've gotta help me." Under the watchful gaze of his keeper, Jeremy rattled off a frantic explanation of where they'd taken him. Please, would she get him a lawyer? Make bail? He hated to hang up and surrender even this fragile link to freedom.

His keeper grabbed the phone from Jeremy's hand. "Okay. Let's go."

A wave of panic jittered through him. "Wait! How can it count if I don't actually reach a person?" Maybe he could try his mother in Florida. No, he'd be too ashamed to tell her his situation. Her only son, a jailbird.

"That's it," the cop said.

"What about legal aid?" Jeremy protested. "Doesn't the court have to appoint an attorney for me?"

"You'll have a chance to arrange all that when you go before the judge tomorrow."

Tomorrow? The pit of Jeremy's stomach chilled. He was about to spend the night in jail.

FIFTY THREE

HANDS TREMBLING, MELISSA DROPPED her cellphone onto the table. All her life she'd turned to her father as her anchor, her rock. She was unmoored now, adrift. No knowing where the treacherous currents might carry her.

Maybe Jeremy had committed a great wrong—perhaps a crime. But she didn't for an instant believe that Howard Milton, the prince of wheeling and dealing, had dimed out her husband as a public service. He'd sounded so satisfied, smug. Mel suspected her father had staged the whole thing to get Jeremy out of the picture, now that...

Her hand dipped to her belly to soothe herself and the tiny being inside. Boy or girl? She didn't even know yet. But her child—hers. She had to be responsible now. Not only for herself—a feat she'd never quite pulled off—but for the baby. She wouldn't surrender this innocent little life to her father without a fight.

Melissa drew a steadying breath. Maybe right and wrong wasn't always a clear-cut matter. The idea of abandoning Jeremy, her baby's father, disturbed her profoundly. Her logic might be uncertain, but her gut was solid on that score. If she no longer trusted her father, she might as well trust her instincts and her heart.

So, a lawyer.

Immediately, Winkelman, her father's attorney, came to mind. He'd represented Jeremy when that girl—the first girl, Mel sourly reminded herself—accused him of sexual overtures. That girl—Heather?—had recanted and there'd been no trial. Which didn't change the fact that Winkelman had been Jeremy's attorney. The one to call now.

But Winkelman was her father's lawyer. Something about that scenario smelled wrong to Melissa. Then it came to her: Winkelman had carried out her father's dirty work, arranged for the private detective to trail Jeremy. She scrunched her forehead, thinking it through. She'd been considering law school. Could it be legal for Winkelman to spy on his own client, like a bounty hunter? Surely lawyers owed their clients some loyalty. At the very least, a duty not to stab them in the back.

A small smile came to her lips. She saw a way to play this. Melissa scrolled through her contacts for Winkelman's office number, then put through the call.

"Peter Winkelman's office," a crisp female voice announced.

"May I speak with him, please? It's Melissa Milton-Barrett."

"Mr. Winkelman is in court right now. Can I have him get back to you?"

"Can you call his cell? I need to talk with him right away. Tell him it's me and that my husband—his client, Jeremy Barrett—has been arrested."

"Oh. I'm very sorry indeed to hear that, Ms. Barrett. I'll try to reach him."

"It's Milton-Barrett," Melissa corrected. "Howard Milton's daughter," she added for emphasis.

"Oh." The woman sounded like she'd sat up at attention. "Don't worry, Ms. Milton-Barrett, I'll make sure Mr. Winkelman calls you as soon as possible."

"Thank you." Melissa gave her cellphone number and hung up.

It took only five minutes for the attorney to call her back.

"Melissa! Peter Winkelman, here. What's this about Jeremy being arrested? On what charge?"

All business, no nonsense. Like her father. Birds of a feather. "I don't know," Melissa said, "but policemen came here to the apartment, looking for him earlier this morning. Then I called him as he was going into school, and they were waiting for him there. He told me he needed a lawyer, then we got cut off. I don't even know where they were taking him."

"Any idea what it might be about, Melissa?"

She straightened up and pushed back her shoulders, channeling the body language of a confident person—maybe the one she grew up with. It helped. "Look, Mr. Winkelman. Peter." You're Howard Milton's daughter. "Some—things—have been going on here."

"Things?"

"Inappropriate things." When he remained silent, she continued. "I believe Jeremy was framed. I suspect you know what I'm referring to."

"Melissa! How could I possibly..."

"Peter, yesterday my father showed me pictures of Jeremy with a girl. His student, he claimed. Today Jeremy was arrested." She omitted the parts about the confrontation in the park and throwing Jeremy out of the apartment. "My father said he got those photos from you."

"From me? Howard told you that? I can't imagine him saying such a thing."

Winkelman tried to sound shocked—indignant—but his voice went high. Melissa heard an undertone of alarm. "Well, he did," she snapped. "He told me all about that detective you hired to set up Jeremy." Her father hadn't put it exactly that way, but this was no time for subtlety. "Who turned in those pictures to the authorities? My father or you?"

"Melissa! Now just a minute." He sounded flustered. "You're jumping to conclusions here, and—"

"Because, if it was you, Peter…"

"It wasn't! I had no idea Howard was planning—"

"Shame on you. You were Jeremy's lawyer, even if my father did pay your fees."

"Melissa, I've represented your father's interests for over ten years now. I'm happy to look out for Jeremy's, as well. So I don't understand why—"

"You know, Peter, I've been thinking seriously about applying to law school. Did you know that?"

"Uh, actually, no."

"I find the whole subject of legal ethics fascinating, don't you?" Enjoying this now.

"Melissa—"

"I wonder what the New Jersey Bar Association would say about a situation like this. I might call and run it by them. For my edification. What do you think, Peter?"

"Melissa, hold on." He drew a breath. "Look," he said, his tone avuncular, "how can I help you and Jeremy in this situation? That's the paramount question here, isn't it, dear?"

"So, you do want to help us." Melissa smiled. Maybe she'd inherited the hardball gene from her father. It might prove useful. "Happy to hear that, Peter. Then you'll continue to represent Jeremy?"

"Of course. Certainly I'll represent him if he needs an attorney." He hesitated. "Will your father, uh, be handling the—"

Ka-ching, ka-ching. Melissa imagined Winkelman running his cash register. "My father will have no involvement whatsoever. Including in the matter of your fees. In fact, I was thinking you might handle this case on a pro bono basis. Under the circumstances."

"Under the circumstances?" Winkelman sighed. "I'd be happy to accept that arrangement, dear."

Melissa celebrated with a silent fist pump.

"But if Jeremy's been arrested, he'll have to make bail. And I gather your father won't be paying the bondsman."

Her glee evaporated. "No, he won't." They were broke. How the hell would she come up with bail money? But she'd made it this far. She'd think of something. "Look, I'll take care of that, Peter. You go see about Jeremy."

FIFTY FOUR

NIKKI EYED THE FOUR adults, all wearing grim expressions, surrounding her in the principal's office. Hardly a comfortable place to be, even under better circumstances. She didn't trust a single one of them. Mr. Donnelly tried to come across all patient and understanding. Who'd he think he was fooling? The pinch of his mouth told Nikki how eager he was to get this whole stinky mess over with. Then there was the Protective Services lady, still with that kindly look on her face that made Nikki want to puke. As for the Prosecutor, Mr. DellaSomething, she found him completely unreadable.

Tell them all about what happened between you and Mr. Barrett.

She'd crafted that story for her own purposes. Now Heather had spilled the beans and spoiled it for her. Nikki's rapid mental calculus computed that she'd have to give it up. But how much should she reveal?

Heather must have told them about the motel, gone and blabbed all the juicy tidbits Nikki had shared last night. Damn! Stupid to expect Heather to keep that stuff to herself. So now the thing was to be consistent. To keep her creds, Nikki had to tell these creeps exactly the same story she'd told Heather.

"All right, Nikki." The detective—Burns—fixed his gaze on her. "I understand you've had contacts with your teacher, Mr. Barrett, outside of school. Is that correct?"

"Uh huh." Of course they knew that.

"I'd like you to tell us about that."

Nikki shrugged. "What do you want to know?"

"Everything," Detective Burns replied. "How often you saw him. Over what period of time. Where you met him."

"I guess it started about six weeks ago." Nikki shot a glance at the prosecutor, who stared back at her, his face implacable. "We met maybe once or twice a week. Usually at the park near school. A couple of times we sat in his car when it was too cold out." Out of the corner of her eye, Nikki saw the principal shaking his head in disapproval. She'd bet Donnelly never sat in a car with a female in his whole stupid life. "And one time he took me to the Watchung Reservation."

The DCPP lady scrawled notes on a yellow pad.

"Now, Nikki," the detective continued. "During any of those meetings, did Mr. Barrett touch you?"

"Touch me?"

"Did he make any inappropriate physical contact with you?"

Nikki cleared her throat. Like being stuck in a roomful of Peeping Toms. "He—uh—kissed me." She'd kissed him, to be precise. But he'd kissed back. She had a fleeting memory. Mr. B had been a good kisser—slow and gentle. Not like those horny boys, always in such a hurry for oral sex. It almost made her sorry to have to ruin him. But, hey, life was a bitch.

"Nikki?" The detective waited.

She'd drifted. "Um, what?"

"You were telling us about him kissing you. Did he ever go further?"

She moistened her lips. "Not until last night."

The Protective Services worker stopped writing. The detective leaned forward. The prosecutor eyed her the way an alpha hyena might stare at a freshly killed gazelle, waiting for the pack of lions to finish gnawing the carcass.

"What happened last night?" Detective Burns asked.

"Well, you know." They did, of course. "At the motel. He tried to rape me." She waited for them to nod and look sympathetic, for one of them to say: Yes, please go on and tell us about it.

None of that happened.

"Good lord!" the principal exclaimed.

The detective shook his head.

"Were you hurt, Nikki?" the DCPP lady asked. "Have you been examined by a doctor yet?"

"Um, no," Nikki stammered. Oh shit.

The woman looked at the prosecutor. "I'll take her to our examining physician as soon as we're done here. I'll call her mother and let her know where to meet us."

Before Nikki got her mouth open to protest, DellaWhatever, eyes narrowing, leaned toward her.

In for the kill.

"Let me get this straight," he said. "You were in a motel room last night with Jeremy Barrett?"

Fuck it. She'd screwed up, big time. They hadn't known about the motel, after all. Now Nikki had no choice but to stick with her story, bull it out. Could she get away with it? That guy who'd punched out Mr. B had taken off too quickly to contradict her version of events. Besides, he totally hadn't seemed like he'd give a shit about saving Mr. B's butt.

But, crap. Now they'd have some pervy doctor poking into her privates. How had she ended up in this mess? It made zero sense for Heather to leave out the part about the motel.

Unless it hadn't been Heather who'd told.

"Nikki." The prosecutor's insistent voice interrupted her thoughts. "Tell us exactly what happened last night. Don't leave anything out."

FIFTY FIVE

HEATHER WAS STUNNED AT the news. Mr. B, arrested. Right inside the main entrance, in front of a bunch of people. And she'd missed the big event, rushing to class at the time.

Poor Mr. B. So Nikki told on him after all.

Heather struggled to make sense of it. She needed her therapist to help her sort out her feelings. If Mr. B did all the terrible things Nikki had told her, then he must be one of those pedophiles. And if she was feeling sorry for someone that skeevy, what did it say about her?

Yet Heather felt a crushing sadness. Such a cool teacher. He'd really cared about the books they studied. And he'd made her feel stuff, see things, in ways she hadn't before. Mr. B was sort of like Gatsby—a romantic, doomed guy. She'd miss him. Was it sick to miss a pervert? Maybe Dr. Goldman could help get her head straight.

The sound of girlie giggles behind her broke into Heather's ruminations. She turned to see three classmates approaching. Easy enough to tell the subject of their intense conversation.

"Maybe he was doing drugs." A tall blonde, who'd never so much as returned a casual greeting from Heather. Blondie and her buddies continued their speculation, ignoring Heather's presence.

"Get out!" This from a whippet-thin girl with long, brown hair. Every time Heather laid eyes on her she felt like she'd just gained twenty pounds. "Mr. B would never do anything like that," the girl insisted.

"Totally not possible," the third one agreed. A look of horror contorted her snub-nosed features. "OMG! You think he's, like, a terrorist or something?"

"Mr. B?" the blonde hooted. "As if! Gotta be drugs."

"It's not drugs." The words tumbled out of Heather's mouth.

Three heads pivoted in her direction. The girls—skinny, blond and pretty—stared at Heather as if they'd discovered a maggot in their yogurt.

Blondie arched her brows, pointedly eying each of her companions in turn before staring back at Heather. "And what would you know about it?"

Heather knew she should back off, but she'd done that one—no, about fifty—too many times with snotty girls like these. "I know plenty."

Snub-nose snorted. "That'll be the day." Snickers from the other two.

"I know why Mr. B was arrested," Heather said. Their scorn drove her over the edge. She knew and they didn't. "He tried to rape Nikki Jordan in a motel last night."

"Bullshit."

"You're crazy."

Heather smiled and saw a hint of hesitation creep into their expressions.

"Exactly how would you know that?" Blondie demanded.

Heather shrugged. "Nikki told me."

"Told you?" The whippet stared at her in disbelief. "Why would she do that?"

Heather raised her chin in defiance. "Because we're friends."

"And I thought Nikki had class," the blonde sneered.

"She does," Heather shot back. "For your information, she and Mr. B had a relationship."

"She told you that?" Whippet said. "And you believed her? I'll bet she was messing with your head."

"Totally," Snub-nose agreed.

Heather was all the way in it now. Weeks of assertiveness training kicked in. "I saw proof. She showed me a picture of them together."

Snub-nose sniffed. "Well, you know, people can do anything with Photoshop."

"Right," Blondie agreed. "But, I'll say this." Her gaze bored into Heather's. "Mr. B is the most popular teacher in this school. If Nikki's the one who got him into trouble, you're gonna be the only friend she has left around here." She turned to her posse for confirmation.

The whippet nodded. "Totally pathetic."

"Totally," Snub-nose echoed.

The three girls walked off.

Heather's cheeks burned as she watched them go. What had she done?

FIFTY SIX

JEREMY LANGUISHED IN HIS cell, more alone than he'd ever been. Hours had passed, at least he guessed so. They'd confiscated his watch and phone. No word from anyone. Was it still daylight? The cell had no window. He felt hunger pangs and wondered about food.

Had Melissa bothered listening to his voicemail, or deleted it? Jeremy could hardly blame her if she'd blown him off. Yet he clung to the desperate hope that she'd come through for him.

He leaned back against the flimsy pillow he'd propped against the wall. The hard, narrow bed—no more than a wooden slab—the sole piece of furniture in the jail cell, unless you counted the ancient, yellowed sink and toilet without a seat. Compared to his present accommodations, the cramped, shabby apartment he and Melissa shared shone like a palace in his mind. Jeremy would have given anything—had he anything to give—to see Melissa's discarded clothing, books and sneakers strewn around this hell hole. He'd have kissed her soiled sweat socks. They'd be an improvement over the sour tang of despair surrounding him.

Would she ever forgive him? He'd betrayed her, beguiled by a foolish dream that had cost him his job and livelihood, covered him in disgrace. He might even go to prison because of his idiotic flirtation with Nikki. They'd never had sex. He'd never even touched her except when she'd initiated a friendly hug.

And that one kiss.

But those photos told another story—assault, the crime specified on the arrest warrant the cops had read him. The charge appalled Jeremy. He'd never manhandled anyone in his life. He even found football too violent.

But he'd wronged Nikki, a child, for all her femme fatale airs. He'd allowed a lonely, needy kid to call the shots in their relationship, instead of being the responsible adult, the professional. He should have protected her, not taken advantage.

A child.

Jeremy thought of the baby Melissa carried. Their child, his. They had a right to depend on him, Mel and his son or daughter. Yet instead of being there for them, here he sat in a jail cell, drowning in self-pity, waiting for someone to save him.

Shame on him.

Beguiled by the prospect of being Nikki's knight in shining armor, he'd grabbed at a second chance to matter to someone. The way he'd once mattered to Melissa. And all the while, his second chance sat right in front of him. He'd been blind.

Footsteps and the rattling of keys made Jeremy look up. A warden approached and, to Jeremy's wonder, unlocked his cell door.

"Let's go. Your lawyer's here."

Elated, Jeremy sprang to his feet and followed the guard to an interview room. Peter Winkelman rose from his seat at a small table as they entered. Amazing how the sight of a balding, portly, middle-aged man could fill someone with such joy.

"Peter!" Jeremy exclaimed. "Thank god."

"I'll be right out there," the guard told Winkelman, angling his head toward the door.

The attorney nodded and gestured to the empty chair opposite his. "Sit down, Jeremy. Let's talk."

The small table held a legal pad, on which Winkelman had jotted some notes. Jeremy sat, heartened to see his lawyer already on the case. He glanced around the interview room, taking stock of his surroundings. Drab and institutional, but an improvement over the cell. No open toilet, and here they had a window— even if it only looked out on the corridor where the guard stood observing.

"Can you get me out of here?" Jeremy asked.

The attorney shook his head. "Not tonight. You'll be arraigned in the morning."

Jeremy noticed a clock on the wall—five o'clock. A lot of hours to wait. But at least he was no longer alone and forgotten.

"You'll be released then," Winkelman continued, "assuming you can post bond for bail."

Jeremy swallowed. "How much will that be, do you think?"

Winkelman clicked his pen. "Depends on the judge. Ten, twenty thousand, I'd guess." He looked at Jeremy. "Melissa's working on that."

Jeremy pursed his lips. "Her father, I suppose." Much as he hated being in his father-in-law's debt, Jeremy would welcome a Get Out of Jail Free card.

"I wouldn't count on that. In fact…" Winkelman leaned back in his chair. "He's probably the one who turned you in."

"Howard?" Jeremy gaped at him. "Peter, what the fuck is going on?"

Winkelman regarded him with a sober expression. "All right, I'm going to come clean with you and you're going to come clean with me. Understood?"

Bewildered, Jeremy shook his head. "What do you mean? I'll tell you everything that happened. You're my lawyer, right?"

"Ye-es." He paused. "But I'm Howard Milton's lawyer, too, and have been for a long time." When Jeremy opened his mouth, Winkelman held up a hand to silence him. "Before we go any further, I have a disclosure to make."

Jeremy braced himself. This could get worse?

"Your father-in-law wanted a private detective to keep an eye on you after Heather accused you of molesting her," Winkelman said. "And I referred him to my best man."

"Oh shit. But—why?"

The attorney grimaced. "Frankly, I chose not to ask too many questions. I assumed he was trying to protect Melissa, in case you really were..." His voice trailed off.

Jeremy nodded in misery. In case he'd really done the things they'd photographed him doing. Doomed all along. "Wait a minute." He frowned. "So you put a PI on me and got me arrested? And now you're here to represent me?" A surge of angry adrenalin coursed through him. "What kind of shyster ambulance chaser are you, anyway?"

"Whoa! Slow down," Winkelman said. "I gave Howard the name of my detective and that was the end of it on my part. Maybe not my best decision, in hindsight. But I had nothing to do with turning you in."

"Then—?"

"According to the prosecutor, the photos of you and Nikki Jordan were sent anonymously to your principal." He looked Jeremy square in the eye. "Melissa thinks it was her father's doing, and I suspect she's right."

Jeremy's head sank to his hands. He struggled to absorb the whole catastrophe, then looked up at Winkelman. "But why are you here now? Did your buddy Howard pay you to make sure I rot in jail?" His voice rose. "Why the hell should I trust you?"

A loud rap on the window. Winkelman waved off the guard outside.

Jeremy lowered his voice. "What are you about here, Winkelman?"

The lawyer leaned in, his face uncomfortably close to Jeremy's sore nose. "Two things, Barrett. One, I'm eating my fee on this, which is the best deal you're going to get in this mess. And, two, I'm going to keep your sorry ass out of prison." Winkelman backed off. "Now, as your attorney, I advise you to shut up and listen."

FIFTY SEVEN

NIKKI SHOVED OPEN THE passenger door as they pulled into the driveway. She'd endured enough of her mother's crap on the drive home from the doctor's office. Blah, blah, blah no business hanging around with that creep. Send you to an all-girl's school and you still yadda, yadda. Ship you off to live with your father if he'd blah, blah.

Like Mom was the freaking victim here.

"You have homework?" her mother asked.

Nikki mumbled a response and stalked to her room. She closed her bedroom door hard enough to send a message: Leave me alone. But not much chance of Mom coming in, once she started on happy hour.

Nikki powered up her laptop, eager to check the social media conversation— and distract herself from the memory of that medical exam. At least the doctor had been a woman. Still, she'd been relentlessly thorough, checking for any and all injuries, not skipping an inch of Nikki's personal real estate. Nothing there to find, of course—no cuts, bruises or scratches to back up Nikki's story. Good thing she'd only accused Mr. B of attempted rape, since the pelvic exam made it plain that she still had her cherry.

Nikki hoped that didn't get around. She tried to give out a vibe of being sexually experienced. It totally sucked how all of this had slipped out of her control. Anyway, on to Facebook. What had they posted about today's events? She brought up her page and checked the newsfeed. Whoa! A shitload of stuff. She began reading.

This is Nikki Jordan's dirty work.

That comment accompanied a photo of Mr. B being led out in handcuffs. The post had drawn 27 likes and a bunch of similar sentiments.

Such a biyach.

Slut will do anything for attention—even ruin a great teacher.

What the fuck? Nikki checked her notifications. She'd been unfriended by at least two dozen people. The only supportive message came from Heather.

Hey, you okay? What happened?

Great question. Nikki ground her teeth. What the hell happened, indeed?

She picked up her smartphone.

HEATHER ANSWERED HER PHONE—gingerly, as if it were radioactive. She checked the caller ID and gulped, tempted to let it go to voicemail. She dreaded the conversation with Nikki. She had to leave for her appointment with Dr. Goldman in a few minutes. At least that gave her an excuse to get off the phone quickly.

"Hey," she said, her voice tentative.

"Are you on Facebook?" Nikki wasted no time on preliminaries.

"Uh uh." Heather had shut it down after a look at the shit storm there.

"How did they know?"

"Know what?" Heather stalled.

"Come on. You're the only one who knew about me and Mr. B. No way would the cops or Mr. Donnelly have told. Admit it. It was you. I know you blabbed to the other girls and said I turned him in. Did you freaking tell everyone? The principal? Protective Services? The fucking police?" Nikki's voice rose. "What did you do to me, you little bitch?"

Heather gulped. Even worse than she'd expected. "I didn't! I swear. I mean, yeah, I did kind of tell a couple of girls at school," she admitted. At Nikki's swift intake of breath, Heather rushed on. "But I never said anything to the principal or police, or anyone like that. I thought you did."

"I told you not to tell anyone!" Nikki railed. "So why the fuck would I?"

"I don't know. Look, Nikki, I'm really sorry. I was just trying to—"

A knock on her bedroom door.

"Heather! Better get a move on. You'll be late for your appointment."

"Coming, Mom," she called out, relieved at the reprieve from Nikki's wrath. "I gotta go. I have to see my therapist."

"Yeah," Nikki muttered. "You need your head examined, all right. But, Heather? This isn't over, you hear me? There's gonna be some serious payback."

She hung up, leaving Heather with plenty of material for her therapy session.

FIFTY EIGHT

"ALL RIGHT, THEN." JEREMY spread his palms flat against the tabletop and stared at his lawyer. "How do you plan to get me out of this?"

Peter Winkelman picked up his Cross pen and rolled it in his thick fingers. "First of all, you need to recognize that you're facing a felony conviction."

"Felony! But I never even—"

"The girl claimed you tried to rape her in a motel last night."

"What?" Jeremy's face flushed. "That's bullshit! I didn't lay a finger on her."

"She told the prosecutor she only managed to get away by socking you in the face." The lawyer frowned at Jeremy's bruises. "And that much appears to be true."

Jeremy slammed the table. "She's lying, Peter!" A sharp rap on the window from the guard outside made him drop his voice. "She didn't break my nose. My friend did it."

Winkelman made a "tsk" sound. "A friend did that to you? Fella, I'd hate to see what your enemies do."

"Yeah, that's really funny, Peter. If you're interested, here's what actually happened." Jeremy gave him a synopsis of the previous night's events, embarrassed at how bizarre and improbable the story sounded. "Call Rick in California. He'll vouch for everything I've said."

Winkelman, who'd scrawled on his legal pad throughout Jeremy's narrative, dropped his pen and looked at him. "That won't do much good."

"What? But Rick's a corroborating witness."

"A witness who left the motel room before Nikki did and can't account for what you might have done to her afterwards," the attorney pointed out.

"With a broken nose? Gushing blood all over the place?"

"Jeremy." Winkelman's tone softened. "It doesn't matter."

"Peter! My ass is on the line." He stared at the lawyer in disbelief. Wouldn't the guy even try to help him?

"Jeremy, I'll tell you exactly what we're going to do. We're going to apply for a PTI."

Jeremy wrinkled his forehead, then winced. His nose hurt. "What's that?"

"A Pre Trial Intervention," Winkelman replied. "A program for first-time offenders. You go into a rehab to deal with your sex addiction."

"What sex addiction?"

Winkelman ignored the question. "Further, you comply with whatever terms the court requires—community service, restitution payments—"

"Restitution? But I didn't do anything!"

"Listen up," Winkelman barked. "They have photos of you smooching with the girl. That by itself is proof of a second degree felony."

"But she kissed me! That's a felony?"

"I don't give a rat's ass whether you were the kisser or the kissee," Winkelman said. "And neither will a judge. Kissing your student, who's under eighteen? Violating the trust inherent in your position of authority over her? Yeah, pal, that's a felony."

"Oh god." Of course his attorney was right.

"The good news," Winkelman said, "is that they did a medical examination. The girl is still a virgin."

Good news? Jeremy felt like shit. Nikki really had been innocent.

"Nor did they find any indication that she'd been subjected to physical force," Winkelman added. "Which leads me to believe the state won't demand a trial."

"But at a trial, we could prove—"

"No trial. Or the pictures will put you in prison."

Jeremy's shoulders sagged under the weight of his lawyer's words. "And this Pre Trial Intervention, you think the court will let us do that?"

Winkelman nodded. "I think I can get them to go for it. And once you complete the program? The charges will be dismissed and you'll have no record of any conviction."

Jeremy sighed. "I guess we'd better do it then."

"You really have no other choice." Winkelman pocketed his pen. "There's a program down in Louisiana. We'll get you in there. All the celebrity sex addicts go there. Costs an arm and a leg," he added, "so you might want to take out COBRA coverage when the school cuts off your health insurance."

"Shit. What will they do to me in this place?"

"Lots of therapy. Twelve step groups." Winkelman chuckled. "Oh, and video surveillance twenty four/seven."

"Video? What for?"

"To make sure you don't jerk off," Winkelman said. "You're about to become a recovering sex addict."

FIFTY NINE

"EVERYTHING IS MESSED UP, Dr. Goldman." Heather twisted a tissue into tight corkscrews, avoiding her therapist's gaze. When the psychologist didn't respond right away, Heather raised her eyes from the mangled tissue.

From her arm chair on the other side of the end table, Dr. Goldman studied her with a look of sympathy. "What's the part that confuses you?"

Heather lowered the twisted Kleenex to her lap and smoothed out the corkscrews. "I don't know." She hesitated. "I guess that I'm not sure exactly what I did wrong." She grimaced. "Or how to fix it."

"What makes you think you did anything wrong?" the psychologist asked.

Heather balled up the tissue and dropped it onto the table. "I keep getting everyone into trouble. First Mr. B, then Nikki." She let out a hollow laugh. "Not to mention me."

"You know," Dr. Goldman mused, "taking on too much responsibility can be as misguided as taking too little."

Heather stared. "Is that what I'm doing?"

"What do you think?"

By now Heather was used to her therapist doing that—making her answer her own questions. Kind of a pain, yet it usually helped her sort things out. "I know I was wrong to lie about what Mr. B did."

Her therapist nodded. "And so you admitted it and set the record straight."

"Yeah."

"How do you believe you've wronged Nikki?" Dr. Goldman asked.

Heather drew her arms across her chest as if shielding herself from the question. She pondered in silence. "I thought for sure she was the one who told on Mr. B." Her forehead creased in concentration. "Who else could have done it?"

"I don't know," her therapist said. "And neither do you. Do you need to fault yourself for an honest mistake?"

Heather unfolded her arms. Her fingers massaged the upholstery of the chair. "But I shouldn't have blabbed everything to those girls."

"Why do you think you did?"

Another tough question. "At first I told myself I was sticking up for Mr. B.

They said he was a drug dealer or a terrorist or something."

"Go on," Dr. Goldman urged.

"And then I thought I should defend Nikki. Because they made it out like she'd invented stuff about him. And I knew that wasn't true."

"Uh huh." Her therapist waited.

Heather's eyes welled. "No, that wasn't it." She pulled a fresh tissue from the box on the table, blew her nose and looked at her doctor. "You know how many times those girls at school just stared through me? Or laughed when I walked past them in the hall, like I was some kind of clown?"

"That must have hurt. I'll bet it made you angry."

"Sure it did," Heather said vehemently. "What makes them think they're better than me? Just because they're..." She bit her lip.

"Because they're what?"

"Thin." The two of them sat in silence until Heather went on. "I wanted to show them."

"Show them what?" Dr. Goldman leaned forward and her leather chair creaked softly.

"That I knew something they didn't. That someone like me could be friends with Nikki Jordan. That I was somebody." She dropped her gaze.

"So that's why you're beating up on yourself?"

"Yeah, I guess." Heather met her therapist's eyes. "And because I made things worse for Nikki. Now she's mad at me."

"I see. How do you want to handle that?"

"Handle it?" The question caught her off guard. It hadn't occurred to Heather that she might handle much of anything about the situation. "Well." She thought. "Nikki said I owe her for this."

Dr. Goldman frowned. "What does that mean?"

Heather shook her head. "I don't know. But she said something like that before, when I met her at Starbucks last night. I got the feeling she was—I don't know—hatching some kind of plot, or something." Heather shuddered.

"And that worries you."

"It does," Heather agreed.

Her therapist glanced at the clock. "Heather, we're going to have to wrap up for today. But I'd like you to think about this: You can't control Nikki. The only person whose behavior you're accountable for is you. That's where your responsibility begins and ends." Dr. Goldman smiled encouragement at her. "Will you remember that?"

Heather nodded, her expression sober. "I'll try."

SIXTY

AFTER A LONG, BLEAK night of searching for a comfortable position that didn't exist on his rock-hard bed, Jeremy had finally dozed off when the sound of a key rattling awoke him. He jolted upright to see the guard opening his cell door.

"Here." The man tossed Jeremy an armful of clothing. His own, but not what he'd worn when they'd arrested him yesterday. "Get dressed. Your lawyer's waiting for you in the courtroom."

The warden locked the door behind him, and Jeremy scrambled out of bed. After hastily peeing, then splashing tepid water on his face at the jaundiced sink, he stripped off the orange prison jumpsuit, wrinkling his nose at the reek of his own anxious sweat. He found a fresh pair of briefs among the things the guard had left and gratefully changed into them. He donned a pair of gray wool pants, wondering how they'd come to be here, slipped on a freshly dry-cleaned shirt, and topped it with a blue blazer he hadn't worn since his job interview at the Forrest School. He smoothed back his hair as best he could without a mirror, feeling almost human.

"Let's go." The guard returned and unlocked his cell. "Arms behind your back," he ordered, producing a set of handcuffs. Reluctantly, Jeremy complied and heard the click of steel as the guard locked them around his wrists. He led Jeremy out of the cell block, down a hallway to a bank of elevators.

They rode up two flights and walked down a corridor, where Jeremy saw uniformed officers and various people in street clothes, ranging from suits— probably lawyers—to jeans and tee shirts. What guardian angel had seen to it that he was dressed respectably for his court date?

The guard brought them to a stop in front of a set of double doors. Jeremy took a deep breath as the man opened one. This was it. His day in court.

As his jailer escorted him down the center aisle, Jeremy's eyes scanned the seats on either side, looking for any familiar faces. With a surge of joy, he found the one he'd hoped to see.

Melissa.

Her gaze lighted on him, and Jeremy grinned. She gaped at him, aghast, and he realized how he must appear to her, handcuffed, his face bruised and swollen.

The pain in his nose had diminished enough that Jeremy hadn't considered his appearance until that moment. No mirror in his cell to remind him. He smiled again to show Melissa he was okay, but the guard hustled him past her, to the front of the courtroom.

Winkelman craned his neck to watch Jeremy's approach from his table at the head of the room. He rose as the guard led Jeremy over to join him, releasing his hands from the metal cuffs.

"Peter." Jeremy rubbed his wrists.

"Don't talk, listen." His lawyer pushed him into a chair and sat beside him. "We're set. I cleared it with the prosecutor."

"You mean...?"

"Just follow my lead."

At the bailiff's cry of "All rise," Jeremy stood and watched the judge enter—a brown-skinned man in a black robe. Not smiling. A fringe of white hair didn't quite reach the crown of his head. As the judge took his seat behind the bench, the bailiff pronounced, "Be seated." Jeremy sank back into his chair.

"Hear ye," the bailiff called out. "This court is now in session. The Honorable Winston Roberts presiding. All having business with the court approach and be heard."

Judge Roberts whacked down his gavel. "The court will come to order." The background buzz of conversation died. "Mr. DellaRocca?"

"Your Honor." Well over six feet tall, a dark-haired man in a blue suit rose and approached the bench. He passed some papers to the judge.

"The prosecutor," Winkelman muttered in Jeremy's ear.

The judge studied the document without expression, then looked up. "Jeremy Barrett? Are you present in the courtroom?"

At Winkelman's nudge, Jeremy rose unsteadily to his feet, nervous and still stiff from his night on a pallet. "Yes, sir—Your Honor." He felt the eyes of everyone in the courtroom bore through him.

The judge stared at him, stone-faced. "You are being arraigned on the charge of felonious assault."

Jeremy gulped.

"Are you represented by counsel?" Judge Roberts asked.

Winkelman was on his feet before Jeremy responded. "He is, Your Honor."

"Has your client been advised of his constitutional rights?"

"He has, Your Honor."

The judge held up the document in his hand. "Does your client wish the court to read the specific complaints made against him, Mr. Winkelman?"

Jeremy drew a sharp breath. Melissa would hear the ugly lies of Nikki's accusations.

"He does not, Your Honor," Winkelman replied, to Jeremy's relief.

Judge Roberts put down the paper. "Very well, then. Mr. Barrett. How do you plead?"

Jeremy opened his mouth and heard Winkelman's words, as though he were a ventriloquist's dummy. "He pleads no contest."

Jeremy nearly groaned. His own lawyer, telling the judge he was guilty?

"Mr. Barrett?" The judge fixed him with a stern look. "Is that your plea?"

Jeremy glanced at Winkelman out of the corner of his eye, caught a quick nod. "Yes," he murmured.

"Speak up, Mr. Barrett," the judge demanded.

Jeremy cleared his throat. "It is, Your Honor."

"The court accepts the defendant's plea of nolo contendere," the judge stated.

"Your Honor." Winkelman looked over at the prosecutor, who nodded back at him. "May Mr. DellaRocca and I approach the bench?"

"Mr. Prosecutor?" The judge arched an eyebrow in DellaRocca's direction.

"Your Honor," he responded.

Both attorneys walked up to the bench. They struck Jeremy as an incongruous pair, his own lawyer half as tall and twice as wide as the prosecutor. He remained standing, shifting his weight from one foot to the other, as he anxiously watched their brief exchange with the judge. The voices were too soft for him to make out the words sealing his fate.

Finally Judge Roberts sat back, nodding to dismiss the two lawyers. Jeremy stood up straight as Winkelman strode over to him, a look of satisfaction on his broad face. "It's a done deal," he stage-whispered.

A low drone of conversation had sprung up in the courtroom during the sidebar and now Judge Roberts banged his gavel to silence it.

"Mr. Barrett." His voice rang out and Jeremy snapped to attention. "The prosecutor has agreed to consider your application for a Pre Trial Intervention Program. During the period required to complete this process, you may be released on bail. This court sets bail at the sum of $100,000."

The figure left Jeremy speechless. How could he possibly pay that? Without his father-in-law on board to bankroll him, he and Melissa were broke.

"Your Honor, the defense has posted bond." Winkelman's smooth tone implied that the huge sum was no big deal.

But it was. Jeremy turned to stare at his lawyer.

"All right, then." The judge's gavel struck again. "Next case."

SIXTY ONE

DAZED, JEREMY TRAILED PETER Winkelman out of the courtroom. All too much to absorb. He had pled guilty—or, at least, not not guilty—to a felony. Yet instead of a return trip to that barren cell, he'd somehow made bail. And, now, there stood Melissa when he emerged through the double doors to the corridor.

A miracle. She'd come through, in spite of everything. "Mel!" He reached to embrace her. She backed away, and Jeremy lowered his arms, crushed. Not such a miracle, after all. Still as outraged as when she'd banished him from their apartment two nights ago. Who could blame her?

But then Melissa exclaimed: "My god!" She stared at his bruised face. "Did the police do that to you?"

"Oh." A reprieve. The sight of his injuries—that was why she had shied away from him. "No." Jeremy glanced at Winkelman, the lawyer tactfully averting his gaze to provide a modicum of privacy for their reunion. What would Peter reveal to Melissa about the events in the motel room? But, no. That fell under attorney-client privilege. It was up to Jeremy to disclose to Melissa that Nikki had been there with him. But not here. Not now. "It was Rick," he said. "He punched me."

"Rick did that?" Melissa's jaw dropped. "Why?"

Jeremy lowered his gaze. "He—uh—didn't like the way I treated you." True enough. He raised guilty eyes to Melissa's. "And he was right."

She regarded him in silence.

"He came back to the motel later," Jeremy added, "and we made up."

"I see," Melissa said. "No wonder he put up the money for your bail bond."

"He did?" Shocked, Jeremy looked from Melissa to Winkelman. Both nodded. "Son of a gun." His friend's generosity moved him.

"Is it broken?" Melissa tapped her own delicate nose.

Jeremy shrugged. "Maybe. I don't know."

"You should get it x-rayed."

"It's okay," he insisted. "It doesn't really hurt anymore." Eagerly, he turned to his lawyer. "What happens now, Peter?"

A flicker of hurt crossed Melissa's face. It dawned on Jeremy that he'd already taken her for granted. Not the way to redeem himself. So many bad habits to break. "Hey." He squeezed her shoulder. "Thanks for calling him for me and saving my stupid, unworthy ass."

"Uh huh." Melissa still looked dejected.

"To answer your question." Winkelman spoke up, filling the awkward gap. "We'll file the PTI application right away. The process will probably take a couple of weeks."

"Weeks?" Jeremy echoed. "Why?"

"You'll be interviewed by a Probation Officer," Winkelman explained. "There'll be a background check. You'd best line up some character references."

"References?" Jeremy's spirits sank. Who the hell would vouch for him now? His mother, if he was lucky.

"Anyone you can line up," Winkelman said. "Your buddy Rick, your minister, colleagues. Work on it," he insisted, as Jeremy looked doubtful. "That PTI is your Get Out of Jail Free card. Don't blow it."

"And if he gets it? The PTI?" Melissa asked. "Then what?"

"If he complies with all of the terms? Treatment, probably a year of probation," Winkelman said. "Afterwards, his arrest record can be expunged."

"Expunged." Melissa's gaze met Jeremy's. "Then you have to do that." One hand brushed her barely rounded belly. "It's our only chance."

A chance! She might forgive him?

"One more thing," Winkelman said. "I'm not expecting any publicity." He sniffed. "It's for damned sure your principal isn't going to want any. But, in the event that anyone from the media approaches you, you have no comment. Got it?"

Jeremy nodded. "Sure." The last thing he wanted, to read about any of this in the papers, or, god forbid, see it on TV.

"I mean it," Winkelman insisted. "If you defend or justify yourself, it could backfire and hurt your PTI application. So, no matter what, you keep your head down."

"Okay," Jeremy assured him. "I will." How hard could that be?

SIXTY TWO

NIKKI'S SHAME FEST ON Facebook proved merely the coming attraction for the total peer blow-off that greeted her at school. Icy snubs in the hallways, whispers and snickers behind her back. Hate notes taped to her locker:

He's better off in jail than with a pig like you.

Thought you were hot shit? Well, you're just shit.

She even found one scrawled in pink lipstick across her car's windshield:

Die, bitch.

At least it was lipstick. The message loud and clear: She'd slimed a favorite teacher and become an outcast.

As she drove home, squinting to see through the pink smears she'd produced by wiping her windshield with a spit-moistened tissue, Nikki fought back hot tears of indignation. So effing unfair. She kept losing out. Dad, so far removed from the picture that she could barely recall the sound of his voice. Mom, more useless than ever since he'd gone. The only fun she'd had all semester was toying with Mr. B, and now that was spoiled. Plus she'd lost all her friends and status.

It totally sucked.

Nikki wanted to hurt someone, everyone. Maybe she'd start with her little brother. When she got home, she saw Brandon's bike outside the house. Little twit still used training wheels. Straddling the front wheel, Nikki gave the handlebars a good twist. Teach him to leave his bike outside. She might have inflicted further damage if she hadn't spotted the envelope on the doorstep. A plain, brown sealed manila envelope with her name printed on it—no stamp or address. Somebody must have dropped it off. She glanced around the lawn and down the street, but saw no one.

Intrigued, Nikki carried the mysterious delivery into the house, dumped her bag on the floor and tore open the envelope. Inside, she found another envelope—standard white, letter-sized. Blank, sealed. With a frisson of anticipation, she ripped open the flap.

She removed the single sheet of paper the envelope contained. She unfolded it with eager fingers, and a business card fluttered to the floor. Nikki perused the typed message on the paper as she knelt to retrieve the card:

You have a story to tell. This reporter will keep you anonymous when he tells it. Will you call him?

The note was unsigned.

A reporter! Why not? She sure as hell did have a story. And nothing more to lose by telling it. A smile rose to Nikki's lips as she read the card and pondered the invitation.

Why shouldn't she? This might lead to even bigger things.

IT TOOK AN AGONIZING forty minutes at the court house to process Jeremy's release. The whole time, he debated over what to say to Melissa. How to beg forgiveness he didn't deserve. Fall to his knees? Take her in his arms? But surrounded—sometimes jostled—by clerks, cops, perps and pervs, this was no place for a confessional.

Would he get another chance?

Her expression grim, Melissa's eyes jittered in constant motion, looking everywhere but at Jeremy. The longer they waited, the more he feared she'd bolt and leave him there to fend for himself.

Finally, his anguish became unbearable. "Mel—"

At that moment, a loud voice called out: "Jeremy Barrett!"

His turn, at last, to retrieve his belongings and get out of there. He turned to Melissa, eyes imploring. "Wait for me?"

Her tight nod made him want to sing.

Minutes later, possessions in hand and wedding ring restored to his finger, Jeremy rejoined her. The tension in Melissa's face melted into a look of relief.

"Let's get out of here," she said.

Last chance. Jeremy summoned his courage. "Please, would you mind giving me a lift to the school? I—uh—need to pick up my car." Please, let it still be there.

"Okay." Her voice cool, expression non-committal.

"Thanks." Thank you, thank you, THANK YOU!

They exited the court house and walked toward the parking deck. Late morning sun warmed the back of Jeremy's neck like a blessing. The breeze held a teasing hint of spring. He darted sidelong glances at Melissa, as they covered an entire block with neither of them saying a word.

Suddenly they both spoke up at the same time.

"Melissa, I…"

"Where did you…?"

Each halted in mid-sentence. Melissa lowered her gaze, gnawing on her lip.

"Go ahead," Jeremy urged. "What were you going to say?"

"I was wondering…" She fiddled with a lock of hair. "Where were you planning to go?"

Where indeed? The thought of returning to the Meadowview Inn made Jeremy queasy. "I—I don't know." He felt lost.

Melissa studied him in silence for a long moment. "You could come back to the apartment, I suppose."

"Mel!" His spirits soaring, Jeremy reached for her.

"Just for tonight." She shied away. "Until you figure out what to do."

"For tonight." Jeremy nodded solemnly, afraid any further display of joy might make her change her mind. More than he'd dared hope for—a chance. "Come on." He offered Melissa his arm, prepared to escort her. "Let's go pick up the car."

Ignoring his proffered elbow, she walked on.

SIXTY THREE

JEREMY FOUND THE APARTMENT even more chaotic than usual. Dirty plates littered the coffee table and kitchenette, shoes and clothing lay strewn around the living room. Today he didn't mind at all. He surveyed the panorama, drinking in the glorious mess.

Home.

Suddenly ravenous, he made a bee-line for the fridge. As he opened it, Melissa called out, "Sorry, I didn't get a chance to go grocery shopping." Sure enough, the refrigerator was nearly barren.

"No problem." Jeremy grabbed a lone apple, noticed an abundance of brown spots, and put it back. "Want me to go pick up some stuff?"

Mel stalked in, scowling. "Why the fuck should I be apologizing to you?"

Her outburst startled him, but he reminded himself of all the grievances he'd inflicted on her. "No, Mel, I'm the one who should be apologizing."

"Damn right. Do you know what you put me through? My blood pressure was already too high, the doctor said. Did you even realize that? It must be through the frigging roof by now." She folded her arms. "And it's your fault."

"I know." He put a tentative hand on Mel's shoulder. When she didn't pull away, he moved closer. Cupping her face in his hands, Jeremy leaned down to kiss the top of her head. "When do you see him next?"

"Tomorrow." She stood, rigid, as he released her face.

"Want me to take you?"

"I want you to make this all go away. Why did you have to do this to us?" Her voice broke.

Jeremy pulled Melissa to him. Her head sank onto his shoulder and tears dampened his shirt. He knew the hour of reckoning had arrived. "Because I was a jerk and made a dumb mistake."

She drew back and glared at him through wet eyes. "That's letting yourself off too easy."

"I know." He sighed. "I'm sorry."

"Sorry doesn't cut it." Her angry eyes burned. "Tell me. Tell me everything that happened between you and that—that girl."

"All right. I'll tell you." He took a breath. "She needed someone to talk to, to listen to her. I thought so, anyway." Jeremy stumbled through a halting account of his growing infatuation with Nikki, their clandestine meetings. Humiliating to expose his foolishness, yet a relief to let it go. "The other day, when you showed up at the park, I'd brought her there to tell her it would be the last time," he concluded.

Her expression stony, Melissa demanded: "Did you have sex with her?"

Jeremy shook his head. "Never."

"But you kissed her, didn't you? Don't lie. I saw the pictures."

The damned pictures. He still had them. "Only that one time, Mel. She kissed me." He lowered his eyes. "But, yeah, I let her."

Melissa eyed him with suspicion, her face hard. "And what else?"

His hesitation gave him away.

"Tell me!"

"All right." Another deep breath, bracing for the worst of it. "She showed up at my room at the Meadowview Inn the other night."

Melissa's eyes went saucer-wide. "You brought her to a motel?"

"I didn't. I swear. She heard you tell me to go there at the park and found me there." He described the debacle with Nikki at the Meadowview Inn.

"You expect me to believe that she forced her way into your room, took a shower and walked out of the bathroom naked?" Melissa stared at him like something she'd scraped off her shoe.

How could he blame her? The story sounded preposterous, even to him. "Call Rick. He'll tell you the same thing."

"Which would only prove you've got a better friend than you deserve," Melissa shot back.

"You're probably right about that," Jeremy conceded. "Look, Mel, you have no good reason to believe me, I know. But I swear, I told you the truth about what happened. That's all of it." He shook his head. "The girl's a budding psychopath. Remember how she taunted you in the park? God knows what she might be capable of." That taunting voice outside his motel room: *Your wife, then.*

Melissa fell silent. Picturing Nikki at her worst, Jeremy hoped. The real Nikki.

Finally she looked up at him, bereft. "I don't know what to believe anymore."

The hurt ravaging her face tore at his heart. Like he'd killed Santa Claus.

"I trusted you!" Melissa cried. "I thought you were different."

Jeremy stared in confusion. "Different? What do you mean?"

She turned away.

"Mel? Tell me." Your turn.

"Different than…" She struck the refrigerator with an open palm, making Jeremy wince. "Than my fucking father."

"What? Mel, what are you talking about?"

She whirled and rushed out of the kitchen.

Jeremy trailed her into the living room, watching in alarm as she paced back and forth. He'd never seen her so agitated. "Mel? Hon? Did he—do something to you?"

"No!" The pacing stopped. Melissa covered her eyes. "Not to me."

SIXTY FOUR

JEREMY LED MELISSA TO the living room. She'd deflated, her agitation drained. He guided her to the sofa. She sank into the cushions, like a rag doll, and he sat beside her, waiting.

A long silence passed before she spoke, eyes staring straight ahead. "Remember the summer we met? That week on the Riviera?"

Hardly what he'd expected. "Of course. How could I forget? What's that got to do–?"

"You remember Lori? My friend?"

"The one getting married."

"Uh huh." Melissa took a breath. "That week in Cannes, Lori told me a secret." She shuddered. "About my father."

A sense of dread gripped him. "Mel?"

"She said he tried to rape her."

"What? And you believed her?"

Melissa nodded. She closed her eyes. "I knew exactly which night Lori meant. It was snowing, so he drove her home from our house in the Range Rover. I had a cold, and he told me to stay home." A tear dribbled from the corner of her eye. "Lori never said anything, but, I knew something happened. She became—distant." Melissa blotted away the tear. "I didn't ask…" Her voice trailed off. "Because… I'd seen things. How he was with my friends. Touching them."

"Jeez." Jeremy stared at her, but she didn't meet his eyes.

"Then a few years later Lori got engaged and we all went off to Cannes to celebrate, before her wedding. Like nothing ever happened. But one night, we'd had way too much wine." She sniffed. "Every night, really. But especially that evening, when she told me what he did to her in the car. Tried to do, anyway." Melissa shook her head. "Only Lori didn't let him." She looked at Jeremy. "She was sixteen at the time."

"Oh no." Jeremy felt sickened.

"That vacation turned into the worst week of my life." Melissa paused. "And then I met you."

He stared at her, hardly breathing.

"You were so sweet and gentle." Her gaze softened. "Funny." She smiled. "You made me feel safe." Her eyes welled again. "You were the anti-Howard, I guess." A tear ran down her face. "Until now."

Jeremy's throat constricted. He felt like vomiting. "Mel, why didn't you tell me?"

"I don't know." She wiped her eyes. "Too ashamed, I guess."

"But why should you be ashamed? It was him."

"It's hard to explain. Too close for comfort, maybe."

"What do you mean?" he asked.

Melissa leaned forward, her head dropping to her hands. "I felt guilty bringing my friends home, exposing them to him. Embarrassed at what he did." Her words came out in a rush. "I even felt jealous, in a way. They were the ones getting his attention." Disgust thickened her voice. "So fucking sick."

"And all these years, you kept this to yourself." Jeremy's brows furrowed. "Why tell me now?"

Melissa stared at him, her expression turning cold. "To make it crystal clear how completely you betrayed me."

Jeremy recoiled, as if she'd punched him. What the hell was he supposed to say? "I wish you'd told me," he mumbled.

"Why?" Her voice edged with disdain. "What difference would it have made?"

"What difference?" Jeremy's old grievances smoldered anew. "Well, for one thing, I'd like to have known that Howard Milton had such big, filthy feet of clay. You know? That he wasn't this great successful guy I kept failing to live up to."

"So you're the victim here?" Melissa sneered. "Bastard! I should be all forgiving and understanding because you needed a little girl to make you feel important?" She gave a harsh laugh. "Well, fuck that. I've had enough of that for one lifetime."

Jeremy flushed. "No, I'm not the goddamned victim. All right?" But he felt like one. Like he was catching his father-in-law's shit, along with his own. "Just, all those times you and your parents treated me like a two-bit loser, you might have at least let me know I mattered." No stopping now. "I mean, compared to Howard the Pervert, I'm practically a saint. But you kowtow to him and act like I'm dirt."

"I do not kowtow! And how many women do you think would let a husband back in the house after—after what you put me through?" Melissa's eyes flashed with fury. "How dare you act like any of this is my fault?"

He had no answer. Suddenly Jeremy felt exhausted, the ordeal of the past two days overtaking him. He needed sleep. "All right," he relented. "I know I fucked up. Epically, okay? Mel, I told you everything. But I haven't slept in two nights, I haven't eaten. My face hurts. I can't think straight and this whole discussion is more than I can handle right now." He rubbed his forehead. Where did they keep the damned aspirin? "Look, you said I could spend the night here. Okay, fine. Invitation offered and accepted. I'll sleep on the couch. I'll even go out for some groceries before I conk out, if you promise to let me back in." He eyed her warily. "Okay? Deal?"

Melissa glared. "Do what you want. I don't care anymore." She turned and walked out. A moment later the bedroom door slammed.

SIXTY FIVE

JEREMY RETURNED FROM THE grocery store with a barbecued chicken, potato salad and coleslaw, saltines for Melissa and aspirin for himself. To his relief, Melissa hadn't changed the locks or fastened the security chain.

He put the grocery bags on the table in the kitchenette, listening for any sounds of her stirring about. "Mel?"

No answer.

He checked the bedroom, found the door closed. "Melissa?" He rapped on the door, lightly. "I picked up some food. You hungry?" He waited. "I got saltines, in case you're nauseous."

Still no response.

Jeremy tried the doorknob. Locked. "Mel? You okay?" What if she'd taken something? Did they have any dangerous drugs in the apartment? "Melissa??" This time he pounded on the door.

"Leave me alone." Although the closed door muffled her voice, he heard the anger, still there. "I'm resting."

Pissed, but alive. She hadn't softened during his absence.

"Okay. Just wanted to make sure you're all right." He pressed his hand against the closed door, wanting to touch her. "There's a rotisserie chicken. I'll leave some, in case you get hungry later."

Silence.

Jeremy gave up and returned to the kitchen, where he expended his last reserves of energy devouring half the chicken and coleslaw, all the potato salad and three aspirin tablets. By the time he cleaned up and put the leftovers in the fridge, his drowsiness had the upper hand.

He found a blanket and pillow in the linen closet, fixed a makeshift bed on the sofa and stretched out, miserable and forlorn. He kept screwing up. She'd opened up to him, made herself vulnerable—and he'd lashed out at her. Idiot. Sleep spared him further recriminations.

IN THE BEDROOM, REST eluded Melissa, despite her weariness. Outrage at Jeremy had given way to anger at herself. His barb about "kowtowing" to her father had hit the mark. And, for all their confessions, she hadn't owned up to stopping her birth control. Melissa tossed and turned, the bed too big and empty. She threw off the covers. How had they accumulated all those lies, so much subterfuge, between them? How the hell would she manage without Jeremy or her parents? Some mother she'd make. Shivering, she pulled the blanket back over her.

No use. No possibility of sleep.

Melissa slipped out of bed, went to the bedroom door and opened it.

Darkness. Silence, except the distant sound of late traffic outside and Jeremy's faint snoring. He rarely snored. His injured nose.

Barefoot, Melissa padded into the living room. She stood beside the couch, watched Jeremy slumbering. The dim ambient light softened his features. She saw the boy she'd fallen in love with that summer.

"Jeremy?" She whispered, wanting yet not wanting to wake him.

He stirred, rolled over. The snoring resumed.

"You can come in to bed. If you want." Still whispering.

His snores grew louder.

Melissa reached toward him, then stopped, withdrawing her hand. "Night," she murmured, and tiptoed back to the bedroom.

SIXTY SIX

JEREMY AWOKE TO MELISSA shaking him.

"Time is it?" he mumbled, eyes half open.

"Jeremy!"

The urgency in her voice snapped his eyelids open the rest of the way.

"I'm spotting." She gripped his arm. "Blood."

He sat up. "Oh, shit."

Melissa's eyes were round with fright. "What should we do?"

He lowered his feet to the floor. "How bad is the bleeding?"

"Not too much. Just a little when I peed."

"Okay." He had no idea how to handle this. "What time is your doctor's appointment?"

"At ten."

Jeremy yawned and scratched his head. His hair stood up in light brown tufts. "What time is it now?"

"About eight thirty."

A fleeting fear of being late for work, then he remembered he no longer had a job. "Listen. This doesn't sound like a 911 situation. Why don't we have some coffee and get dressed. Then we'll head over to your doctor's office. I'll take you there. Sound okay?" He brushed back an unruly lock of her dark hair and she didn't resist.

"I guess. There's coffee in the pantry, if you want some, but I'm doing herbal tea." She paused. "Thanks for getting the saltines." She got up from the bed.

"Are you nauseous?"

"Not yet." She headed out of the bedroom.

Jeremy stood and stretched. Spotting. Weak tea. Morning sickness. How the hell did women do pregnancy, anyway? He used the bathroom, threw on a clean pair of jeans and a sweater, and joined Melissa in the kitchenette five minutes later.

She sat at the small, round table, staring at the daily newspaper, her face ashen.

"What?" he asked, alarmed. "Mel, what is it?"

She pointed at the paper with a shaking hand. "Read it for yourself."
Warily, Jeremy leaned in to look. He spotted the article on the open page.

High School Student Reveals Details of Sexual Assault by Her Teacher
By Stuart Kinkaid, Staff Writer

In an exclusive interview with the Star Ledger, 16-year-old Traci (not her real name) disclosed the events leading to the arrest yesterday of Forrest School teacher, Jeremy Barrett (33) for felonious assault. "He lured me to a hotel room and attacked me," the Forrest junior alleged. "If I hadn't managed to hit him in the face with a beer can, he would have raped me." Several students and faculty who observed Barrett's arrest confirmed that his face was severely bruised.

Traci acknowledged that she and Barrett, who resides with his wife in the Hillcrest apartment complex, fell into a pattern of meeting secretly outside of school. "At first it was like he was helping me cope with stuff, but then it got more personal," she stated. "He got my cellphone number and kept texting me, wanting to meet. Then, the other night, he called me from the Meadowview Inn and said his wife threw him out. He begged me to come over there. I felt sorry for him, so I went."

According to the manager of the Meadowview Inn, Barrett was alone when he registered for a room there on the night in question. However, he confirmed that he directed a young woman matching Traci's description to Barrett's room shortly after he checked in. "She claimed to be his daughter," the manager said. "If I'd realized what was going on, I'd have called the cops."

Barrett was arraigned in Union County Criminal Court yesterday morning and is currently free on bail. He could not be reached for comment.

"Oh shit." Jeremy looked up from the newspaper to Melissa's stricken face. "This is a pack of lies, Mel. I told you what happened. And what does he mean, I couldn't be reached for comment?"

"Well, have you charged your phone since you got home?" Melissa's voice was cold.

"Fuck," Jeremy muttered.

Her lip quivered. "Did you spend the night with her at that motel?"

"Of course not! I spent the night there with Rick, remember?" A thought struck him. "How did the Star Ledger find her, anyway? Her identity was supposed to be confidential."

Melissa frowned. "Wait a minute." She reached for the paper then gave Jeremy a knowing look. "Kinkaid. I've got a pretty good idea how he found her. My father has Stuart Kinkaid in his back pocket."

"But—how?"

"The way he gets to everyone. The way he got you. By gathering dirt on them, with the help of Winkelman's PIs." She sank into her chair.

Jeremy glowered. "Maybe it's time he got a taste of his own medicine."

"Don't," she warned. "You'd be poking a rattlesnake." Her expression turned to one of alarm. "My appointment! We've got to get moving." She stood.

"Right," he said. "I'll grab the car keys." He went to the living room for them, glanced out the window and froze. "Oh, shit."

"What?" Melissa asked, shrugging on a jacket.

"Two news vans, in front of the building."

"Oh god." She stared at him with frightened eyes. "I have to get to that appointment. What are we going to do?"

Jeremy debated. "Do you feel able to drive yourself there? I could try luring them away from here. It's me they want."

"But Winkelman said not to talk to the press."

"I know." He approached and drew her into a brief embrace. They needed to be a team now, in spite of everything. He had a chance to take care of her. "I'll come up with something. I won't tell them anything, I promise." He gave her a searching look. "You okay to drive?"

She nodded.

He picked up his jacket. "Watch out the window. When they follow me away from here, go for it."

"But where will you—?"

"I'll figure it out," he said, with more bravado than he felt. "I'll call you later." He kissed her quickly and left.

SIXTY SEVEN

NIKKI SMIRKED AS SHE read the Star Ledger article. Too bad the reporter couldn't use her real name, because she was a minor. How would the story go over at school? Nikki had holed up in the bathroom that morning, convincing her mom she had a stomach bug, so she wouldn't have to face more bullshit from those bitches. But they'd be kissing her butt now that she was famous.

Anonymously famous, anyway.

The phone rang and she ignored it. Let Mom get it. Nobody Nikki wanted to talk to called on the land line. She debated—cut the article out of the paper, or download the online version? Her mother came into the living room before she decided, face beet red with fury.

"Suspended! That asshole principal of yours just called."

"Suspended?" Nikki echoed. "How come?" She bolted upright on the sofa.

"What exactly is going on with this Facebook stuff? Donnelly said he did this for your sake. A week's leave from classes. Some crap about a cooling off period."

"Then it's not a suspension," Nikki protested.

"Leave, suspension, whatever." Her mother reached for her coat. "I asked you about Facebook, Nikki. What's going on?"

"Oh." Nikki folded the newspaper. No point in letting Mom see. "Uh, some of the girls are kinda mad at me."

"Mad at you?"

"Yeah. Mr. B is a pretty popular teacher."

Her mother buttoned her coat. "This whole thing seems completely inappropriate." She pursed her lips. "I wonder if we should get a lawyer?" She pondered, then shrugged and reached for her purse. "Well, your father needs to step up for a change. I have to get to work. You stay in today, young lady. You've caused enough trouble."

"Whatever," Nikki mumbled. Like she couldn't make trouble from home if she wanted?

"And be nice to your little brother. Make him a snack when he gets home."

Nikki rolled her eyes. Piss on that.

"I'll see you tonight." Her mother left.

Nikki heard the garage door close and went back to reading her interview. Cool that the reporter named the development where Mr. B and his wife lived. But no apartment number.

Fortunately, Nikki knew who to call for that information.

"OH, MY GOD!"

Heather looked up from her cereal as her mother nearly spit out her coffee. "What is it?" she asked.

Her mom had the morning paper open, stared at it like the neighbor's dog had pooped on the page. "A serial pervert! That weasel! I knew it."

"Cereal pervert?" Heather stared in confusion at her bowl of corn flakes.

"Look." Her mother turned the newspaper toward her and smacked the page. Heather read the article about Mr. B, her breakfast turning to dust in her mouth. Holy shit.

The call from Nikki came a few moments later.

"Did you see the Star Ledger?" Nikki asked.

"Uh, yeah. Is that you? That Traci they talked about?"

"The one and only." Nikki sounded smug.

"But—did you really tell that stuff to a reporter?" Heather asked. "I thought you didn't want people to—"

"Listen," Nikki interrupted. "I'll fill you in later. Right now I need you to do something for me."

"Can it wait? I need to finish my breakfast and get to school."

"Heather! I said I need this now. Can you go online and find Mr. B's apartment number for me?"

Heather got a bad feeling in her gut. Forget breakfast. "You mean, where he lives?"

"Duh! Yeah. The article only gave the development. Hillcrest Apartments. Come on, you know how to look up stuff like that. It'll only take you a minute."

"Okay." Arguing with Nikki would only take longer, with the same result. "Call you right back." Ending the call, Heather opened the online White Pages on her iPhone. But she didn't like the whole thing. Whatever Nikki might be up to spelled trouble.

NIKKI DIDN'T EVEN NEED Mr. B's apartment number, after all. When she pulled into the Hillcrest Apartments she spotted two news vans. Only one reason for them to be there. She pulled into a nearby space and watched from the driver's seat.

Perfect timing.

Mr. B came out of the building Heather had sent her to. Reporters and camera crew streamed from the vans, closing in on him like a pack of jackals.

Showtime.

If only she could go join the fun. But if mom caught her act on the nightly news? Her funeral. Nikki settled for remaining a spectator, lowering her window to listen.

"Any comment on the Star Ledger story?" The reporter shoved a mic at Mr. B's face. "Did you sexually assault your student?"

Nikki beamed. Her! Even more famous. She saw Mr. B shake his head. Lot of good that would do him. He glanced at the camera, looking awkward and uncomfortable. Good. Nikki hunkered down so he wouldn't see her.

He raised his hands to silence the clamoring reporters. "Look, you want a story? Follow me."

Interesting.

Mr. B headed over to his Honda, got in and pulled out. The news people scampered into their vans and took off after him.

About to take her place at the back of the motorcade, Nikki noticed a woman emerge from the apartment building and look around cautiously. It took Nikki a moment to recognize her.

Mr. B's pregnant wife.

She walked quickly to her car, the Ford Escape Nikki remembered from the park. The woman started the car and drove off.

Nikki had a wonderful idea.

SIXTY EIGHT

JEREMY PULLED OUT OF his development, the two news vans on his tail. Now what? Where to take them? Drive around in circles? He had to give Melissa time to get out unseen.

Damn his no-good father-in-law, who'd put them in this mess. Jeremy knew Howard Milton meant to drive a wedge between Melissa and him, sink his claws into their child. By revealing the ugly truth about her father, Melissa had given him the green light to despise the deceitful, controlling bastard, guilt-free at last.

Coming to a decision, Jeremy veered into a sharp right turn. Ready to poke the rattlesnake.

He pulled onto the entrance ramp to Route 78, checking his rearview mirror to make sure the vans followed. He floored the Honda's accelerator and, twenty minutes later, pulled into the Miltons' driveway. Jeremy bounded from the car to the sound of the van doors slamming. The news crews' footsteps thundered behind him as he stepped up to the front door. He rang the bell, then glanced over his shoulder.

Cameras running. Now, what? Time to improvise.

"This is Howard Milton's house, right Jeremy?" a reporter asked.

Must have checked out the address on her smartphone. Insane to bring them here. Winkelman had warned him to keep his head down and instead he'd invited the media to cover his half-assed showdown with Howard.

"What's his role in all this?" the other reporter asked.

"He's my father-in-law."

"Is he expecting you, Jeremy?"

"Nope." He gave the doorbell another furious stab. His own wellbeing didn't matter anymore. All that counted was Melissa and the baby. Jeremy prayed she'd made it safely to the doctor's.

The door flew open.

Howard Milton gaped at Jeremy, then took in the cameras and microphones. He scowled. "What is this?"

Jeremy drew a breath. I'm doing this for you, Mel. Please know that. He turned to the news crews. "You want a story? Talk to him." He pointed at Howard. "I'm just a pawn. He's the chess master."

Suddenly everyone was shouting at once.

"What does he mean, Mr. Milton?"

"Can you elaborate on the charges against your son-in-law? Did he assault a minor student?"

"Jeremy, what are you accusing him of?"

"Over here, Mr. Milton!"

"Get off my property!" Howard roared. "Turn off those goddamned cameras!"

"Go ahead," Jeremy yelled to the news crews. "You want the lowdown on messing with teenage girls? Ask him! The expert."

"You are all trespassing," Howard snarled. "I'm going to call the police." The cameras continued to roll. "And you," Howard fumed at Jeremy. "I'll see your ass in jail! I'll make sure you don't get within a mile of that child, Barrett!"

"My child, Howard!" Jeremy shouted. "And it's you who's not getting near them. Melissa might be smart enough to leave me, but she's not dumb enough to come back to you."

"We'll see about that." With a black look at Jeremy, his father-in-law pulled out his cellphone.

"Try it, Howard, and I'll take you down with me." Jeremy wheeled, pushing past the news people. He'd made a mockery of his lawyer's instructions. Headed for jail, no doubt, prison even. He needed to get away before the cops came. The reporters fired questions as he rushed down the steps.

"What child, Barrett? Are you and Howard Milton fighting over a teenage girl?"

"Melissa? Is that her name? Another one of your students?"

"No comment," Jeremy muttered. He kept going, fleeing the apocalypse he'd unleashed, praying the reporters wouldn't follow. To his relief, they went for the bigger game, converging on his father-in-law. Hurrying to his car, Jeremy heard one of them ask:

"Are you and your son-in-law involved in child pornography together?"

Jeremy didn't know whether to laugh or cry, only that he needed to get out of there and call Melissa.

SIXTY NINE

IN HER OBSTETRICIAN'S WAITING room, Melissa avoided the eyes of the other women, feeling as if she wore a neon sign—Pedophile's Wife. Stupid, really. If they'd even read the newspaper article about Jeremy, how would they spot her as his wife? Not like the receptionist gave out name tags.

But the receptionist knew. When Melissa checked in, the Star Ledger sat open in front of her. Under the woman's intent gaze, Melissa's face flamed. She'd taken the most isolated seat available and hunched over her cellphone, wishing it had an app for invisibility. In her haste to dodge the news vans, she'd arrived early. Now her wait in the reception area dragged on for a seeming eternity. About to venture over to the magazine rack, Melissa caught sight of two women across the room whispering to each other. One of them glanced her way and Melissa nearly bolted.

"Melissa?"

The nurse spoke softly, but Melissa started as if a firecracker had popped. Thank god for those HIPPA laws prohibiting medical staff from using patients' last names. She stood and scurried after the nurse to the examination area, feeling like she had a searchlight tracking her.

Out of the waiting room, at least.

Following the usual drill, Melissa stopped at the powder room and left her urine sample, then went to the nurse's station to weigh in and have her vitals checked.

"Everything okay?" The nurse smiled and strapped the cuff around Melissa's arm. She pumped it up without awaiting a reply. Maybe she hadn't read the paper yet.

"I'm having some spotting," Melissa told her.

The nurse frowned, keeping her eyes on the sphygmomanometer. "When did it start?"

"This morning. Lucky I had the appointment today."

"All right." The nurse removed the cuff. "Let's get you into a gown and the doctor will be right with you."

Melissa followed her into an examining room and changed into the obligatory paper gown when the nurse left. It crinkled as she boosted herself onto the examining table and sat, legs dangling off the side, awaiting the doctor. Why did they always keep the place so cold? She massaged the goose bumps rising on her bare arms.

A quick rap on the door, and her obstetrician breezed in, frowning at her chart.

Not a good sign. "I'm spotting," she said.

"How heavily?"

"A little when I urinated this morning. "What does it mean, Doctor? Is it serious?"

"Probably not," he reassured her. "I'll take a look. I want to re-check your blood pressure first."

Shivering, Melissa extended her arm. Her readings must be through the roof. She took slow breaths while the doctor took a reading from her left arm, then repeated the process on her right.

"What did you get?" she asked as he removed the cuff.

"One eighty over ninety two."

Melissa's eyes welled. "That's bad, isn't it?"

He patted her arm. "Let's take a look and see what's going on. Then we'll talk."

She nodded, turned and slid her feet into the stirrups.

On cue, the nurse came in. The doctor gloved up and carried out the pelvic exam without comment. Melissa concentrated on the ceiling, her breathing— anything but those probing fingers. She especially didn't want to look down and catch sight of any blood streaks on his latex gloves.

Finally he nodded to the nurse and snapped off the gloves. "All right, Melissa. Go ahead and get dressed, then we'll talk in my office."

In her obstetrician's inner sanctum Melissa fidgeted in the chair beside his large, mahogany desk as he finished writing in her chart. Her eyes flitted over the diplomas and certificates on the wall, trying to summon hope from all that framed paper.

He put down the pen and looked at her. "Well—"

"Am I having a miscarriage?" Her voice quavered. Might be for the best.

"Very unlikely." He gave her a reassuring smile. "A little spotting at this stage is not unusual. And you had a normal ultrasound last week. There's a difference between spotting and bleeding. What you're experiencing is common during early pregnancy. Bed rest usually helps." He paused. "It's your hypertension that worries me."

She had an impulse to apologize, as if her high blood pressure reflected a personal failing. "I—I'm under a lot of stress right now." She reached for a tissue from the box on his desk.

"I can understand that."

He knew. "Maybe you saw the Star Ledger this morning," Melissa ventured. "The article about my husband?"

His mouth tightened in a grim line. "I did. I'm truly sorry for what you must be going through. Especially at a time like this."

Melissa wept into her tissue. A time like this? Putting it mildly. Alienated from her parents, no job and no idea if her marriage might survive. Crazy to think of bringing a child into this mess.

"I'd like to start you on an anti-hypertensive," the doctor said. "We want to nip this in the bud before it can develop into something serious."

"You mean pre-eclampsia." Melissa blotted her eyes.

"That's right." He reached for his prescription pad.

"Doctor?" She hesitated.

"Yes, Melissa?" He looked up from his writing.

"I, um, I might be having second thoughts. About the pregnancy, I mean." She lowered her eyes.

"I can understand that." He paused for a beat. "Perhaps some counseling...?"

Yeah, right. That would fix everything. "If I— if I decide to terminate...?"

He leaned back and put down his pen. "You're twelve weeks along. While a pregnancy can be terminated into the third trimester, you're right at the milepost for a D&C."

She looked at him quizzically. "What does that entail?"

"The cervix is opened with a dilator," he explained. "Then a curette—a thin rod with a sharp edge—is inserted into the uterus to dismember the fetus."

Melissa cringed at the ugly image.

"Finally, the fetus, placenta and uterine lining are suctioned out with a cannula."

"I see." She swallowed. "Could—could I be asleep for that?"

He nodded. "Sure."

"And after twelve weeks?"

"Then it's the second trimester. We're into either a D&E, a two or three-day procedure because the dilation takes longer..." He paused. "Or a prostaglandin abortion."

"What's that?"

"The hormone prostaglandin is injected into the amniotic sac, inducing violent labor."

"My god!" An even more repulsive prospect—painful delivery of a dead fetus. Melissa's stomach roiled.

"Please," he said, "don't be alarmed. "You needn't go through all that—or any of it. I wanted to be sure you understood the options. We can safely do a D&E

up to 24 weeks. But if you wanted a minimally complicated procedure, it would be best to do it this week."

"I see." Fear sent a rushing sensation through her ears, like ocean waves. An abortion. This week. How do you make a decision like that?

Alone. Getting pregnant was her idea, not Jeremy's.

"Think it over, Melissa, and let me know." Her doctor handed her the prescription he'd written. "In the meantime, take this. You'll need it if you plan on carrying the pregnancy to term."

She took the script, feeling light-headed. "And if I don't plan to?"

"Then call me before the end of the week, and we'll get it done."

SEVENTY

JEREMY SPED AWAY FROM his father-in-law's house, leaving behind the news vans. Hearing no police sirens, he hoped Howard hadn't made him the target of an All Points Bulletin.

Although he wanted to return to the apartment, Jeremy knew he'd better stay away, rather than risk drawing reporters to swarm Melissa after her doctor's appointment. He decided to put a few miles between himself and the Miltons before calling her.

Pulling out his cellphone, Jeremy remembered he hadn't charged it before he'd run out of the apartment. Luckily, he kept a spare charger in the glove compartment. While his phone charged, Jeremy pondered his next move. Even without the media in tow, Melissa might not welcome his return. The Star Ledger story this morning hadn't helped his cause any. Quite a stretch to expect one's wife to shrug off a public scandal. Better let Melissa set the pace for a reconciliation. Give her space, if she wanted it. For now. Suck it up, find the cheapest motel in the area, and wait.

At least until the credit card charges got denied.

Jeremy preferred not to dwell on that prospect. Instead, he focused on clothing and toiletries. He'd rushed out that morning without any. Should have taken a minute to pack his overnight bag.

Then Jeremy remembered. He'd left his bag and clothing at the Meadowview Inn when he'd gone to school, expecting to spend the night there, rather than in jail. What if the motel continued charging his Visa card?

Resigned to a return visit to the scene of his alleged crime, Jeremy headed for the Meadowview Inn to reclaim his belongings and settle the account. The idea of facing the manager there sucked, but what choice did he have?

He parked in the motel lot and entered the lobby, looking around for reporters. All clear. Jeremy approached the front desk, hoping he'd find someone other than the manager on duty.

No such luck.

"So it's you!" A wizened old guy who'd run the place since Day One glared at him.

Jeremy gave him a nervous smile. "I—ah—left my things in the room the other day, and I wondered…"

"Yeah, you did that," the manager sneered. "Did a lot of other nasty stuff in there, too, according to the newspapers."

Coming here now struck Jeremy as the stupidest thing he'd done all morning, which was saying a lot. "I meant to check out, but—uh, something came up."

"Ha! It sure did, mister." The manager's lip curled, as if Jeremy gave off a rank odor. "All right, you wait a minute." He vanished into the office, leaving Jeremy to worry whom he might phone. The cops? The press?

He considered leaving his stuff and making a run for it, but the manager returned with his overnight bag. He heaved it at Jeremy, showing more strength than his skinny frame suggested.

"Take yer shit and get outta here!"

Jeremy caught the bag before it hit him in the face. Everything hit him in the face these days.

"And don't come back here, you pervert!" the manager shouted. "Ever! This is a respectable place. You hear?"

"Yeah, thank you." Jeremy took his bag and hurried out. Thank god for the empty lobby. He'd meant to settle his bill, but now just wanted to get out of there.

Jeremy tossed his bag in the trunk and drove out of the parking lot. Free on bail, with every right to be out in public, yet persona non grata wherever he went. Like a criminal at large.

Like being naked in the middle of a crowded street.

He drove to a nearby Starbucks. Too self-conscious to sit inside, Jeremy used the men's room and got a latte to drink in the car while he called Melissa.

"Hey," he said when she picked up. "How'd it go? What did the doctor say about the spotting?"

"He doesn't think it's that big a deal."

Her voice sounded distant. The connection? "Anything he wants you to do?"

"Bed rest. And he gave me a prescription for blood pressure meds."

"Yeah? So your pressure's high, huh? You were worried about that," Jeremy recalled.

"Well, he's worried about it, too." She sounded flat, almost mechanical.

"Mel, would you like me to come back to the apartment? I could take care of you. Do the shopping and stuff so you can rest." A long silence. "Mel?"

"I need some time, Jeremy."

"Hey, look, I can understand…"

"I—I have to think things over. I think it's better if you stay someplace else, for now." She ended the call without saying goodbye.

SEVENTY ONE

TO NIKKI'S DISMAY, INSTEAD of impressing her friends, the Star Ledger article only lowered her plummeting stock on Facebook. By afternoon, her few remaining friends bailed on her.

Shit.

But what else could you expect in a community like this, populated by snooty princesses with pokers up their butts? How cool it would be to blow this wimpy scene and take off for someplace like, say, California. Or maybe Costa Rica?

As if.

What sixteen-year-old could pull off a stunt like that by herself? Then, in a stroke of genius, Nikki edited her fantasy. A travelling partner! Someone mature, experienced enough to manage the logistics.

Like Mr. B.

Except he might be pretty pissed with her now. And, he had a shitload to answer for. But, what was that saying? To screw up is human, to forgive, divine. What did he have to hang around New Jersey for, at this point? Only a bitchy wife, and she'd already kicked him out. And the bun in her oven he didn't want. Remove them from the picture, and Mr. B might be persuaded to run away with her. And maybe she'd let him.

That notion turned Nikki's thoughts back to the brainstorm she'd had that morning, watching what's-her-name—Melissa?—walk to her Ford Escape. Big, dumb car. Exactly what she'd expect a cow like that to drive. There must be a way to do it. And Nikki had the ideal candidate to assist her.

Heather, queen of the geeks. Who still owed her.

HEATHER GRIPPED HER CELLPHONE so hard her fingers hurt. "You want to blow up Mr. B's car? Nikki, are you for real? That's crazy."

"No. What's crazy is he's getting away with rape."

"Attempted rape," Heather corrected. "Isn't that what you said? And how is he getting away with it? Won't he go to jail?"

"He should, right?" Nikki demanded. "But the Prosecutor told my mom he'd probably go to some kind of rehab instead."

"No shit! Is he a drug addict?"

"No, dork, a sex addict. Did you forget how he came on to you?"

"But I told you about that," Heather protested. "He didn't."

"So you're letting him off the hook, too? You're gonna drink the freaking Kool-Aid and let him get away with it?" Nikki adopted an injured tone. "I thought you were my friend, Heather. First you ratted me out to the other girls, and now you abandon me in my hour of need." When Heather didn't respond, Nikki added: "How would you like it if I told everybody about the love notes you wrote to him?"

That was Nikki's best shot? She'd already done that. And she, Heather, had survived. She'd feared Nikki would try to rope her into some kind of revenge plot. But this? Way sicker than anything Heather had imagined.

But, then, who had an imagination equal to Nikki's?

Well, perhaps she did. What had Dr. Goldman told her? You can only be responsible for your own behavior. But she'd given Nikki Mr. B's address. That made her responsible, right? Heather glanced over at Pretzels, in his crate, but the guinea pig offered no opinion.

"Heather?" Nikki pressed. "I'm waiting. You with me or not?"

Heather decided. "Okay."

"All right!" Nikki crowed. "How should we do this?"

"Umm." Heather pondered. She needed to buy time. "Let me do a little research on line. I'll get back to you."

"Good, real good. You're great at that stuff. But be quick, okay? They could ship him off to rehab any day now."

"Okay. What kind of car does he drive?"

Nikki hesitated. "Don't you know his car from school?"

"Uh uh. It might make a difference in how we blow it up." God, was she actually saying that?

"Oh, right. It's a Ford Escape."

"Okay," Heather said. "I'll call you later with the plan."

"You better."

Heather ended the call and looked at Pretzels. "Guess that's the Nikki version of thanks, huh?"

SEVENTY TWO

JEREMY CHECKED INTO THE Budget Inn, over by Newark Airport, the rock-bottom, cheapest motel he found. His Spartan room featured a TV, a cheesy print of one of those kids with huge eyes, and a cramped bathroom with threadbare towels. First a jail cell, now this. He prayed he'd awaken without itchy red bumps. Prayed even harder that his stay here would be brief.

Lying on the worrisome bed, Jeremy picked up the remote to catch the local evening news. Two stations had covered his escapade at Howard's. Would they broadcast it?

To his relief, the lead stories had nothing to do with him. One network opened with a busted water main in South Orange. The other led with a hit-and-run in Cranford. Flipping back and forth between the channels, Jeremy dared to hope he'd make it to the sports and weather.

No such luck.

"And in a bizarre development..." the anchor said as Jeremy switched channels. His own image came up on the TV screen, pointing at his father-in-law and ranting. Shit. He looked deranged. What had he been thinking?

The coverage segued to Howard Milton's distinguished face, his expression somber. "Sadly, my daughter's husband has suffered a mental breakdown stemming from recent events."

Bastard. Jeremy gnashed his teeth.

"I'm relieved to say he will be entering a treatment program immanently," Howard continued. "On behalf of my family, I ask you to respect our privacy at this difficult time."

Jeremy felt like hurling a shoe at the TV, picturing all the people he knew who might be watching. Especially Melissa. He half expected banging on the door and cops ordering him to open up.

Instead, his cellphone rang.

He muted the TV, retrieved the phone from the nightstand, and glanced at the screen.

Winkelman.

Jeremy didn't want to hear what his lawyer would say about his television debut. But he didn't dare blow him off.

"Hi, Peter."

"What the bejesus were you thinking?"

Winkelman's voice was so loud that Jeremy held the cellphone away from his ear.

"I know," he acknowledged. "I screwed up. But—"

"Howard Milton was a millimeter away from getting a restraining order against you. He can have you thrown back in jail. Do you realize that?"

"Peter, do you realize the things that man has done?"

"Spare me," Winkelman responded. "Anyway, you may be a schmuck, Barrett, but you're a damned lucky one."

"Huh?" Luck struck Jeremy as something in short supply these days.

"The only thing your father-in-law wants less than seeing your ass in a cell is media attention. He sent the prosecutor a heartfelt character reference on your behalf this afternoon…"

"He what?"

"…along with his personal, equally heartfelt, request to expedite your PTI application."

"Holy shit."

"And your father-in-law being the influential person he is, DellaRocca chose to honor his request." Winkelman paused. "You're on your way to rehab, mister."

Jeremy gulped. "When?"

"Day after tomorrow."

"Where?"

"The place we talked about, in Louisiana." Winkelman chuckled. "Trust me, you'll have a great time."

"So…?"

"So, I have your plane ticket. The terms of the PTI state that I'm to take you to the airport and see that you board the flight. You'll be met by a representative of the facility when you land."

"Uh huh." Jeremy tried to get his mind around it.

"Where are you staying?"

Jeremy told his lawyer the location of his motel.

"Perfect. Stay put. I'll pick you up there at 7:30 AM sharp, day after tomorrow."

"But—"

"I mean it, Jeremy." Winkelman sounded dead serious. "Don't budge from that motel room. Order room service."

"I don't know if they have it."

"Then use the vending machines. You've dodged enough bullets. Don't push your luck. You hear?"

"Roger that," Jeremy said, resigned.

Winkelman hung up.

Jeremy tossed his phone onto the bed. He got up, ran his hands through his hair, and paced over to the window, a short distance in his tiny room. He pulled back the drapes and stared out at the bleak view of I78.

Good news, right? And Winkelman had a point. He'd dodged a bullet. All he had to do was get on a plane, get off in fucking Louisiana—a place he'd never for one moment contemplated visiting—and suck it up for thirty days of so-called recovery. Not too much to ask, given what he'd done. All he'd put Melissa through.

Melissa.

He'd be leaving her for a month. How could he go, with everything up in the air between them? She was spotting, her blood pressure too high. She might lose the baby. Anything could happen in a month. And he'd be incommunicado in that wretched place. Not even able to take her phone calls, if she needed him.

Unbearable. He had to at least see her before he left. He'd promised Winkelman he wouldn't leave the motel. But maybe Melissa would come to him. If he explained. Begged.

Jeremy speed-dialed, only to get her voicemail. "Sweetheart? Mel, I heard from Peter. The PTI went through and I have to leave day after tomorrow. Look, I'm worried about you. About us. I have to see you, Mel, please. Will you call me?"

He ended the call and stood, gazing around the narrow confines of his room. It looked like a long night ahead.

SEVENTY THREE

FINALLY THE CALL CAME, as Nikki was finishing dinner. If you could call frozen fish sticks and crinkle-cut fries from the microwave, dinner.

"I have to take this," she told her mother, rushing from the kitchen table. "It's about my school assignments."

Her mother frowned at the plate Nikki left un-bussed.

In her room, Nikki closed the door and spoke into her phone. "So? Did you figure it out?"

"Yup." Heather's voice held a note of pride. "It's kinda complicated, but extremely cool."

"Great!" Nikki cackled. "Tell me."

"Well…"

Rolling her eyes at Heather's geeky tone, Nikki held her tongue. Her own lame tech skills forced her to rely on Heather's.

"Do you know what an ECU is?"

Nikki scrunched her forehead, thinking. "Is that like a hospital facility? An extensive care unit?"

"You mean intensive care unit," Heather corrected her. "And that's ICU."

"All right. So tell me what it is, already."

"An ECU is a car's electronic control unit," Heather explained. "Sort of command central for controlling the vehicle's functions. You know, brakes, steering, the engine?"

"Oh, sure," Nikki said. "I get it. So…?"

"So, it turns out, even your average hacker can use a car's onboard computer to disable it."

"Yeah?" Nikki was all ears. "How?"

"What the hacker needs to do—and it's not all that complicated—is to upload a—" Heather cleared her throat. "A self-erasable attack code."

"Christ, Heather! We're not the CI-fucking-A. How are we supposed to—"

"The code gets recorded onto a CD," Heather went on. "It just takes a few seconds of audio signal that gets uploaded into the ECU when someone puts the disk into the car's media player. Then, bingo! The driver loses control of the brakes, the steering, whatever. The car does whatever the attack code tells it to do."

Nikki absorbed this information. "Seriously? That's really possible?"

"Absolutely. I checked it out online. Not only that, but there's research demonstrating it works on the exact car Mr. B drives."

"You mean…" Nikki stopped before blurting out a Honda. "It works on a Ford Escape?"

"Yup."

"That's—that's pretty fucking amazing, Heather."

"Isn't it? Much better than blowing up the car, right? It'll look like the driver's fault this way."

Nikki swallowed her irritation. Know-it-all. "So, we make this CD with the attack code, and…" She stopped. "Wait, do you know how to do that?"

"No, but my cousin Martin does. He's, like, a genius with computers. I checked with him, and he knew all about this stuff. It's a snap, he said."

"Can we trust him?"

"Absolutely. I know a few things he wouldn't want his mom to hear about."

Nikki nodded eagerly. Everything was falling into place. "Okay, so how do we, you know, execute this?" The word had a nice military ring.

"Execute?"

"Get the CD in there." Dork.

"Oh," Heather said. "See, that's the beauty of it. All we have to do is leave it there. Say, tape it to the windshield. Maybe put a note on it, like Play Me, or something. Mr. B finds the CD, he's bound to be curious. He puts it into the media player, and—pow! Lights out."

"Awesome. When can I have it? The CD?"

"Mmmm…"

Nikki made gimme motions at her phone while Heather contemplated the question.

"I'm sure Martin can have it ready in 24 hours."

"By tomorrow night, then?"

"Sure."

"Promise?" Nikki pressed.

"Promise."

"Heather? You've done a truly primo job. This time, I owe you one, buddy."

"Hey, Nik, no problem. Glad I could come through for you, girlfriend."

Ending the call, Nikki was too stoked to mind Heather's pushy use of "girlfriend." Her plan was going to work. The wife and rug rat? History.

Mr. B was hers.

SEVENTY FOUR

MELISSA'S SPOTTING STOPPED BY late afternoon. The baby's fate now lay within her own hands, rather than nature's. The conversation with her obstetrician replayed as a continuous mental loop, and she remained torn over whether to schedule the abortion. She'd resolved to make the decision alone, and soon enough to avoid a difficult, later-stage termination. Melissa planned to hole up in the apartment, think it through over the next 24 hours, decide and move on. If she chose abortion, she'd tell Jeremy when it was a done deal. Either road guaranteed guilt and regret. But which carried the greater risk? To deprive Jeremy of his child, or corral him into obligations he probably didn't want? No way would she raise a child alone. Besides, it looked like she'd need to start searching for a job.

Despite her preoccupations, a corner of Melissa's mind nudged her toward the TV when the local news hour came around. To watch, or not to watch? God only knew what she might see—perhaps Jeremy making headlines that would send her blood pressure into the stratosphere.

She turned on the news. She had to know. And there he was.

Melissa stared, transfixed by the confrontation between her husband and father. A modern-day David and Goliath battle. How had Jeremy summoned the gumption to take him on? She feared his victory would be short-lived. Howard the giant brought machine guns to stone-fights, even if he had to hire them.

Shuddering, Melissa heard her own name thrown into the mix, heated words exchanged about the baby. Would the media come after her now, forcing her to deal with her pregnancy in the public eye, like some reality TV contestant?

She turned off the television, got up and drew the blinds, wanting to hide. Her cellphone rang and she let the call go to voicemail. Again it rang, followed by the chirp of an incoming message.

Melissa turned off the phone, went to the door to ensure it was locked, the chain secured. Too nervous to sit, she paced the small living room, fingers raking her hair. She had to think. Decide.

She went to the kitchenette, filled the kettle and started the water heating while she pulled out a bag of herbal tea. Chamomile might calm her. When the kettle whistled, she poured the water with a trembling hand and carried the mug to the table. She inhaled the fragrant steam and exhaled deeply, her heartbeat gradually returning to normal.

The doorbell rang and Melissa nearly spilled her tea.

I won't answer it. Whoever they are, I won't buzz them in. Jeremy had the only key besides her own. With the safety chain fastened, even he couldn't get in, unless she let him.

Loud pounding began downstairs. Melissa heard it, even with the upstairs door closed. Not Jeremy, then. He'd have unlocked the downstairs door and come upstairs. The pounding grew louder, more insistent. Melissa put her hands over her ears to block it out.

Abruptly it stopped, followed by voices below. Melissa's heart thudded in her ribcage. Her downstairs neighbor must have opened the door. Footsteps raced up the stairs.

She got up from the table, eyes darting frantically around the apartment. She felt an impulse to hide—in the bedroom closet, or the shower, with the bathroom door locked. Frozen in place by the table, Melissa gasped when the knocking began at the upstairs door.

She tip-toed over to retrieve her cellphone and turned it on. The pounding ceased, replaced by her father's voice from the other side of the door.

"Mel? I know you're there. I saw your car outside. Open this door at once!"

The rage in his voice made her weak-kneed, but Melissa remained silent. She wouldn't let him in, no matter what. If he tried to break down the door, she'd call 911.

More knocking. "Listen to me, Melissa. You need to come back to the house with me. Now." Her father's voice softened. "Sweetheart, you shouldn't be alone at a time like this. It's not good for you or the baby."

So the carrot now, instead of the stick. Melissa bit her lip to keep from answering. She felt like an ostrich, hiding her head in the sand and pretending to be invisible.

"Be rational. Do you have any idea how you've worried your mother?"

So much for the carrot. Melissa shook her head in disgust. Recognizing his guilt-trip tactic made her feel stronger. She remained mute, remembering the threats her father had hurled at Jeremy on the newscast. You won't get within a mile of Melissa or the baby. With a shudder, she imagined herself imprisoned in her old bedroom at the house.

"Very well." The calm in her father's voice struck Melissa as even more ominous than his rage. "You're forcing my hand. If I have to come back here with a locksmith and a psychiatrist, I'll do it. Think it over, Melissa. I'll be expecting your call." His footsteps thumped down the stairs.

When the downstairs door slammed, Melissa hastily scrolled through the contacts in her cellphone and called her obstetrician. Following the after-hours voicemail menu, she pressed the prompt to leave a message.

"It's Melissa Barrett. Please call me as soon as you can. I want to schedule the procedure we talked about."

SEVENTY FIVE

MELISSA PASSED A FITFUL night on the sofa, afraid if she slept in the bedroom she might miss hearing her father return. Hearing his approach might not save her, but she kept vigil anyway. At dawn, she sank into exhausted slumber until her cellphone startled her awake—disoriented to find herself in the living room, daylight seeping in beneath closed blinds.

Warily, she checked her screen. Her obstetrician's office. At once, Melissa wakened fully, memories of the previous evening flooding her. They'd returned her call about scheduling the abortion.

Her mouth nearly too dry for speech, Melissa listened and nodded while the nurse confirmed the arrangements. A D&C tomorrow at 9:00 AM, at their surgical center in Mountainside. Melissa needed to arrive an hour early, sign consent forms and prepare for the surgery. No food or liquids after midnight tonight. Someone had to drive her home after the procedure. Her pre-op bloodwork and EKG to be done at the hospital today.

All happening so fast.

Melissa hung up and a wave of nausea sent her sprinting for the bathroom. Arising from morning sickness or terror, either way, it would be over tomorrow.

Feeling better, she made her way to the kitchenette for tea and saltines. The doorbell rang and she dropped the newly filled kettle into the sink with a loud clatter, sloshing water over the countertop. Her phone chirped with an incoming text and Melissa's hands went cold. Back under siege.

She hurried to the living room and checked her phone. A message from her mother:

I'm downstairs. Buzz me in.

Melissa debated, then texted back:

Alone?

At the affirmative reply, she took the chance and buzzed open the downstairs door. She unlocked the apartment door, but kept the security chain fastened while she waited to see who came up the stairs.

Footsteps too light to be her father's.

Her mother's worried face appeared at the partially opened door. Melissa whimpered and unlatched the chain. "Mom!" She sank into Beth Milton's arms.

"Sweetheart." Her mother enfolded her. "Are you all right?"

"Uh huh. Not really," Melissa amended in a small, frightened voice.

"Come." Beth led her to the sofa. "Sit down. Have you had breakfast?"

Melissa almost smiled. Such a Mom question. "I was making some tea."

"Just the thing. You rest. I'll get it."

"And maybe some saltines?" Melissa didn't care if she sounded about twelve years old. Having her mother take charge made her feel safer than she had in days. As Beth went for the tea, Melissa realized she was dangling from a precipice, desperately wanting to let go, fall and have somebody there to catch her.

"Here, dear." Beth emerged from the kitchenette, bearing a steaming mug and a plate of crackers. "See if you can get some of this down." She handed Melissa the tea, put the saltines on the coffee table and took a seat beside her on the sofa.

Melissa took a sip of the hot herbal tea. When her stomach didn't protest, she drank some more. Slightly fortified, she asked: "Where's Dad?"

"At home." Beth studied her daughter's face. "I convinced him it was better if I came alone."

Melissa put down the mug and reached for a cracker. "That's for sure. God, Mom, he was like a crazy person last night. He was threatening to, I don't know, have me committed or something."

Her mother made a soft clucking sound. "He's terribly worried about you, Melissa. We both are."

"Well, that makes three of us."

"And all this—" Beth hesitated. "Stress you're under. It can't be good for the baby, either." She grasped her daughter's hand and fixed her with imploring eyes. "Dear, wouldn't it be best to come home? At least until everything is sorted out?"

Melissa shook her head. "I can't, Mom. I can't come home." She took a breath. "And I can't have this baby."

Her mother gasped. "Mel! Oh, darling, you mustn't say that."

As Beth released her hand, Melissa held on, squeezed. "Please, Mom! Listen to me. I can't do it. I can't bring a baby into this mess, or take care of it. I can't even take care of myself right now."

"But you don't have to," her mother insisted. "Do it alone, I mean. Daddy and I…"

"No." Melissa dropped her mother's hand. "I'm not going to be a child having a child, Mom. If I can't do it on my own, I won't do it. Period."

Her mother gave her a searching look. "What are you saying, Melissa?"

She held Beth's gaze. "I'm scheduled for an abortion tomorrow."

Her mother paled. "Oh, no."

"I am, Mom. I'm having a D&C. I'm going for the bloodwork and stuff this afternoon."

Beth's eyes welled. "My grandchild." Her voice broke. "But what does Jeremy say about all this?"

Melissa looked away. "It's not up to him." She swallowed. "He didn't want the baby, anyhow."

"Melissa, men don't always want a child, at first. But they come around. Does Jeremy know you're having this—procedure?" Beth uttered the word as if it left a foul taste on her tongue.

Melissa sank back into the sofa and crossed her arms. "He's leaving for that rehab tomorrow. When he gets out, I'll tell him. I'll say I had a miscarriage."

"Oh, Melissa." Sorrow thickened her mother's voice, clouded her face.

Melissa leaned forward, her head sinking onto Beth's shoulder. "Mom? Please, will you help me? I need someone to drive me tomorrow."

"To the abortion?"

Melissa cringed at her mother's tone.

"Please, Mom. They won't let me drive after the procedure. I need you."

"Melissa, I couldn't. Don't you have a friend you can call?"

"They don't know." Melissa flushed. "I don't want them to. Please, Mom."

Beth shook her head. "Don't ask me to do this."

"Mom?" Melissa clutched her mother's arm. "Please don't make me ride home with some cab driver. Help me. I can't do this alone."

After a long moment, Beth sighed. "What time should I pick you up?"

SEVENTY SIX

HER SUSPENSION ALLOWED NIKKI to sleep late. While eager for Heather's status report on the promised killer CD, she didn't expect a call until the school day ended. So she slept in until noon. As the afternoon stretched on with no word, Nikki grew as taut and jittery as an unwalked dog. When at last the call came at around 4:00, she pounced on her cellphone.

Heather.

"Well?" Nikki demanded, too impatient for any preliminaries. "Is it ready?"

"All set," Heather assured her. "I'm going over to Martin's to pick it up. Want me to come by your house from there?"

Duh. "Yes! Bring it." Like she hadn't made it clear she wanted the thing ASAP?

"No problem. I should be there in about an hour."

"Look, are you totally positive this will work? Tell me exactly what it'll do."

"Well, like I told you…"

Another geek lecture. Nikki seethed, but had no choice except to hear her out.

"You leave the CD on his car…"

Her car, Nikki mentally corrected.

"Leave it somewhere conspicuous, like the windshield, with a note," Heather went on.

"Right, I know that part," Nikki snapped. "What happens when he plays the CD?"

"Okay, so the self-erasable attack code will upload through the media player into the computer, and—"

"Wait a minute," Nikki broke in. "What does that mean—self-erasable?" "The code is set up to wipe itself out after the CD plays," Heather explained. "No evidence that way."

"Smart." Little witch thought of everything. "So—I shouldn't listen to the CD, then?"

"Right, or it will erase. Also, Martin programmed it to take effect a couple minutes after it uploads. That way, Mr. B will already be driving, instead of pulling out. You see?" No missing the note of pride in Heather's voice.

"Yeah, got it. Good thinking." Nikki pictured the steep hill outside Mr. B's apartment complex. "Then what?"

"Then...da da DAH!"

Nikki ground her teeth. "Yeah?"

"All hell breaks loose."

"And? What?"

"The brakes and steering will be completely disabled, the engine will race... and—pow! Mr. B is road kill."

Exactly what Nikki wanted to hear. "Way impressive, Heather. You sound pretty hot to settle your own score with him, huh?"

"Well, you know. After the way he led me on."

Nikki snickered. "All that therapy must be working. You didn't used to be this bold."

"I guess we all have to grow up sometime," Heather said. "Anyway, I already gave you his address. Couldn't take the chance you'd botch the job and figure out a way to blame it on me."

Jeez, Heather really grew a set of cojones. Maybe she should pin it on her, get her out of the picture. "Guess there's the chance Mr. B might take someone else out with him, though," Nikki said. "Another driver or pedestrian, right?"

"Well, yes. There could be civilian casualties," Heather agreed. "Is that going to be a problem? I mean, do you want to go ahead with this, anyway?"

"Yeah. Affirmative." Nikki giggled, echoing Heather's military-speak. "So you'll have it here by dinnertime?"

"That's a promise. See you soon. Over and out."

"Yeah, out." Nikki ended the call, grinning. "Lights out," she whispered.

SEVENTY SEVEN

JEREMY FELT THE WALLS of his motel room closing in on him. Eighteen hours until Peter Winkelman came to take him to the airport, and a mix of boredom and anxiety had him crawling out of his skin. He'd passed the time watching TV and playing games on his iPhone. And he'd Googled the website for the rehab facility.

Some of what he read ntrigued him. They offered yoga, meditation and something called Equine Assisted Therapy that involved horses, but not riding. What the hell would you do with a horse, if not ride it? The prospect of daily group and weekly individual therapy made him more leery. And Twelve Step groups. "Hello, my name is Jeremy, and I'm a sex addict." He still didn't buy the notion that he was an addict. But he'd read the web page section that listed symptoms of sex addiction, and a couple of them hit home. His infatuation with Nikki had produced plenty of adverse consequences and he'd kept meeting her in spite of them. But he'd have stopped, if only...

Too much to think about. Time enough for that when he got there. Instead, Jeremy went for a brief workout in the motel fitness room, despite his lack of sneakers and sweats. Returning, he stripped off his sweaty clothes and it dawned on him. He'd never get through a month of rehab with the meager supply of clothing in his overnight bag. He'd still heard nothing from Melissa, and decided calling or texting her again would be an exercise in futility.

Under a hot shower with anemic water pressure, Jeremy pondered his next move. No question of buying new clothes, with his bankroll and credit running even thinner than the shower stream drizzling down on him. He'd have to go to the apartment and pack a bigger bag. Give Melissa a heads-up that he was coming.

A convenient excuse to call her, he knew. But suppose she told him not to come? Or said okay, then stayed away when he did? Neither scenario sat well. He needed the clothes, but also wanted to see Melissa.

What the hell. Easier to ask forgiveness than permission, isn't that what they say? Jeremy decided to take his chances. He'd show up unannounced and hope for the best.

Assuming Melissa hadn't changed the locks since yesterday.

Dressing in his last clean outfit, Jeremy remembered Winkelman's injunction to stay at the motel. No point in seeking permission there, either. No point in mentioning the visit to his lawyer, at all. Jeremy collected his phone, jacket and keys. As an afterthought, heading out the door, he stuck the Do Not Disturb sign on the knob. In case of unexpected visitors.

In the light mid-afternoon traffic, he made it to the apartment in a hair over half an hour. Jeremy parked and looked around. No sign of Melissa's car. He felt a pang of disappointment, but decided it might be better this way. In and out, with no awkward confrontation.

But no chance to say goodbye.

He mounted the stairs, his feet leaden. At the top, he rapped lightly on the apartment door before using his key. If Melissa was there, he'd give her a heads up before barging in.

No answer.

He entered the silent apartment. No trace of Melissa in the flesh. He lingered in the living room, gazing at the familiar disarray. Mentally, he photographed the bits of Melissa's clothing strewn about—shoes, a shirt, an empty mug with her lipstick on the rim. He'd savor those images during his exile. Would she be here when he returned?

He went to the bedroom to pack.

Robotically, Jeremy stuffed a duffel bag with jeans, shirts, socks and underwear. Since he'd be in the Deep South, he threw in a few pairs of shorts and tee-shirts. Added his sneakers. The website mentioned a state-of-the-art fitness center.

His packing finished, Jeremy looked around the bedroom for anything he might have forgotten. He had an impulse to take something of Melissa's as a token to cling to during their separation. He smiled, picturing the red garter he'd slipped onto her thigh the last time they'd made love. Where would it be? Had she kept it?

Probably not the thing to bring to a sexual addiction facility, anyway.

Forlorn, Jeremy sank onto the bed. Laying back, he rolled over and pressed his face into Melissa's pillow. It hurt his injured nose, but he didn't care. He wanted to inhale her scent, carry it with him. Anything to fill the void.

Time to go.

Already he'd pushed his luck, coming and staying this long. Jeremy hoisted the duffel bag and carried it out of the bedroom. On the verge of leaving, he paused. Why not leave her a note? She'd see his things missing, might worry. Only common courtesy, he rationalized, to confirm he'd been there and spare her further worry.

Glad for the excuse to write Melissa a last note, Jeremy went to the kitchenette for the shopping list pad. He'd only written "Dear" when a key rattled in the door.

He looked up. Melissa stood in the doorway.

SEVENTY EIGHT

MELISSA GLARED AT HIM. "What are you doing here?"

Jeremy froze like a kid caught with his hand in the cookie jar. He gestured at his duffel bag. "I needed to pack some things. Didn't have enough to get through a month. I called and sent a couple of texts. But you didn't answer." Christ, now he sounded petulant.

"I told you, I need some space." Melissa unbuttoned her jacket, avoiding Jeremy's eyes.

"I get it. But I've been worried. You still having the bleeding?" Jeremy took a step toward her. She looked pale, tired. Wanting to reach for her, he held back, sensing she might bolt like a frightened deer.

"No. It stopped." Melissa brushed back a stray lock of hair from her forehead.

Jeremy stared. "What's that on your wrist?" He pointed at the plastic band she wore.

"Nothing." Flustered, Melissa tugged at the patient ID band until it tore off. She crumpled it in her hand.

"Mel? Were you at the hospital?" Jeremy peered at her face, but she still avoided his gaze. "What's wrong?" he pressed. "What's going on?"

She shrugged. "Nothing. Some tests my doctor wanted. Bloodwork and stuff." Melissa stuffed the crumpled band in her jacket pocket and dropped her coat on the sofa.

Jeremy didn't buy it. She looked furtive, guilty even. Why? "How come he ordered the tests?" Emboldened, he clasped her shoulder, turning her to face him. "Don't shut me out, Mel."

Her weak smile looked more like a grimace. "I'm not. It was just routine. I told you, Jeremy, he's worried about my blood pressure. He wanted to check my hormone levels."

His eyes remained glued to her face. "And? Were they okay?"

"He'll let me know. It takes a day or so to get the results." She wriggled her shoulder from Jeremy's grasp.

His hand trailed down her arm, unwilling to release her. "Look, I'm leaving tomorrow. Peter's taking me to the airport pretty early for a ten o'clock flight."

Too early. Too soon. "Once I'm at the facility, they won't let me have my phone. If you find out the results, would you call, or text me? Please? Maybe I'll get the message before..." He broke off, helpless at the prospect of being incommunicado.

For a moment, Melissa's mask slipped and he saw his own pain reflected in her eyes. But only for a moment. "Okay," she said. Don't worry. I'm sure everything will be fine."

"Yeah." He nodded. If that's the way she wanted to play this. "I'm sure you're right." He forced a smile. "Hey, it's nearly dinner time. Wanna go out? Have a sort of..." He made air quotation marks. "Last supper?" Bad choice of words. "A farewell dinner, I mean." His eyes beseeched her, a lost puppy, begging to be taken home and fed.

"I can't." Melissa pulled away her arm. "I'm really not hungry. Still a bit queasy."

"Okay," Jeremy relented. "I understand." But suppose he never saw her again? "How about if we sit and talk for a while? Here, or wherever..."

"I'm really tired."

In other words, no. She didn't want to be with him.

"I had a pretty stressful day," she added.

Jeremy looked away, well aware of all he'd contributed to her travails. "Did you—?" He hesitated. "Uh, any further trouble with the news people after I left?"

She shook her head. "No. You?"

He shrugged. "Nah. Not after..." Had she missed his debacle on the evening news?

"I saw it," Melissa said.

He flushed. "I made quite the jerk of myself, huh?"

"Not entirely." She gave him a small smile he wanted to bottle and take with him. "It might have been your finest hour."

"Mel..." Jeremy moved toward her.

She shied away as if he held a cattle prod. "You'd better go."

His eyes refused to release her. "Take care of yourself, huh?"

Her smile faded. "Sure. You, too."

He nodded at her belly. "And the baby."

"Uh huh." Melissa's eyes glimmered.

What did her unshed tears mean? Jeremy longed to kiss her goodbye. Her rigid stance warned him not to try. "Okay, then. Bye." Grabbing his duffel bag, he hurried out before he lost it and wept like a child.

Jeremy drove back to Newark under a darkening sky. Melissa needed space and he owed her that. Somehow, he'd make it through the night, get on the plane tomorrow and do the rehab stint for his so-called sex addiction.

For all the sense that made.

How did someone who'd barely had a sex life qualify as a sex addict, anyway? He'd only slept with—what?—two or three other women, besides Melissa. A rank amateur. They'd laugh him out of the treatment facility.

He pulled into the motel lot and turned off the engine. A troubling thought occurred to him. Suppose they assumed he was lying, or in denial? Or both? If they considered him treatment-resistant, they might refuse to discharge him at the end of the month. Should he invent some racy exploits to confess in group therapy? As a lit teacher, he could come up with some hot stuff, ala D.H. Lawrence or Henry Miller. Fifty Shades of Jeremy Barrett.

Jeremy got out of the car and took his duffel bag from the trunk. He stood a moment in thought, then slammed down the hood.

No.

Done with lies. He sucked at it, anyway. Striding toward the motel entrance, Jeremy raised his head and straightened his shoulders. He'd be totally open and transparent at that treatment center. Maybe they had something to offer him. He sure as hell had plenty to learn. He'd keep an open mind.

He'd blown his old job. His new one—cleaning up the mess he'd made. As Jeremy stepped through the doors into the motel lobby, his duffel bag, and the rest of his burdens, felt lighter.

SEVENTY NINE

BACK IN HIS ROOM, Jeremy finished off the Pork Lo Mein and spring rolls he'd ordered in. Not four-star cuisine, but probably better than he'd get in rehab. He tossed the empty containers in the wastebasket. What next? He'd spoken with his mother, laid out clothes for tomorrow, already packed the rest of his things.

Adjusted his attitude, he hoped. Any loose ends, for this last night of freedom? Rick.

Jeremy owed him a call. He'd still be in jail if not for his friend and needed to thank him. He picked up his phone. Late afternoon in California, assuming Rick had made it back. Good time to call.

"Hey, pal! How's the nose?" Rick greeted him. "You ever get around to having a doctor check it?"

Jeremy grinned, hearing his buddy's voice. "It's fine. No worries."

"Then I won't be getting any medical bills?"

"Nah." In a serious voice, Jeremy told him, "I already owe you, big time. I don't know what we'd have done if you hadn't come through with bail."

"You'd do the same for me."

Jeremy bit back a wisecrack about his poverty. "I'll find a way to pay you back, Rick."

"No rush. So what's going on?"

Jeremy took a breath. "I'm on my way to a rehab in Louisiana tomorrow."

"Rehab? For what?"

Jeremy explained the PTI arrangement his lawyer had brokered.

"Pretty good deal," Rick observed. "How's Melissa taking all this? She sounded really rattled when she phoned, after your arrest. You guys patch things up?"

"Uh, let's say it's a work in progress," Jeremy acknowledged. "I can only hope having the space while I'm away helps her sort it out."

"She will. And when you're sprung from rehab? You going back to teaching?"

"Not at Forrest, for damned sure. In fact, I doubt I'll teach." Until he'd said it, Jeremy hadn't known he'd decided that. "Time for a fresh start, maybe."

"Huh! In that case…"

"What?"

"My company is opening a sales office in the southeast. Think you might be interested in becoming a rep?"

"Selling software?" Jeremy blurted, incredulous.

"Why not?"

"For starters? I've never done it."

"Neither had I, when I started," Rick said. "You'd be a natural. Quick study, strong platform skills. Better money than teaching."

"But—where are we talking about?"

"South Car-o-lina," Rick drawled. "The Lowcountry. Spanish moss, warm winters." He chuckled. "Grits."

Grits? "Rick, I don't know what to say."

"Say you'll think about it. If you want, I'll set up a meeting with the regional manager when you get out of rehab. You're practically next door, down there in Louisiana."

A second chance? "Jeez, Rick. I will. I'll think about it. If Melissa is open to it. Gotta be a better place to raise a kid, right?" South Carolina.

"Talk to her." Rick laughed. "Sell it to her. Be good practice. Let me know."

"Yeah, I will. Man, thanks for saving my ass again."

"You can save it yourself," Rick said. "All I'll do is open the door. See ya."

Jeremy ended the call in a daze. A new life in a new place. With his wife and child. The old saying—one door closes, another opens. Perhaps enough to see him through the month ahead.

MELISSA FORCED DOWN SOME tea and nibbled a slice of toast. For dessert, she filled a small dish with applesauce, managing a few spoonsful. Last supper, Jeremy had said. More so than he realized.

Their baby's last supper.

Melissa pushed away the applesauce and got up from the table. Right not to tell him. He had enough to deal with.

She carried the dishes to the sink. A done deal, anyway. She'd made the choice, scheduled the procedure for the morning. Procedure. Nice, safe, clinical word. But, for the best. Not cut out to be parents, either of them. Not now. Maybe never.

Melissa swiped away a tear with the side of her hand, wishing to brush away her despair as easily. All those high hopes, back when she'd stopped her birth control.

Idiot.

She went to the living room and burrowed through a stack of books on the coffee table. Keep busy. Don't think about tomorrow. Selecting a thriller she'd borrowed from the library, Melissa carried it into the bedroom. Read for a while, go to sleep early. Wait for Mom to come for her in the morning.

Then—over. All over.

HER HANDS ENCASED IN latex gloves, Nikki hefted the CD in its plastic case. So light, for a tool of destruction. Heather had come through, all right. She and that geek cousin of hers. Handy having a sociopath in the family.

Everything set for tomorrow.

Nikki peeled off the Post-It note she'd inscribed with a red Sharpie, and affixed it to the case holding the disk.

Listen to me.

She grinned. Short and sweet. She'd printed, not that the cow knew her writing. Nikki slid the CD into her bag with care, wanting it in place when she left in the morning. She pulled off the latex gloves, tossed them into the purse as well. Heather or Martin's fingerprints already might be on the CD. Not her problem, as long as hers weren't.

Nikki set the alarm on her cellphone for 5:00 AM. Crazy early, but the pre-dawn gloom would provide cover while she positioned her booby-trap under the wiper blade on the driver's side windshield of that bitch's car. Then Nikki would back off to a safe vantage point to watch the fun.

It promised to be one hell of a show.

Nikki turned off the light and crept into bed. Way before her usual bedtime, but no taking the chance she'd oversleep for her dawn mission. All that remained now—to get her beauty sleep.

EIGHTY

WINKELMAN'S CALL CAME BRIGHT and early the next morning.

"Rise and shine, sex offender!"

Jeremy marveled that his attorney sounded so cheerful at 6:30 AM. Probably generating billable hours already.

"I'll be by to pick you up in an hour," Winkelman said.

"Why so early?" Jeremy asked. "My flight is at ten and the motel is so close to the airport planes are practically landing on the roof."

"I'm taking you out to breakfast. A man can't start recovery on an empty stomach."

"Depends what he's recovering from. Anyway, my car or yours?"

"Leave yours at the motel," Winkelman said. "Give me the keys and my secretary will drive it back to your apartment."

"Like valet parking, huh? Okay, on my way to the shower. I'll be ready."

As Jeremy started for the bathroom, his cellphone rang. Melissa, calling to say goodbye? He grabbed his phone from the night table and checked the screen.

Not Melissa. Beth Milton.

Jeremy frowned. Why would his mother-in-law phone? His considered ignoring her call, but there might be an emergency with Melissa. Or maybe her test results.

"Hello, Beth," he said warily.

"Jeremy."

Her urgent tone commanded his attention. "What's wrong? Has something happened to Mel?"

"Oh, god. I hope I'm doing the right thing."

"Beth, what is it? Tell me." Anxiety chilled the pit of Jeremy's stomach.

"She's going for an abortion. Now. This morning."

"What?" Stunned, he sank onto the bed.

"She asked me to drive her, because of the anesthesia. I didn't want to." Beth's voice broke. "I told her I would, but I can't go through with it. I won't help her destroy my grandchild."

"But—why? Why would she do that?" And not tell me? Jeremy flashed back to the hospital band he'd seen on Melissa's wrist yesterday. Tests, she'd said.

Pre-op tests.

"She doesn't think you want it, Jeremy."

Her words knocked the wind out of him.

"And frankly I don't know whether you do or not," Beth went on. "But you're the only one who can stop her." She choked back a sob. "Please, Jeremy! Go!"

"What time are you due to pick her up?" He pulled on the pants he'd laid out.

"Seven fifteen."

Less than half an hour from now. "Does she know you're not coming?" He zipped up the trousers, cradling the phone against his neck.

"No. I—I haven't told her yet."

"Don't. Stall, Beth. Let her think you're coming. I'm on my way."

He didn't wait for her reply. Throwing on the rest of his clothes, Jeremy grabbed his duffel bag and rushed out the door. Let Winkelman and rehab wait. First he had to save a life.

Maybe three.

EIGHTY ONE

"MOM, WHERE ARE YOU?"

The second voicemail Melissa had left, along with a text. Now she was worried. Beth Milton, going incommunicado? Unheard of. Granted, her mother disapproved of distracted driving, and might ignore a call while behind the wheel. But she despised tardiness. Inconceivable for her to be ten minutes late without calling.

But missing in action, on this of all mornings.

Melissa raised the blinds and peered out the living room window. Where was she? This was hard enough, without Mom going psycho on her.

Fifteen minutes late now.

Her mother didn't want to be involved with the abortion. But standing her up for the appointment? Unthinkable. Had something happened to her? Melissa's anxiety cranked up a notch. Rather than stand there, staring out the window, she decided to go wait downstairs. Then they'd be off the instant her mother pulled up. Melissa grabbed her jacket and purse, hurried downstairs.

What if her mother let her down? She'd drive to the procedure and call someone to take her home afterwards. A taxi, if necessary. One way or another, she'd get this wretched thing over with today.

OUTSIDE THE BARRETT'S APARTMENT, Nikki sat, on stakeout, in her car. From a few doors down, she watched the apartment entrance with the bitch's Ford Escape parked in front. It now sported the lethal CD beneath its windshield wiper. The Deathmobile, armed and ready.

Let her have an early errand. Come out soon. At least Nikki's suspension from school—or excused absence, holiday, or whatever the fuck—gave her a pass on classes. How I spent my summer vacation.

Would the lazy cow make her wait all day?

At that moment, Nikki's target appeared. Mrs. B emerged from the building.

Yes! Nikki wanted to pump her fist, except she was keeping a low profile. The car. Get into the freaking car, dummy.

But Mrs. B stopped on the front steps of the apartment building. She stood there, shifting from one foot to the other, scanning the street with an impatient frown.

Waiting! The goddamn bitch won't even drive herself. Frigging princess. Nikki clutched the steering wheel. C'mon. C'mon!

Mrs. B pulled out her cellphone. Too far away to pick up the conversation, Nikki saw by her scowl that she didn't like what she heard.

The person who was supposed to pick her up? Don't wait. Nikki silently mouthed the words. Get in the car, bitch.

Mrs. B ended the call.

Nikki held her breath. Would she wait, or go?

At last Mrs. B shook her head. She walked toward the Deathmobile.

EIGHTY TWO

"GO, GO, GO!" JEREMY nudged the Honda up to 85, weaving across the westbound lanes of Route 78, passing, not bothering to check his rearview for cops. Thank god for the lighter rush hour traffic on this side. Going the other direction, he'd be a dead duck. This way, he might reach the apartment in time.

But cutting it mighty close. He glanced down at the dashboard clock. Only five minutes until Beth's arranged pick-up time. Wait, Mel. Wait for me.

Without warning, traffic came to a dead halt. Jeremy braked hard to avoid rear-ending a mini-van in front of him. With a screech of tires, the Honda stopped inches from its bumper, drawing a glare from the driver in his rearview and a blast from his horn.

Pounding the steering wheel in frustration, Jeremy craned to peer around the mini-van. Traffic stalled in all three lanes, but he couldn't make out the cause. Shit! Move, damn it.

He pulled out his cellphone and called his mother-in-law. "What's going on?" he asked when Beth answered.

"She's calling, texting, leaving me voicemails. She's so angry, I—"

Jeremy cut her off. "Have you talked to her?"

"You said to stall, so no. But I have to tell her something, Jeremy," Beth protested. "I can't leave her hanging. She must be worried sick."

"No. Don't call her until I tell you to." Cars ahead inched forward. "I have to go. Wait for my call." He dropped his phone onto the passenger seat and eased the Honda forward a couple of feet. "C'mon, move," he muttered.

A siren screamed on Jeremy's left, growing louder as a police car sped past, roof light flashing red and blue, traveling along the median. Must be an accident ahead. Had he not been stuck in the center lane, Jeremy might have veered over to the median and followed the cop. For the moment, he had to crawl forward with the other cars and wait for an opening.

Precious minutes ticked by. Trapped behind the van, Jeremy had no view ahead. Finally, on the right, he spotted the exit sign for Route 24. Work his way over, and he'd escape.

His fellow motorists had the same idea. Cars oozed their way toward the right lane, slowly at first, then faster as drivers used the right shoulder as a makeshift exit ramp.

Jeremy nosed the Honda over. A horn blared in protest as he accelerated to cut off a Mercedes to his right. Tough shit, buddy. He claimed the lane. No need to look in the mirror at the middle finger pointed at him. Reckless, Jeremy pushed his way onto the shoulder and followed the line of cars to the exit lane.

7:37.

As Jeremy's eyes flitted to the dashboard clock, his cellphone rang. He picked it up and glanced at the screen, in case Beth had called with an update. But, no— Winkelman. Jeremy let the call go to voicemail. Peter would be having a shit fit over his absence. Nothing Jeremy could do about that right now.

As the traffic edged onto Route 24, the logjam gave way and Jeremy gunned the Honda, making for the exit leading to Springfield Avenue, and the apartment.

At 7:45 he hit Springfield Avenue. Melissa had waited for her mother half an hour by now. But still waiting? He grabbed his phone, risking a brief glance as he redialed his mother-in-law.

"Jeremy?" Her voice high with panic.

"Okay, call her now. Tell her you're on the way. Say you'll be there in five minutes."

"But—"

"Tell her to wait, dammit!" He hung up, accelerating way beyond the local limit. He'd make it. If she waited, he'd get there.

7:51.

A loud bang from the front right tire, then the smell of burning rubber. The steering wheel in Jeremy's hands lurched to the side.

"No!" A fucking pothole.

Although tempted to keep driving, he knew by the feel that the wheel rim had taken a hit. Spewing curses, Jeremy pulled to the curb. An incoming text chirped from his cell. Beth? He looked.

Winkelman.

You're going to jail, pal.

Jeremy slipped the phone into his jacket pocket and got out of the car. A glance at the front passenger wheel confirmed his suspicion. His ride had gone lame.

He clenched his fists. Too late. He'd blown it again.

No. He wasn't about to rot in prison with a bellyful of regret. Fuck it. He sprinted toward the apartment, a quarter mile away.

Jeremy jogged now and then, but the cold of winter had shut him down. Lacking speed and stamina, he used desperation as fuel. The first two blocks left him panting, but he kept his pace. At four blocks, Jeremy's right calf seized up in a cramp. He stumbled, regained his footing and kept going.

His cellphone rang and he pulled it out on the run.

Beth.

"I spoke to her. She won't wait. She's driving there, Jeremy. Hurry! For heaven's sake, stop her."

"On my way," he rasped. Wait for me. Melissa, please wait.

A low growl behind him made Jeremy wrench his neck around. A boxer, frothy saliva flicking from its jowls, lunged at him. Jeremy yelped, then saw a slender young woman clutching a leash as the dog strained against it.

"Sorry," she said.

Too winded to reply, Jeremy waved her off and gimped onward.

Finally, the last block. Jeremy labored up the steep hill to the apartment development, wheezing and clutching at a stitch in his side. Lungs burning, he reached the top. He jogged into the complex. Scanning for Melissa's car, he missed the curb ahead and ran into it. He went down, his left ankle twisting.

"Melissa!" Jeremy's eyes watered at the sharp pain. Too winded to talk, he croaked. "Mel!"

Too late?

Hands braced against the pavement, he forced himself to his knees. He wobbled to his feet, cramped right leg taking the weight off his injured left ankle. "Melissa!" He stumbled forward, each step sending an electric jolt though his ankle.

He saw their apartment. Her.

"Mel!" His last shred of energy in that cry.

Walking toward her car, she stopped. Turned.

"Mel, wait!" Gasping, he hobbled toward her.

EIGHTY THREE

HIM!

Through her windshield, Nikki gaped at Mr. B as he shouted his wife's name and limped toward her. Had she been waiting for him? Why the fuck did he turn up now, with the bitch about to get in her car? And she looked surprised to see him here. Expecting someone else, maybe? Two-timing him? Unable to hear them from her car, Nikki hunkered down in her seat to watch the action.

"MELISSA!" JEREMY LABORED TO catch his breath. "You're still here. I'm not too late."

She stared. "What are you doing here? I thought you were flying to Louisiana."

"I am," he panted. "But your mother called me—"

"Called you?" Her eyes narrowed with anger. "What the fuck is this? Where is she?"

Jeremy had enough breath now for full sentences. "She told me you're going for an abortion." He gripped Melissa's arms, afraid she might flee. "Mel, why? How could you do this without telling me?"

Instead of struggling against his hold, Melissa went slack, staring at him with eyes full of pain. "How can we have this child? You never wanted it. You think I don't know that?"

"That's not—"

"No, listen to me." She pressed a hand against his chest. "I didn't get pregnant by accident. I stopped my birth control pills."

He stared, speechless.

"I didn't give you any choice then." Melissa dropped her gaze. "So I didn't think it fair to burden you now."

Jeremy tightened his grip on her arms. "Listen to me. I want the burden. It's my choice, too." His face drew close to hers. "Melissa, I love you and I want our child."

Tears dampened her eyes. "How can we? We've made a mess of everything. How can we take care of a baby?" Melissa's voice grew high and tight.

Jeremy cradled her in his arms, like a frightened child needing comfort.

"Because we can. We will." He stroked her hair. "Don't you see, Mel? This child is our chance to grow up. Get it right. Have something in our lives that matters. The baby is our second chance."

She sighed. "Jeremy, isn't that a heavy load to place on a kid? Saving its parents?"

"No." His voice carried new certainty. "Because we're the ones who'll bear the load. Look, I spoke with Rick last night. I've got a shot at a sales position with his company."

Her eyes widened in surprise. "In California?"

"No, South Carolina."

"South—"

"Come with me, Mel." Jeremy grasped her hands, as if ready to lead her there right now. "Let's get out of here, make a fresh start."

"But—the baby! My parents…"

"People have babies in South Carolina, too. And some distance from your parents wouldn't hurt either of us at this point, would it?"

Melissa looked down at their joined hands, then back at his face. "You're serious?"

"Meet me in Louisiana in a couple of weeks. They have family sessions at the program. Help us get off on the right foot. And then we'll go see about the job." He grinned. "It'll be like summertime down there." Releasing her hands, he held her face and looked deep into her dark eyes, finding a glimmer of hope there. "Say you will, Mel. If we blow this chance, we'll blow everything. Fail ourselves and our child."

"But Jeremy, do you really think…?"

"Melissa, I know." Never more sure of anything. "Promise you'll come. You and the baby. Make the flight reservation today."

"I—" Her eyes widened in alarm. "Oh my god, Jeremy! When is your flight? If you don't get on that plane…"

He smiled gamely. "I'm not going anywhere until you promise me."

"Jeremy!" Despite the protest in her voice, she smiled back.

"Hey." He sensed victory. "What should we name it?"

"Please! You'll miss your flight!"

He stood firm. "Answer me and I'll go." He wanted a name, needed to know how to think of his child during the weeks ahead.

"All right," she conceded. "Michael, if it's a boy?"

Jeremy nodded. His father's name. "Definitely. And if it's a girl?"

"I don't know." Melissa's eyes softened. "Maybe…Hope?"

"Hope." He tried the sound of it in his mouth. "That's good." He thought for a moment. "Or maybe Faith."

"Faith." She nodded. "I like that." She held his gaze a moment, then gave him a push. "Now, get out of here." Melissa looked around. "Where's your car, anyway?"

"I—uh—blew out a tire down the road."

"Then, how…?"

"I ran it." Jeremy shrugged. No big deal. "I'll have Peter take care of it. Could I borrow yours?"

"The Escape? Oh. Here." She handed him the remote. "Now, go!"

"Thanks. I'll make sure Winkelman gets it back to you. He'll handle every-thing, once he finishes ripping me a new one and putting what's left of me on the plane." Jeremy hugged her tightly, then pulled back and kissed her. "I'll see the two of you in Louisiana."

He turned and headed toward the Escape.

EIGHTY FOUR

NIKKI WATCHED THE WRONG Barrett approach the Deathmobile.

She considered jumping out of her car, running over and stopping Mr. B before he drove off. Before the brakes gave out, the steering failed and the engine accelerated as he hit that steep downhill run outside the complex.

She'd meant it to be her, not him.

But, in the end, Nikki didn't. She stayed in her car, watched him discover the CD and remove it from under the wiper blade. Watched him take it with him into the Escape.

Too bad.

But, after that nauseating embrace with wifey, Nikki saw no point in saving him. Pussy-whipped chicken shit. Unfuckingworthy. Best to let him go. At least she'd leave the bitch a widow.

And besides, Mr. B wasn't the only good-looking teacher at Forrest. That music teacher, Mr. Cascone? Pretty hot.

Nikki waited as Mr. B started the engine. Watched him look over the CD and insert it he drove off in the Deathmobile.

Licking her lips, she started her car and followed.

JEREMY STARTED THE ENGINE, eyeing the CD he'd removed from the Escape's windshield.

Listen To Me?

What the hell? Some advertising ploy? He frowned. Or a half-assed attempt by his father-in-law to intimidate Melissa. Good thing he'd been the one to find it and spare her. He inserted the disk into the media player. Better give a listen and see what the bastard was up to. Jeremy pulled out and drove through the development, heading for the street.

Nothing to fear from a stupid CD.

Jeremy no longer feared his father-in-law, or rehab, or a new job—or anything much, now. Whatever. Bring it on.

He'd face it, his heart finally at peace.

EIGHTY FIVE

HEATHER EXPECTED THE CALL. She found the message on her iPhone after her second period class. Blowing off Bio lab, she slipped out of the building and found a secluded spot to return the call.

"It's me, Heather. How'd it go?"

"It didn't, that's how. A total bust."

"No kidding? What happened, Nikki?"

"Nothing! Fucking zilch. I planted the CD on the windshield, like we said."

"Uh huh, and...?"

"He took the disk, he got in the car..."

"You sure you had the right car?" Heather asked. "The Ford Escape? It makes a difference."

"Of course I had the right car," Nikki snapped. "Think I'm some kind of retard?"

"Just making sure. So, then what?"

"So he started the car. I watched him. He looked at the CD and I'm sure I saw him put it in. Then he drove off."

"And?"

"And I followed him all the way to the expressway, but nothing happened. You fucked up, Heather. Your goddamn booby trap didn't work."

Heather smiled. "But it did, Nikki."

"Are you deaf? I told you—"

"The trap worked, Nikki." Triumph rang in Heather's voice. "It caught you."

Nikki received the news in stunned silence. "What do you mean? What was on that CD?"

"Us."

"What?"

"I recorded our phone conversation yesterday. Remember? How you'd plant the disk, about the attack code." Heather paused. "How you wouldn't mind a few civilian casualties? Ring a bell, Nikki?"

"You recorded that? How?"

"On my phone. There's an app, you know."

"I didn't," Nikki muttered.

"So I made the recording and burned a CD of it. That's what Mr. B heard when he played the disk."

"Shit!"

"Along with a little introduction, warning him that if anything happens to me, he should turn over the CD to the police," Heather added. "An insurance policy, you might say."

"You little bitch!" Nikki snarled. "You tricked me."

"True that," Heather agreed. "But now I'll be a hundred per cent honest with you, girlfriend. See, I'm recording this conversation, too. Right now. So if anything happens to Mr. B?" She paused. "Or his wife? I'll play our little talk for the police. Understand, Nikki? I'll tell. I'll tell on you."

Acknowledgements

Thanks to Kevin Garrigan, Meghan Sheena Hyden and Dr. Randy Simon for encouragement and feedback. Randy also provided invaluable subject matter expertise on the NJ child protection system. If the story strikes any false notes in that arena, the fault is mine. My fellow scribes at New Providence Writers helped give shape to the first draft of the novel. Sidney Nesti's razor-sharp critiques made this a far better book than it otherwise would have been.

Kudos to Michael Yuen-Killick for his stunning, insightful cover design, and to Jane McWhorter for the interior book design. Heartfelt thanks to my publisher Deborah Herman, for believing in me and taking me to the next level.

Finally, appreciation and love to my husband Dan Hansburg. So glad we made our journey to the beautiful South Carolina Lowcountry. The best is yet to come.

About the Author

Freda Hansburg is a psychologist and co-author of the self-help books *PeopleSmart* and *Working PeopleSmart*. *Tell On You* is her debut novel. Freda and her husband live in the South Carolina Lowcountry, where she is working on her next novel and her Pickleball game.

www.fredahansburg.com
www.facebook.com/Freda HansburgAuthor
www.twitter.com/fredahansburg